THE VAW JOURNAL

VOICES OF AFRICAN WOMEN

TITLE:
The VAW Journal
Voices of African Women

PUBLISHER:
I, AFRICA™ Publishing Services
www.iafrica54.com | projects@iafrica54.com

COVER IMAGE BY:
Tamary Kudita

DESIGNED BY:
Cláudia Cassoma

EDITED BY:
Cláudia Cassoma & Lauretta Onwuegbuzie

ISBN: 9781734877694 (Vol.1 — First Edition, 2020)

DISCLAIMER: Feelings, opinions, and/or any ideas expressed in this publication are those of the authors. They do not necessarily reflect that of the I, AFRICA™ organization or its publishing annex.

THE VAW JOURNAL

VOICES OF AFRICAN WOMEN

ACKNOWLEDGMENTS

by: Roberta Ezike

We would first like to thank all of the women who participated in this work. We thank you for believing and trusting our vision when we said we wanted to create an anthology that would highlight the stories of African women through their own artistic lens. Without their submissions, this book would not be possible.

We also want to extend our deepest gratitude to the founder of Malaika, Noëlla Coursaris Musunka, for agreeing to speak with us about African Women identity. Who she is and what she fights for greatly speaks on the themes we chose to highlight in this edition and we could not have chosen a more perfect voice to feature in our book. Thank you, Martha and Jaime, for promptly helping us schedule our delightful conversation with Noëlla. We are grateful for the connection.

Last, but certainly not least, our warmest and biggest thank you goes out to all of the African women from the continent, for whom and by whom this work was inspired. We draw motivation, peace, love, and courage from you daily. This anthology is dedicated to you.

INTRODUCTION
by: Ida Adjivon

"The rights we want: We want to choose our husband, we want to own land, we want to go to school, we don't want to be cut anymore, we want to make decisions, we want respect in politics, to be leaders. We want to be equal"   —   **Rebecca Lolosoli**

The voices of African women have often been left out of conversations that particularly affect them. The world seems to be so threatened by *her* voice that it tries its best to shut it down.

The intention behind this journal is to create a platform for the voices of African Women. In the first edition of this art collection, we hope to showcase pieces that outline identity and its development as recounted by African women. We seek to understand how African women see themselves; their internal and external difficulties when living out their dreams, hopes, and lives in this identity.

This year has been plagued with many hashtags that should not have existed, like: #justicefortina and #justiceforuwa. We cried justice for women whose voices the world tried to take from them and some of which it succeeded to take. But we will not let their voices fall silent.

We will fight!

The brutality in the case of Vera Uwaila Omozuwa affirms the necessity of this art collection. Vera was a twenty-two year old student who sought the quietness of her empty church in Benin City, Southern Nigeria, to study. She was found hours later raped and killed. Unfortunately, there are many Vera(s) on the African continent that we never hear about. That we never get the chance to mourn. That we never get the chance to protect.

The lack of support for survivors of rape and the culture that supports the persistence of these, and all acts of violence, whether physical or emotional, against women needs to be explicitly addressed and changed.

Even in Rwanda, a country heralded for being progressive when it comes to gender equality in the government, still has a culture that requires the notion of gender equality be parked at the front door. Powerful, outspoken and outstanding female leaders who call the shots every day in their offices, still find it difficult to assert themselves in their own homes - some out of fear for their own safety.

This should not be the case!

I, AFRICA™ was founded with the intention to amplify the voices of those whose stories have been told on their behalf, whose voices have been suppressed, and who have been made to believe that they are not worthy. This initiative is also led by four Black Women who know each and every one of these circumstances and decided to use these experiences to empower everything we do.

Let's take Cláudia, our Program Director. She was born and raised in Angola, South-West Africa. She left for the United States at the dawn of her womanhood to pursue better professional training, but she has achieved much more than that. She is a part of a number of projects and has founded SmallPrints, an organization focused on the well-being of every Angolan child through education. Regardless of her current location, she always does her all to contribute to the development of her home country.

Our Communications Director, Lauretta, was born and raised in Nigeria where she is currently studying to practice law. She is passionate about her continent, her people, and the preservation as well as the sharing of authentic African stories. She finds peace in meditation, reading, self-reflection, and writing with the ultimate goal of being a better version of herself everyday so that she can make an impact on the African continent.

Like Lauretta, Roberta, our Executive Coordinator, is also Nigerian. Roberta, however, was born to Nigerian parents who emigrated to the United States twenty-four years ago. She draws inspiration from her parents' bravery to leave their home and family and go to a foreign country for the sake of providing the best for their children when their country, at the time, could not. Their decision to cross borders has motivated Roberta to honor them by striving for the best both academically and professionally. At I, AFRICA™ she works to draw attention to the stories of people like her and her immigrant parents.

I, on the other hand, was born in Togo, where I enjoyed most of my childhood surrounded by extended families and a multitude of neighbors with kids my own age. When I was about twelve years old, I emigrated to the United states, where I currently reside. Learning a whole new language was, simultaneously, exciting and daunting but I met lifelong friends in the process. I have had the pleasure of living on two continents and within two different cultures, which create a form of dissonance at times, but has made me into who I am.

Our individual stories are vastly different. But etched into each, is our identity, our personality, the source of our dreams and our hopes. The differences in our stories are important as they individualize us, and the similarities connect us.

Take some time to read the stories in this book to learn about the identity of the many voices of African women. Listen to the voices of these audacious African women sharing their vision of a better, stronger, more inclusive and reverent world for all women. For a moment, forget everything you know about what it means to be African, or to be a woman, and see it only through their eyes. Do not judge them for freely and explicitly talking about sexual freedom, allow them to tell you how they see themselves in the world, and contemplate the stories they tell you – stories they know the world would not believe. Find the differences between yours and their identities, but more importantly find the places where you connect. Let these works of art: each poem, essay, short story, drawings, and paintings, for a brief second, challenge the way in which you have thought about African Women.

No nation can survive much longer in negating or subduing the voices of its women or menacing their existence. Not in Kenya where Rebecca Lolosoli and her community are literally fighting against the patriarchy by establishing their own women-only community; not in Nigeria where atrocities of rape are no longer tolerated; not in the Democratic Republic of Congo where Noëlla Coursaris Musunka is fighting for the right for girl's education through her all-girls school, Malaika; not even in Rwanda where traumas of a past genocide is slowly but surely being healed through shared stories, policy changes, and sentences against the perpetrators. Not anywhere.

We, African Women, want the space to create our own identities, we want the space to be feminist without being called a "foreigner", we want to assert our place in the world, to be leaders in our own right. We want to not be forced into marriages just for the purpose of bearing children; often, before we are done being children ourselves. We want to be equal. Take heed and join us or move out of the way. We are no longer asking. We are simply informing you.

I, AFRICA™ STAFF

Ida Adjivon
Executive Director

Roberta Ezike
Executive Coordinator

Lauretta Onwuegbuzie
Communications Director

Cláudia Cassoma
Program Director

CONTENTS

—

SEXUAL FREEDOM

sub-theme

Untitled

[Munira Maria Makerow]

Motive of my feelings.
Rape.
Molestation.
Blind eye.
Dark skin is a sin.
Muscular bodies are.
Too much of an omen.
Especially from women.
Abandoned feelings.
Self-dried tears.
Mocking cliques.

Sexual Freedom

[Sinenhlanhla MlilowokuNqoba MaPhezabantu]

[Teresa Taimo]

Entre Gemidos
Da Mulher Casada
e outros Gritos Mais

Toca-me Ricardo, surpreenda-me. Torço em silêncio, enquanto acompanho a mão de Ricardo, que calmamente passeia pela minha cintura, calejada pelo amarrar da capulana. Prendo-me no momento, agarro as palavras e finjo sono pesado. Permita-me viver o namoro de amor com sexo nesta madrugada. Continua, Amor, não para. Esqueço que Ricardo é um homem de negócios e tão ocupado que entre o trabalho e seus amigos me perdia em pensamentos e num "eu te amo" acostumado. Lhe desejo com todo o meu ser, meu coração bate a mil por hora, queria encostar meu corpo no dele mais do que já estava, naquele instante sentirá a cama de casal grande.

*Tira do meu corpo este vestido de seda vermelho que a capulana de flores acesas esconde sua sensualidade. Digo sem tabus! Queria que ele virasse para mim e me desse beijos apaixonados, que trinca-se meu beiço no canto inferior esquerdo, e depois no direito suspirando ares de paixão ,queria sentir o afago macio de seus dedos aveludados e delicados.

*deixa-me sentir o calor dos seus sussurros na minha nuca, tira de mim esta capulana que amarra os calores do meu desejo, me deixa despir sem medos. Me provoque! Junte, meu peito com suas mãos de homem, que sabe o que quer, me dê calafrios e arrepios. Meu amor reinicie em mim a paixão do bem fazer, vamos fazer como nós últimos dias dos nossos primeiros dias, vamos fazer como dois estranhos que não tem nada a perder, Amor, me ame como se eu fosse uma forasteira ou uma mulher da rua que não a casaste, não quero que me enlouqueças , quero que me toques lúcida, não quero que me aqueças porque isso fazes as noites todas ,me esfrie Ricardo ,me esfrie como a lua faz a terra depois de um dia ensolarado. Revele em mim o Ricardo selvagem que há em ti, faça-me o que fazes as outras, o que fazes aquelas que não te preocupam e fazes tanto para satisfazê-las, faça-me melhor que elas,me faça mulher ,sua mulher!

Sabes Amor, Me imagino lhe falando friamente.

*Estou cansada de gemidos vazios e de suores sem prazer. Enterro neste quarto meus desejos e faço da cama minha guilhotina, Ricardo, estou cansada de apertar os travesseiros com a frustração de não poder ser, há mais de uma década nós conhecemos e há mais de uma década não me beijas com paixão, encostas em meus lábios uma vez a outra e mais nada, não tocas nos meus peitos desde o nascimento de Junior, não beijas minha nuca, não acaricias meu corpo, não variamos as posições sexuais, não temos mais sexo no princípio da noite porque adormeces cedo e cansado quando das por ti já é madrugada e te limites a introduzir sem preliminares. Lá Se foram os passeios a sós, juntos só em festas familiares, xitiques e cerimônias fúnebres interrompendo os meus pensamentos, Ricardo desce minha lingerie lentamente.

Naquele momento, o ar faleceu-me, pois, eu não queria gozos apressados, nem fingir orgasmos, ,queria libertar a mulher que há em mim, quero orgasmos múltiplos e verdadeiros.

*Amor, chamo-o com a certeza de querer mudar o rumo da nossa vida sexual, e de repente lembrei da vizinha Mayazi, esposa do Nguito mecânico do bairro ,que perdera seu lar por tentar implementar novas posições sexuais . Lembro como se fosse ontem ,quando no silêncio da madrugada ouvira Nguito aos berros questionando Mayazi onde aprendera as posições que tentara implementar, tia Munemwase sogra da Mayazi chorava desesperada ,gritando não só pelo filho e pela nora,chorava seus anos sexuais reprimidos pelo seu medo de falar ao marido o que desejara e como desejara.tia Munemwase aprendera desde cedo que sexo é só para satisfazer os homens e para a procriação, ela entendia a nora e também sabia que a sociedade as reprovaria , de mãos atadas ela assistira, Nguito que arrastava enraivecido a sua esposa nua pela cabana afora lhe expulsando de casa sob acusação de ela ter cometido adultério. Eu não queria isso para mim, mas estava cansada de aprisionar os meus gemidos na hora dos prazeres, queria me libertar ,passar para cima ,para esquerda,para direita ,trepar as paredes , beijar o corpo dele e fazer qualquer coisa mais que me satisfizesse. Queria me expressar sabes!sim, falar que lhe amo,falar que lhe quero ,falar que lhe desejo enquanto ele me penetra profundamente. Desta vez, diferentemente de outros suspiros ,suspirei com prazer acabara de atingir orgasmos múltiplos em pensamentos. Só em pensamentos.

*Sim minha querida,respondeu carinhosamente o Ricardo. Está tudo bem? Prosseguiu.

*Te amo, respondi a seco.

*Também te amo Malize, respondeu afastando para um lado a lingerie cuja a cor ele desconhecera e uma vez mais penetrou-me e afogou o meu ser mulher na rotina dos meus medos.

They said I lost my identity when he tore my clothes apart.
And only to think that my soul could not react,
but turned on itself like a tortured snake.
My inner body swelled at every morsel of pains
In my father's tongue, the truth was a bad taste.

I became a lifeless flower, whose beauty was stolen in a gust
The river flowed like a stream of glass,
lancing the holes in my skin
As teardrops seeped out of my wound as blood.
Barefooted, ragged with neglected hair,
I was tossed to suffer my curse.

I am only human whose fate met dusk.
Walking on the lane to home,
he devoured my bones and flesh.
Yet when I spoke, I was muffled the cause of my plight.
From the other side of the world, I sat to find hope again.
But life is a mere dream, a fleeting shadow on a cloudy day.
Just like them, I want to be seen as a human whose Identity carried
weight.

Identity

[Ifunanya Juliet Ottih]

[Eugenia Shaw]

Hair Up

Hair drawn up, to the top of your head.
Afro puff sits tall; your neck is long....
My fingers are drawn to it.
Stroking, caressing, playing a rhythm on the nape of your neck.

Your hairline soft.
Wispy, soft, curly hair, caressing my fingertips.
As I play, your perfume engulfs me, intoxicating me.
I lean in; inhale deeply....
Committing your scent to memory.

I want to taste your ebony neck;
Make you giggle, the way you do when I do.
But, we're in public.
So I content myself with just stroking and touching.

You lean into my hand and sigh...., turn and look at me.
Your brown eyes speak volumes, and my heart skips a beat.
There is a twang in my groin.
I smile into your eyes as I think of the promise of pleasures to come.

Hair up, I love your neck.
Don't take it down before I cum.

Untitled

[Paloma Peyron]

[Vivian Ibemere]

Chapters and Verses of a Girl's Journey

I watched as my sister-in-law, the head of the women furiously unwrapped the razor to be used on my longish hairs. Since their sudden arrival, not a soul produced any sympathetic words to me rather they added to my wounds.

"Come and sit down, let's scrape your atrocities away," she hissed. I kept wondering the reason behind their acrid attitude. These were the same women who dished out words of advice the day I was sold to my beastly husband. The day my life came to a halt. They gathered and filled my head with donts leaving me naked with no choice of my own.

"As a woman, it is your husband's duty to carter for all your needs so do not make him angry," my mother cautioned.
'What if he makes me angry?' I thought. None said anything about the husband making me angry. No one gave him the kind of instructions I was given; lengthy and lurid enough to be drafted into a constitution. So many donts.

"Don't say NO to your husband. Always be in the mood, force the mood even," Mama decreed with a deadpan face as she rend my ears. She was my father's elder sister and fond of calling me a stubborn girl because I wanted to complete my secondary studies.

"Don't wake up late, serve his food early and always." I looked up at the speaker who shot me a sour smile. She was pale and I guess from working herself to death.

That day, I concluded marriage was another form of slavery. The women around me the day my father made a fortune off my head, looked scared as they spoke, but here they were with tongues sharper than the razor they came with.

"Don't give birth to only female children mix it up. If possible give him a son first!" my aunt said as if she was the goddess of male children. She should thank her stars that the Almighty Allah blessed her with seven boys.

There are things that shouldn't be heard from a woman's mouth especially the issue of bearing male children. Common sense toppled with the teaching of my Basic Science Teacher, made it vivid that it wasn't in anybody's might to determine the sex of their child. But there they were, dishing out nonsense in the name of wise counsel.

"Don't go out without his permission. In fact come to think of it, where will you be going to apart from the market because I am certain your husband will treat you like a queen?" I wasn't only going to be a slave but a prisoner too. My heart was swollen from the horrifying pictures my mind created.

"Don't show your anger, endure everything as women do." I couldn't let this slide, as I opened my mouth to say something, my mother pinned my lips with her fingers and said "...don't talk back at your husband. Listen and say nothing."

"What?!" I heard my chest pound. These people cared less for my happiness. They just wanted me out of the house because I was up to age as claimed and wouldn't want people to say they didn't abide by the custom. A custom that was unfair to girls like myself. I have been paralyzed by the custom of my people, made to marry a man older than my late grandfather because 'they'—the wise women, said he trickled of money like water and my father was stone broke.

The so loving husband according to the women who had never shared a roof with him, was my nightmare. Every night he would barge into the room, unclothe me without my consent and roughly make his way inside of me with fiery breathe against my stiff body: wooden as a board, threatening to kill me if after his irksome effort I gave birth to another female child. Afterwards he abandoned me like some piece of rubbish. I never had a say. They said I shouldn't talk back and this silence ate me up. Twice, I had ran away from the beast to my father's house: the only place I knew to run for safety but I was brought back even after showing them my bruised bag of bones. "You'll get used to it," my mother said as she held me by the hand back to the house of horror. "I got used to it, your sister did. So yours won't be any different."

I was alarmed when I heard her. Deep down I knew I couldn't bear 'it' any longer. Why drag my life down in the dumps when I have neither flawed the rules nor said anything noxious to my two-faced husband who was sweet-tempered to the world and short-tempered with the one who lived under his roof. I was being maltreated for birthing female children.

Now, they stomped in with wrathful faces and bunched lips, sucking air through their teeth as if to say I never kept to their words. I was a living dead because I listened to them; like a bare tree waiting for a heavy wind, I stood. The death of the man that killed me brought them to his house like a vulture perceiving a carcass miles away. Their eyes pierced my soul accusingly.

"I hope you're now happy? You've achieved nothing as a married woman. You didn't even give him a son to follow his footstep," that was the voice of my sister-in-law. Her last statement made me glad that a male child didn't come out from my abused marriage. I wouldn't have the heart to see my son walk same path as his monstrous father. My own child was still a stranger to me. Each day I stare hard into her face with mixed feelings hoping she doesn't turn out to be like her mother, who failed to stand on her ground.

They believed I killed my husband, no one remembered that he was sixty-four when he married a white fourteen year old girl. I won't forget. My solace knew no bounds that he was gone for life and perhaps scraping off my hairs will steer me into a fresh start; fresh voice, fresh ground and chiefly, a fresh self.

Supression

[Nguseer Gavar]

[Sankofa Umbi Umbi]
Sobre Choros e Gritos

Eu sentia me suja,
Por azar ou sorte eu era dita cuja
O cheiro do corpo dele
Estava na minha pele,
Era nojento, mesmo com o corpo limpo minha alma estava
Imunda a boca muda.
De ódio, raiva e rancor.
Somos Mulheres, adolescentes e crianças.
Então digam...

Será que o lobo abusador
Estaria sem temor
Disfarçado nas vestes da ovelha
Nas vestes de Pastor, Activista popular,
Protector, Pai, irmão, tio,
Da família o amiguinho,
O exemplar vizinho
& Até com sacro sacramento camuflado na batina preta
Em cima do altar.

Na linha da hierarquia, do chefe do colega
Que alega
E alicia, como se meu valor estivesse no corpo bonito?

São órgãos de um corpo que não
Te deram permissão

Sequer autorização
Se o abutre for da família a orientação
É regra, normalização
Sem excepção.
Como se não bastasse o trauma, as escolhas também ficam condicionadas
A Voz silenciada
A coragem anulada

Entre choros de menores de 14 anos
Estão as suas parafilias, pedófilia!

Entre adultos, não importa
Se a pessoa foi para o teu quarto
Tipo arrastou o pato
Se deitou na tua cama
Se é esposa ou namorada
Se disse que queria ser papada
Quando ela disse NÃO é NÃO.
Se ela diz NÃO é NÃO.
If She say NOT is NOT.
E mesmo quando não tiver voz para dizer.

Presta atenção.
Oral, toques íntimos, introdução forçada de objetos, dedos, não é ciência
É violência, com nome e sobrenome
Abuso sexual, no seu tipo mas grave é estupro.

O sistema capitalista alimenta
Seu comportamento orienta
Com a pornografia
Dotada de códigos
Mulheres e crianças
Abusadas, em posição de submissão
Tornando te em um robô
Reproduzes o comportamento
Abusivo, invasivo, instintivo e destrutivo
Do filme porno...

Achas uma afronta ser barrada
Por isso te satisfaz que seja forçado
Com agressão física e verbal
Nada justifica sua actividade irracional
Doentio animal.
É um corpo não um esgoto
Para depositar o teu lixo
Seu escroto.
If She say NOT is NOT.
Boca tapada gemidos e choros,
Sobre esses gritos e choros digam-nos nos
Se o abuso fosse devidamente denunciado & Severamente
condenado?

[Gugu Ngwenya]

Morning Glory

My nature screams profanity,
My body implodes slowly ,
Rivers flow downwards to the sea.
Gushing waters hitting against rocks.
Ride my wave, release my tide.
Strick my rock,
Religiously,
Turn your staff into a snake.
Answer my prayer.

[Lizelle van Dijk]

Memories Of An Unremarkable, Twenty-Something Suburban Girl

1

I wasn't born screaming (if I am to take my mother's word for it). Her body was wrapped around my neck, suffocating my breath, turning my small lungs into purple silence. The cord that connected me to life swivelled around me and deprived me of my first taste of oxygen. A machine fed and granted me life outside of her womb; pumping breath into my chest and forcing my lungs to expand into voice. I screamed, a short piercing sound followed by cries.

After that I hardly made a noise. I never cried or screamed from the racket of the people at our house during the late night parties my parents loved to host. I just remember my grandmother, sitting in the corner of our spacious living room on the old grey couch. She was silent too. She only talked to answer questions. I use to imagine that old age had rendered her back to quiet internal reflections of the bodies that talked and twirled around her in our home to the langarm-sokkie treffers. I thought she was content when my infant eyes observed her during these parties, seated quietly on her own. Her name was Elizabeth Maria, but people called her Mary because it was more convenient, or maybe just because they heard others calling her Mary. She never contested to this renaming.

She was the best cook, according to my mother. If you wanted a good Sunday lunch of boudvleis en soet wortels or sweet tamatiebredie, my grandfather's farm house in Vredenhof was the place to be. There Mary would spend her Sundays cooking the soft red meat that her husband brought home from their butchery for my mother and her brothers. It was the best of times, my mother assures me, except when my grandfather drank brandy.

"It's a thing, you know, us Swanepoel's can't drink brandy. Just look at your uncle, that night he drunkenly slammed on your grandmother's front door. Heaven knows what for, but your poor grandmother was too scared to even open the door. She just stayed quietly in her room and waited for your father to arrive and take your brandy-drunk uncle home". (Perhaps, dear reader, there is no truth more difficult to face than the darkest, most abject one about the one's you love). I wonder what my grandfather did in their Vredekloof farm house when he drank brandy.

A few years later I visited my grandmother in Huis André Van Der Walt, where I was meant to say goodbye to her frail cast-off body. She was screaming, crying, fighting with the nurses. Dad told me she was forgetting, she can't remember who she was, who I was, who anyone was. Her voice frightened my mother, and it frightened me. I think now, reader, that she had found her breath again. It was no longer suffocated in a silence of remembering – in a violent melancholy wholly inexpressible by words. Her piercing voice named the person she was at the beginning of her breath, not the one people decided to call her afterwards.

After the machine breath bled out the suffocating purple silence in my infant body at birth, my mother decided to name me Mary. I carry my grandmother's voicelessness with me.

2

Shit!

They won't stop. They keep opening the bathroom door. My one piece bathing costume is wrapped around my lower legs; I can barely reach the door to push it closed. I beg again and again and again for them to leave me alone, but they only laugh at my still boy-like body. It's a game to them. My new-found embarrassment ferments and grows into a desperate scream. They only laugh.

I'm screaming. I'm crying. I'm shitting. I pull up my bathing costume – bright pink with yellow flowers – and run outside. The other kids stay in the bathroom, they're growing taunts follow my small body. I forgot to tie the knot at the back of my neck, and the costume flaps down to my stomach as I run crying to my parents. We're at a family gathering at my aunt's house. The older people glare at me.

"What was that for? You don't scream like that!". My father doesn't ask me why I'm crying, why my boyish chest is open and why I still stink of shit. "Don't act like we haven't taught you manners, Mary. I didn't raise you like a boy, damnit!"

My mother covers me up with a towel. "You should apologise, sweetheart. You gave us all a fright with that sudden shout".

I try to explain that my cousins kept looking at me, that they wouldn't leave the door closed. I did ask them nicely, really I did! But they didn't listen. My parents don't listen either. I gulp down my tears.

Reader, I'm sorry, I promise I won't scream again.

3

My mother's best friend lives with us sometimes. She married too young, got knocked up, and then decided she was unhappy. Now her ex-husband is a gospel singer and remarried to a younger, prettier version of his first wife. My mother often defends her best friend's early life choices. "It's because she wanted to get out of that house, Mary, her parents were fighting all the time. She could have done much better, though, than that pretentious asshole. Poor aunt Jen and her son hardly get any money from him".

I told my mother that aunt Jen's son touched me. He hadn't done it before, reader, just this one time when we were watching TV. He offered a piece of his blanket and I moved over. I froze when he put his hand on my leg and moved it slowly towards my inner thigh. I just stayed quiet. I waited; waited; waited for his hand to go away. It didn't. I said I needed the bathroom, stood up and struggled to unlatch the sliding doors of the living room. He helped me get the doors open.

I probably shouldn't have moved closer to him.

I didn't say anything until I reached my mothers' room. I showed her where his hands were.

"He's a bit older, sweetheart, hormones all over the place", she laughed faintly, "Let's not tell your father though, your poor aunt Jen doesn't have anywhere to go if your father kicks them out". She wiped away my tears before my father saw them.

4

We were drinking at Speakeasy after work. I had my usual few black label drafts while you drank two double brandies and coke. The boys were surprised when you came back to the table with the two drinks for yourself. I smiled at their comments - it seems like anything other than a pink cocktail or vodka and sprite is a weird drink for a woman. You smiled unabashedly and jokingly challenged the brandy drinking men to an arm wrestling contest to test if you're man enough to be allowed to drink brandy. I decided a while ago that I like your choice in alcoholic beverage - you were always charmingly unafraid of people's opinions about your brazen behaviour, and the strong liquor reflected that.

We left the bar together after last call. I drove you home. You were probably a bit drunker than me - you didn't flinch when I leaned over to kiss you. It was soft, slow.

You didn't talk to me for two days after that night at Speakeasy. I woke up at eleven on Monday with a Whatsapp message from you:

"I need to talk to you, let me know when you have a moment".

I responded, adding one too many emojies to seem nonchalant. You immediately replied:

"LOL. Ok, so, you know what happened the other night? I'm not sure if I'm overthinking it. I just don't want you to feel like I don't love you or anything. I'm not sure what happened, like how that happened. I don't want you to think differently about me. Like I love you, but that was just drunk fun, right?"

I wanted to tell you you're beautiful, it wasn't just drunk fun, I wanted to kiss you.

But instead I answered: "Haha don't worry. It was all the jägerbombs we drank, waaaay too many".

"Phew, ok. It was a fun night. Like, I don't feel awkward or anything. You're still my best friend."

When I introduced you to my parents back in high school they immediately liked you. I didn't tell them that you let me grow like unwanted weeds, your hands pulling at the strands of my voice, forging new breath unknown to my childhood memories. You didn't wipe away my tears. You held my hand whenever I was angry; you let me scream if I needed to.

"Don't even worry about the other night". I selectively place a few laughing emojies before hitting send. I wanted to add that I'm not sorry I kissed you, but I thought I'd rather leave it for another day.

Untittled

[Ruina Carim]

[Mahafuza Abdulrahman]

The Monster

On that heinous night you shrouded me off my dignity and
ruptured My whole life
I bleed like watermelon
despite the tears rolling down my cheeks you keep on riding on me
because you re a filth
my eyes got puffy and red
A part of me has been torn apart
the pluck in his eyes shows he's a monster
He played his game to him I was a chess
i was so helpless as I watched My dignity taken away
A pride that will never be mend
whenever he feels a thirst, I was his prey to quench his thirst of lust
As tears keep rolling down my chins just like an ocean
I can still dirty hands penetrating through my poor skin
I can hear the echoes of mockery all around me
my breath got stuck at the back of my throat

I can't hold myself

the hours you spent strumming me will not make you a macho man

You murdered my innocence and took my sanity away

No matter how many times I bath I still stinks

is the season of hunger where dogs eat their own

HIS words are ruthless and cruel, but your words make the spark
inside of me grow to a raging fire my body isn't yours to swallow

All the metaphors remain thesame

Why did you choose me to satisfy your deadly lust

Because I was born with a vagina or because I have legs with a space
between them or I look sweet for a taste

Are we turning into a statistic

You deserve to die and your body devoured by animals

pieces of me are still lying on the floor

Tell me what to do

should I disperse them to the winds of insouciance or will you keep
them safe for me in your heart

When I talk about my trauma am not asking you to carry it or relieve
me from it am just asking you for

your time to feel a little light in my heart so that I can reclaim my
own body

Even the words slices my tongue each time I try to talk

Now I speak, for I'm done being weak

stop invading our privacy

we'll take control of our own bodies and uphold our pride and
dignity

It's time to raise

it's time for justice

we are the voice of the raped

49

[Charanee Marimuthu]

The Temptress

I am stuck.
Stuck in your intoxicating energy.
Fueled by the of crumbs of lust.
Drawn in by your gaze.
Is this love?

Your touch is raw electricity.
It catches me off guard...
My knees are weak.
My mind is blank.
I am incapacitated.

Dying to be with you.
Compelled to please you.
Drawn in to this trap.
Caught in your web, a happy victim,
ready to be feasted on by your toxicity.
I cannot a escape.
I don't want to.

Feast on me, you're all I desire.

[Vimbainashe Takarwa]
Memories, Dream And Nightmares

She remembers the darker nights,
 The ones haunted by his touch.
 A touch so defiling that it left her very soul dirty.
She remembers these nights and the pain,
A pain she hardly knew how to speak of,
She remembers the shame she left with the pain,
 Memories so treacherous.
She recalls the shackles of his actions,
How they made her fear the intimacy she also craved.
She recalls how the memory frequently stole from the present moments.
How one touch could have her back in a dark place.

 She recalled being his victim long after his deeds.
She remembered too the helplessness,

The frustration of never healing,
She felt the frustration of moments never lived,
Of the lies her body had to tell,
She hated that she could still feel the shackles of his actions,
She also felt them loosen shockingly with time like a new dawn.
She could wiggle free of the death grip.
With the right embrace and emotions,
The chains that had her stuck in the cold broke.

This stranger brought with him bliss,
His touch healing wounds inside and out.

She felt in those moments an escape from the pain that haunted her.
His kisses the very medicine her soul needed,
His touch leaving her body trembling and craving more,
She remembers the darker nights but she has more now.
She has now a dawn to the dusk,
the nightmares still come but they no longer reign eternal.

The bliss has erased his touch,
The stranger has given her hope.
Drunk and high on his touch and the feel of his skin,
With him, every moment is pure ecstasy.
In her waking moments, he is only a thought away and when she
sleeps memories of him chase her nightmares away.
Now she knows its possible that pleasure and pain are the same coin,
She found in his touch what she had lost the very same way.
He might not be forever but his memories are,
She knows memories, dreams and nightmares are.

[Aisha Mohammed]
Reckoning

Rana thrust this child into this
Place.
Naked, nipples throbbing
crying lava out of her eyes
She danced on the threads of it's heart
when she got strong enough to walk,
teasing the fragile thing with her feet
Tip toeing nervously
On it's blood afraid to sink in.

Demons wrapped their whips around
her thighs when her body blossomed.
They ripped her legs apart,
and stared at the petals in her core
Mocking it passing it amongst themselves
they turned her into their garden,
revelling in her sweetness
whenever they could.

The demons moved into her,
swam in her head
till she could no longer
see without their tails blocking her eyesight

One day when she looked at this place
With her eyes bloodshot and her petals

Dying,
she realized
her blood was lava,
and Rana made her heart out of
Ice and Earth.

She drew her blood,
carved daggers out of it
And cut the threads,
Grabbed the heart and took a bite of it
She stopped tip toeing,
Dipped herself into its blood.
slayed the demons
hung their heads, her trophies
On her skin.

[Oluwamayowa Somoye]

Freedom

I want to be free,
To chose when I have sex,
Not because God would smite me
If I do before marriage
And I would live in bondage forever.

I want to be free,
To choose when I merge my soul,
Not because I must be pure
on my wedding night
to avoid my husband's ridicule.

I want to be free,
To choose when to fulfill my needs,
Not because of family scorn
or fear of disownment by father
for being the town slut.

My virginity should not be the price,
My show of gratitude,
that he designed to love me
and offered to be my husband
or buy from my father.

My virginity should not be my worth,
My only contribution to marriage,

The reason I am loved,
Proof I can be a good wife
or mother to my children.

I want to be free,
To explore my body
or hide it beneath clothes
without fear of ridicule,
Without shame,without judgement.

I want to be free,
To completely own body,
Not my father before marriage
or my husband once say I Do
until my dying breath.

I want to be free,
To choose to be celibate
or explore my body,
Sadly,this is not my decision
my culture decides for me.

[Rumbidzai Zamukudzi]

Bird set Free

As I entered marriage, I thought it was a land of milk and honey. We had been in courtship with my husband for six months. He had shown me exceptional love. I never had an iota of doubt in my mind. I met Simba when I was 20 and he was 30. He made his intentions clear that he wanted to marry me. I never had thought of marriage lately but I saw it as a way to move out of my parents' house with an abusive father, a drunkard and bedswerver. I had seen my mom crying countless times. I took the idea of getting married as a way to rescue me and my family. My boyfriend was well up and I knew he could provide for us.

I had confided in Simba about all my family secrets he felt so remorse and offered to help my mom and siblings out as soon as he would marry me. The day came, I was so excited, lobola was paid and I moved in with my husband. To my surprise he was renting a 2 roomed shared house. At first I thought we were going to visit maybe one of his family but got shocked when he told me that was his house. That was where we were going to stay. I pinched myself, I thought I was dreaming. The place was so scattered with dirty clothes everywhere and it was so smelly.

"Are you joking Simba, is this a prank, it's fine you got me. Just tell me it's a joke". I said this looking straight into his eyes hoping he will smile and say it was a prank, I thought he wanted to test if I had loved him for his possessions or not but no it was reality. I had to Live in a place which looked like a pig pen. I thought of going back home but I knew my dad would beat me to death, he wouldn't accept to pay back my lobola. I had to endure the suffering. I looked straight into Simba's eyes tears flowing on my cheeks, I was seeing a monster, it was never the sweet guy I had met. His face had changed. " Them slay queens, you like flashy stuff isn't it, where do you think I would get all those expensive cars in this bad economy huh, you fell for my gold not for who I am. Stop crying, you have to start cleaning maybe. The place is so bad isn't it". He said this as he took the car keys and went out.

I kept on standing, I couldn't find a better place to sit, everything was everywhere. I felt so weak, this was supposed to be our honeymoon phase but it had already started on a bad way. I had nothing to do had to pick myself up and be a strong woman. I started packing the stuff back to their positions. The room was overcrowded. I tried my best and as I finished I just sat on a scrap bed which would fall down in a couple of days. The blankets were so smelly and tattered. I couldn't wash them the day I arrived as they wouldn't dry up. I kept on sitting waiting for my husband to come, tears still dripping off my eyes.

Time went so slow, watched the dirty clock hanged on the wall clocking as I counted every minute which passed by. I was hungry but there was nothing to eat in the house. I had to wait for my groom to come who was nowhere to be found. It started to get cold then I took my jacket and warm trousers and put it on as the night kept on going the coldness was getting worse I had no option than to get into the tattered blankets. I don't know how I fell asleep I just remember being waken up by Simba's hands touching my breasts. I checked on the clock and it was already 1:00 am. I couldn't believe it, he was smelling alcohol all over. No this wasn't the man I fell in love with at a church conference. He had told me he never had tasted alcohol. I had promised myself not to marry a drunkard as my dad was one and judging from his behavior drunkards were not an option for me.

I tried to stop him from touching me with his filthy hands but he didn't listen. He said it clear that it was the reason he had paid lobola. He had to do whatever he wanted with my body. Taking me as an object he would buy in a shop. I felt so devalued. He ordered me to remove all my clothes, married women shouldn't sleep with clothes. I had to know that and follow his rules. I refused but he grabbed my tiny body and said softly in my ear that I belonged to him and if I don't listen he will beat the hell out of me. I became so scared started to remove all my clothes and he forced himself inside me. It was painful, I cried but it never moved him. He finished, pushed me to the wall and shoved me under the blankets as he hold me in his arms. I thought of an escape plan, I couldn't endure this suffering, I was too young for it. The next morning Simba woke up, prepared and he left the house. There was nothing to eat, no entertainment as I reached my bag to take my phone it was nowhere to be found. I knew he had taken it. I thought of going back home. I just put on my clothes and took my bags went to a taxi rank then I left.

The problem came when it was time to pay, I checked for my wallet, it was nowhere to be found. I felt like a fool. I kept on searching the whole time but the conductor told me not to waste his time. I started to cry tried to explain what had happened but my words reached deaf ears. I was thrown out of the taxi. There was no way I would go without my documents. I walked for about 15km and I couldn't walk anymore a Good Samaritan just stopped and took me home.

I was so tired and hungry, when I arrived Simba was in the house sitting on the bed. He just looked at me and laughed. " You thought you would run away from me. I knew you would try it and from now on you will be in a house arrest". These words came to me as a sharp sword piecing through my body. " I will not run away Simba, at least let me wash the blankets, they smell so bad, you can put me on house arrest when they dry". I said this avoiding eye contact with him. He looked at me so furious, " So you mean I'm not human enough to use those blankets huh, you will use those dirty blankets, I'm going out now, there is your food". He said this as he walked out of the house and locked the door.

I just sat down my back against the wall, I was now a prisoner. I didn't deserve this, it was to early for a new marriage. I lost appetite, I became so pale, got pregnant in no time and bore a baby boy still I was under arrest if I wanted to go out Simba would accompany me. If I had to visit my family he would be with me so that I wouldn't be able to say a word of what was happening until one day I wrote a letter and just left it on the couch when I visited my mom. Lucky enough she read it and in no time police officers were on my door step Simba got arrested and I was free again.

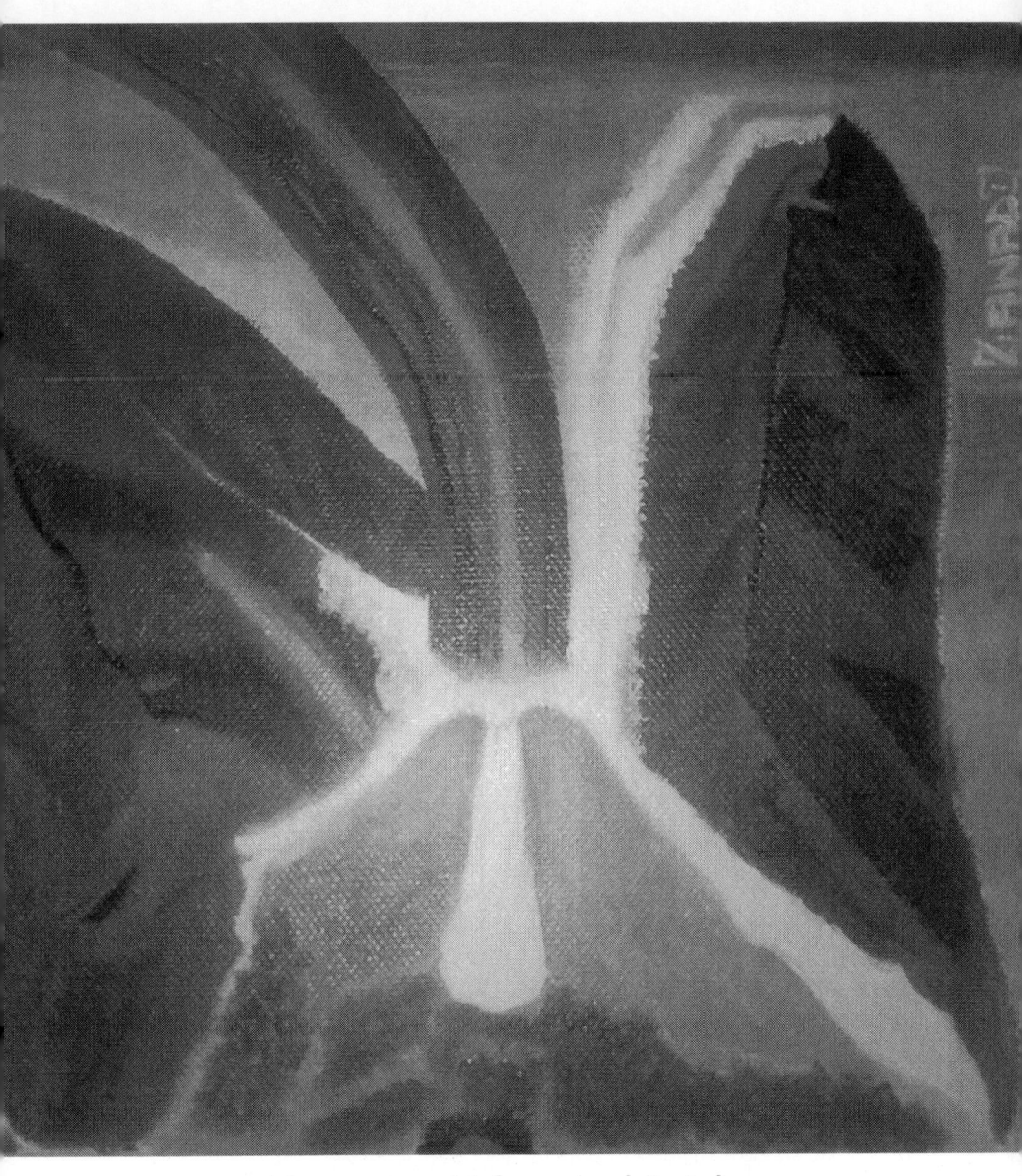

Mountains, Vulvas And Rainbows

[Zawadi]

[Ladunni Peace]

Set Her At Liberty

Love is not a crime
So why tie down our arms
Like we are meant for the cage?
Love won't breathe in a suffocating cage
Why give rules that tightens our wrists harder than a rope will?

We have the key to freedom
But our hands are still cuffed
Our hearts are kept stuffed
As we aspire that someone may be our Messiah someday

The land is a cage that enslaves
How then can the key be used
While our hands are tightly together
And we become birds that sing in the cage?

Even in our chamber
While we adore our rose flower
And our hearts leap it's forever ours
We remember the shattering truth

Why can he and why can't she inherit her father's name?
Our opinion stays in our minds
Why are we not the owner of our chambers
Until we reproduce him
Why can't we own our chamber when she is born?

Why call us princess
When we are no more priceless ?
You go into us without consent
And come out smiling
While we gaze up at you with a wry smile
We are subjected to endure all
Our will never prevail
But his will always reign

Our reality has now transformed
The sky now seems dusk and shadows gets long
We have been punctured a million times
We assumed a position and place
But alas! It's a perforated place
We showered love on him
But he does not show us we deserve same love

Despite our desperate plight
We will sacrifice even our last breathe
To make sure we are free
Though our ship journeys slowly in the sea of despair
And the sailing to freedom does not seem to lead to the shore
Yet I glimpse a glimmer of hope
We will in no time tell the story of liberty
We will be translated into the realm of freedom and peace

We are females
we are not futile
While our hearts beat fast
And our nose breathes its last
Our hands will fight manfully
And not in vanity
In guarding her to everlasting freedom and liberty.

[Ammywrites]

Freedom!

Redemption
Redemption

.

.

.

Redemption is all WE seek
Redemption, to embrace the warmth of manly chivalry.
Redemption,
To walk graciously in the dark,
With OUR head high,
Singing songs of liberty.

Redemption is what WE ask for
Redemption, from the shackles of sexual slavery.
Redemption,
To dress with a skirt so short,
A gown too long,
And yet, be bold in the face of dark alleys.

Redemption is what WE pray for
Redemption, from the tangles of despondency.
Redemption,
To say NO with a slur,
And we mean it.
Redemption,
To heed to our NO,

And let us hang on our shoulders,
Our bag of EGO-
Without even a scratch to it.

Redemption!
Redemption!
It's called CHOICE.
Either drunk or sober,
We say NO, we mean NO.

[Charanee Marimuthu]

A Poem To My Unknown Lover

If you could understand my love for you.
You would see that it goes beyond what you are.
Beyond your intoxicating eyes.
Beyond your perfect aging skin.
Beyond your scent, gender, and appearance.

It sees you,
naked in your vulnerability,
opening your mind, and heart to only me.
Standing there, with the trust and naiveté of a child.

And that is why I love you.
Infinitely.

[Tshepo Moyo]
Draw Blood

When I was 5 my mother told me to
punch till I drew blood.
I didn't get why she was so mad.

When I was 12 a man said I looked sexy in shorts.
I stopped wearing shorts. Or playing outside.
I closed my legs, I sat like a lady.

I wear shorts now.
I walk at night.
I drink tequila.
I reject nice guys.
Someone told me I was asking for it.

I remembered then,
My mother said...
"When a boy tells you he owns you punch till you draw blood."

[Lucy Mwimbilizye]
My Life, My Choices

There some things in life you don't have to wait someone to fix them for you,it's a matter of taking actions towards what bothers you. In the end I had to make some tough decisions,after all it was my life and my choices.I had to follow my heart desires and marry the man I am inlove with,In my community I am disgraced to the family but sooner or later they will get used to it and life will get back to normal.

I was sixteen when I first got married,Ofcoarse i was young but my father was to decide everything for me back then.It was a beautiful morning when he came with another man who was almost of his age.its our tradition that younger ones have to greet their elders shikamoo meaning "Am below you".I gave the man my Shikamoo and he replied with just a wierd smile.My mother and my siblings where all called and my father said"Flora you are know grown up, the man I am with is your husband,I have taken two cows from him already and tomorrow we shall have your wedding celebrations.

"I replied with okey Papa.Deep down i said to myself "it's okey Flora by the the way the old man will die and you will marry anyone you love,you can't be against your dad's will so just accept the marriage".

It has never been easy and it will never be easy marrying a person who you don't love at all,One year of marriage but it seems I have married him forever.There is a guy at a near by street, I think I am into that guy and the way he looks at me says it all.Silly me,am still married remember!My husband says he married me so that he can just have sex with me,he doesn't need children because he as children older than me already.

I have no power and control over my body,I am a sexual slave.My job is to satisfy the old man with his needs.So let's talk about the guy who lives in the next street,He wants me to stand for my own decisions and happiness and I have decided to divorce my husband.It doesn't make any sense if you are married and not happy,If you are in relationship so as to please your parents.

The old man said he will kill me if i don't return the cows that my father took as my bride price.I and my new husband sold our properties and gave him back his cows.He is now planning to marry another woman with the cows that I have returned.Ofcoarse am not jealous but I feel sorry to his next bride,.My father doesn't believe in true love but I had to show him that true love exists.

I thank Victoria Woodhull she paved a way for us in breaking chains of own sexual slave,I am now in a relationship of my own will.I hear advice you dada meaning sister don't let your economic situation inslave your body don't let your social condition enforce you to a relationship that you don't want because you have the right to marry and be with who you want.

[Pétala Preciosa]
Me Condenas

Me agrides
Com letras tortas chamas-me sexo fraco
Para alimentares esse teu machismo antiquado
E sobressaíres nesse seu mundo quadrado
Me condenas, mesmo sabendo que de fraca não tenho nada

Marcas-me como um animal
Abres caminhos frescos no meu rosto
Desmontas os meus braços e pernas feito uma boneca
Crias em mim tatuagens deformadas da minha horrível escolha
Me condenas, e te esqueces de que os machistas não brincam com
bonecas

Te divertes com a dor que espreme os meus olhos
Usas a tua força para me incapacitares
Afogas os folhos da minha auto-estima
Porque te sentes ameaçado
Me condenas, mas não deixarei de ser essa grande MULHER

Sentes-te mais homem quando pincelas
O meu corpo de palmadas doloridas e socos?
E quando fechas a porta para que os meus gritos sejam ocos
A sua ideia é matar-me sem que haja testemunhas?
Me condenas, mas um dia tu irás viver nas celas

71

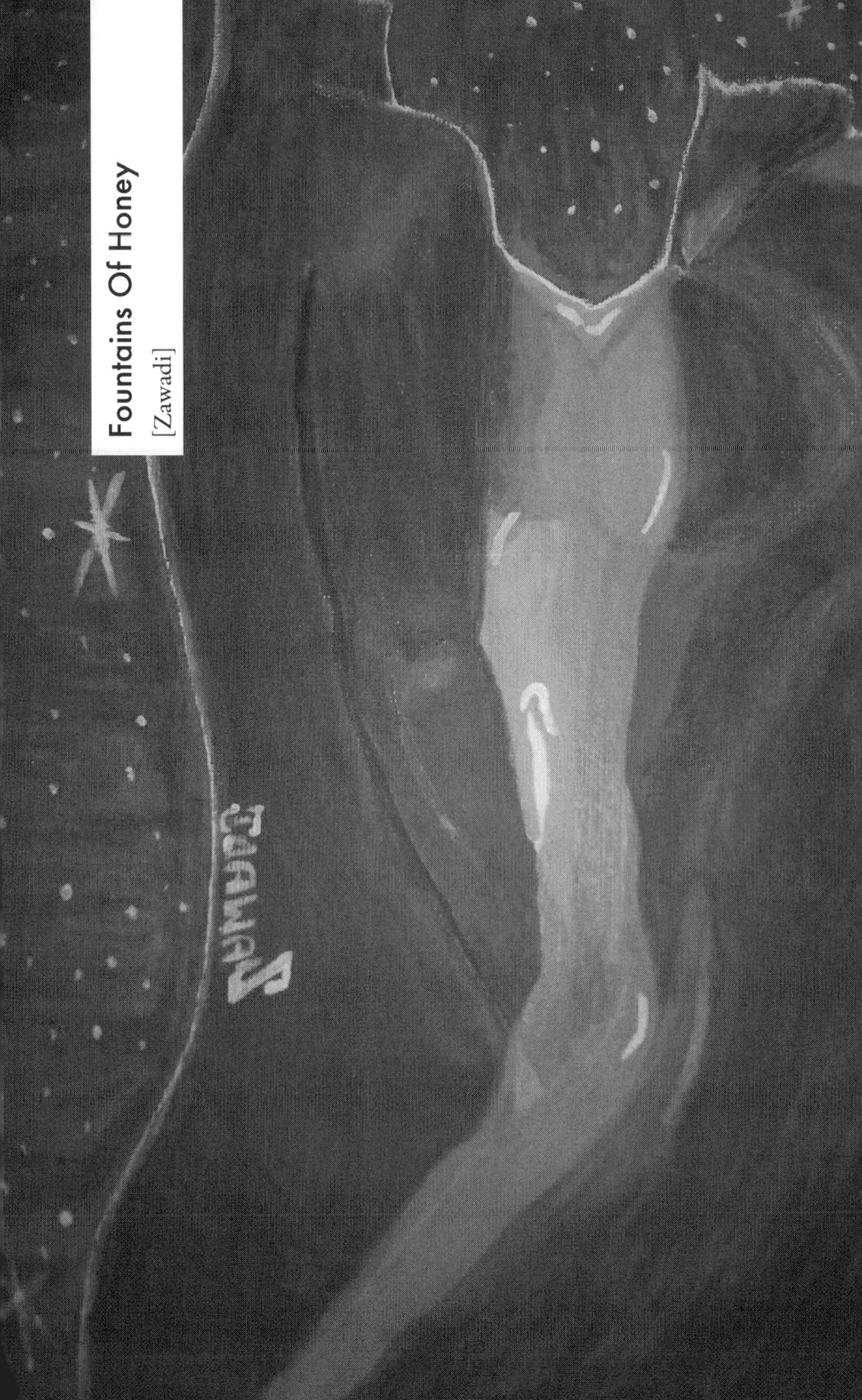

Fountains Of Honey

[Zawadi]

[Mojisola Esther]

Sexual Freedom

Own your body let it be free
Don't violate your pride
Don't let anyone do,
Culture, Norms nor, 'it's the thread'
Don't make the stats rise
Dear sis you're priceless
Beauty lives in your abode
I hear cries of my sister's every time:

The aura and face leave a pain my heart
The darkness and force come into my body
Seems like dead is friendly,
I'm a girl child who had grown up wanted
I didn't have strength not voice to cry out

We didn't know our lives were in danger
Our culture cuts us
So we shouldn't enjoy it- sex
The lips of our body isn't ours
It's for him

I'm to face down and not up
Because I belong there, down
I don't have a voice

Education? No we are for the kitchen and other room
Death lives we us daily
It starts from the heart that bleeds

Our mouths are cover with different covering
We dear to speak out
Even when we are hurting
We dare not talk

What's freedom?
Do we know it?
Sexual life isn't discussed openly
We have no say about it

Here come a body sister,
The body of many sisters like you
Women that fight emancipation,
the body of one voice
Voice for you sister
We are here to set you free
But freedoms starts with your voice!

[Chelsy Maumbe]
Virginity

My virginity is no product
for a patronizing, patriarchal society,
Upheld by the dry and brittle hands
of my cruel old ubabakazis
Jealous of my succulent womanhood.
They defend their men.

Its unwarranted absence is LOUD.
An undesirable act of violence
grabbed from me in the middle of the day,
without concern for my consent,
by uncles who claim to protect.

It is marred by the uneven edges
of broken bottles,
the jagged teeth of eroding knives
used countless times to silence girls like me.
Unwillingly,
we meet a rite of passage,
So soon after the gods
have given rein to our wombs,
bursting with fertility.

My virginity is a defiance!
against a patronizing, patriarchal society.
The spark that now lights the fire

to stop the rape of 1 in 3.
To never let
the daughter of tomorrow
lie on her back,
feet in the air
Losing a part of herself
For the pleasure of a man
playing god with a whole universe
between her thighs
In the name of tradition.
She depends on no man!

*ubabakazi – term used to say Aunt in Ndebele.

You sit back and cross your scrawny legs.
You draw out and light up old, mottled cigars.
Smoke goes up like in blood sacrifice to the deities that oppress.
You pat your bellies and roll your tongue.
You bellow out in a voice as if thunder.
You ask why this gender still goes on about equality.
You say a lot has already been done. You do not see the need for more.

When your daughters come back with their faces torn apart, you say they need to learn to be more submissive.
You pretend you do not see the old brown marks that stretch across her back to her shoulders.
You say the world used to be better in the days when everyone was ready to be ordered about.

Just wait, every oppression is about to burn to ashes like it was lighted up by your old, mottled cigars.
And then when we gather here we would talk about how gentle the air of freedom is like.
We will talk about emancipation and all the good it brings

Old, Mottled Cigars

[Henrietta Enam Quarshie]

[Thandokuhle Sibanda]

A Kind Of Love

This is what happens to the universe,
When your soul and mine intertwine
All things birthed from its core become one
what is of the skies and the galaxies comes down
to be embraced by that which belongs to the earth
this passion knows no bounds
Now understand why it is forbidden
It's heat and weights is something the universe yet to adjust to
It's strength and uniqueness is something it's people are yet fathom

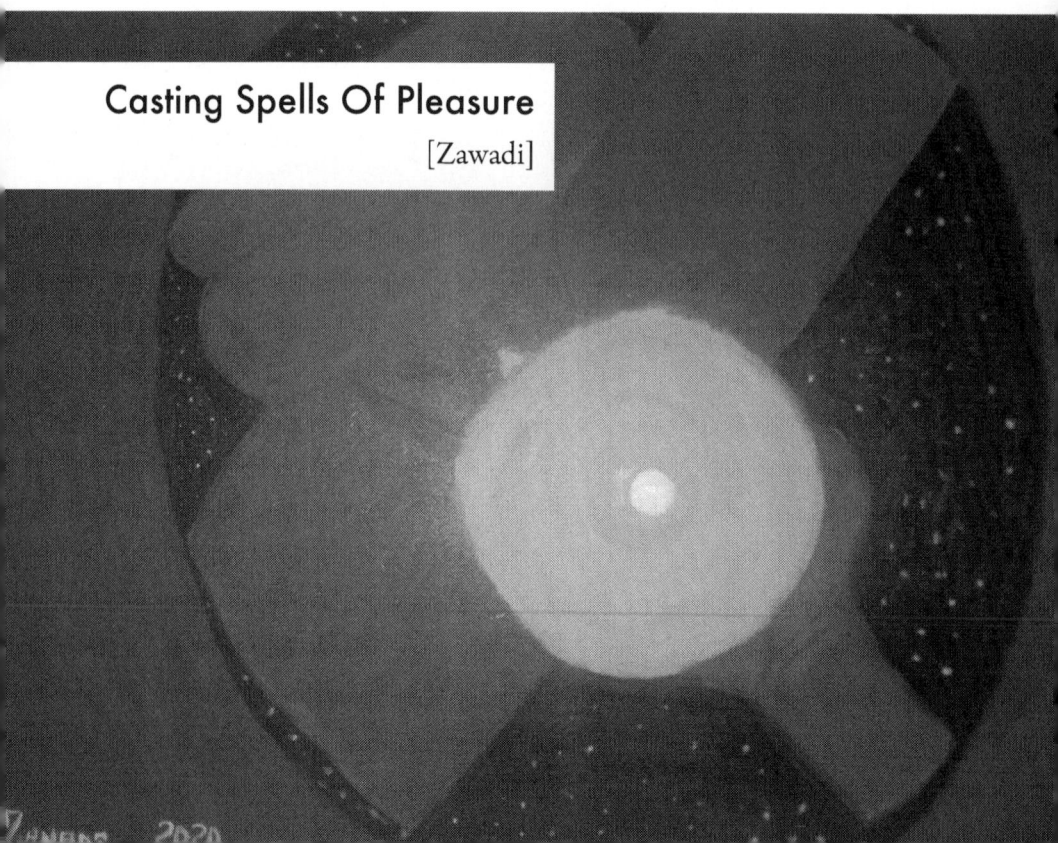

Casting Spells Of Pleasure
[Zawadi]

[Adedoyin Adebiyi]
Rose Tinted Glasses

If I had been told that I would be standing here, amongst a group of women and men protesting about Male and female sexual desires I would have laughed at them and said they were crazy, why? Because I have always been giving as much as I was receiving, all my relationships involved control on both parts and it never occurred to me that soome people out there aren't so lucky.

Kunle and Maria are a feminist power couple in the office who everyone including me thought he was in it because she gave out the best sex. But my world was rocked when he brought in a book to the office on a faithful Thursday that was so misogynistic and patriarchal with a hint of matriarchy that had half of us in the office angry beyond compression.

The book spoke about women and how they should be submissive and all that shebang and how whatever the man said goes and how women who were seen as equal by their men were going to hell and there was an uproar in the office. It spoke about how if the man wanted sex even during her period when she was in pain and tired she was never to refuse him because that and childbearing was our main goal in life. But half of us in the office disagreed because women should have the right to control their own fertility and to bare as many or as few children as they wish. Women should have the right to refuse or to initiate sex inside or outside marriage, on the same basis as men. It was our bodies and that was when I realized that I had been shelthred all my life. The way it was for me, I was a drop in a sea of ocean.

And that was why I was standing under the sun, under abay bridge chanting, 'Both men and women should strive to eliminate the social conditions which currently make it necessary that a woman barters her sexual freedom for economic or other reasons - in marriage or in prostitution."

We all probably looked stupid but at the end of the day I felt like I had done a good job by following k and m on one of their rampaged accross the town to educate young girls who were busy giving birth every year not because they wanted to, but because their husbands said they would have no time to cheat on them if they were always pregnant and surrounded by kids. While we were talking a woman came to ask about contraceptive's and her husband threatened to send her back to her parents if she so much as dared to get one before hissing at us and walking away angrily. Male and female sexual desires should be seen as the creation of social processes, and therefore open to change: not given by biology I soon learnt.

That was when I realized that kunle and Maria were heroes, facing such people everyday and still staying through to their beliefs both as feminist and Christian's, preaching God whenever they joined us for lunch and how we were all different yet the same in Christ.

It was right there in my sight and I refused to see it because of my rose tinted glasses, whenever Aisha came to me and complained that she had never had an orgasm and I laughed it off that maybe she was asexual, whenever Oyinyechi would run out of the room saying she was tired and her husband would tell her to shut up and come back inside and I would think, not my business. It was always there, the signs that we were leaving in a world far from peace, equality and sexual freedom and I choose to ignore it. But on this hot afternoon, holding a sign that said, 'sexual freedom for both sexes' and chanting loudly, I realized if I of all people could do this, then maybe just maybe we are going to get there.

End Rape Culture

[Oyindamola Adisa]

[Oyindamola Adisa]
Consent

i'll let a smile wake me up, that'll be my own
i'll assure i recognize the one in the mirror
the color of my dress will be solid me

no fear will push me away from dawn
no other false breath will destroy my inner
i'll let a smile wake me up, that'll be my own

as sun resumes and i ready for bunches to see
as i go by them with a skin that's a winner
the color of my dress will be solid me

every day i'll build up my own throne
every step will be a mark of my in hero
i'll let a smile wake me up, that'll be my own

i'll let a smile wake me up, that'll be my own
the color of my dress will be solid me

intimate covenant

[Cláudia Cassoma]

[Valerie Asiimwe Amani]
Salma in Bloom

[Dikun Elioba]

Living with the Memory of Love

No one should come in between us
he says
with his palm across my
mouth to silence all words
and his warm breath rushes swiftly across the skin of my neck
his heart beats become more heavier as his wishes spill
from his mouth in the evening
it is the peak of discovering love and the words
"I love you" feel as permanent as his touch
your body is the bridge between me and the world that it feels like
no one break into
I wonder what has happened to us now
as your aura still lingers within my skin

I wonder why you left and are no longer here
the image of you still engraves
delicately and both sharply
into me like the parting of braids
on top of my scalp
I yearn for you to enter-
a place where no one has gone
Innocent and ripened
an appetite still lingers
within the strain of my words
saliva of yearning boils in my mouth
the body is like a shell
inside is a swarm of butterflies
like the resounding inside of a seashell
an echoe of desire still lives
and unweaves itself in the turmoil
of memory

[f.gabdon]

Self Love as Healing

1.

Truth is, I crave people.
I crave the memories,
the moments, the feelings.

My entire body almost wills itself back to people and places. Some
nights, I have to tell it to be still.
To hold still a moment.

Have you ever had to do that? Talk your body and heart out of
somebody? Soft like a whisper, warm winter shower, reminding it;

"they are not good for us baby.
they don't love us like we love them.
they don't need us the same.
we can't go back there again."

· Self love as healing

[Catherine Mazhandu]
Situationships

" It's okay, I'll pick up the morning after pill on my way from work" I reassured him for the hundredth time.

"What brand do you use? I can pick it up for you, so you won't forget"

I used all my energy to make sure my face did not betray that my mind was racing with a million questions and scenarios. Today's pillow talk clearly wasn't going to be full of compliments on my flexibility from the night before. "Umm I'm gonna take a shower and head to work. I'll see you later" He picked up on the exit cue in my voice and I watched him pick up his clothes and get dressed. I waited till I heard the front door close before let my face do what it had been dying to do – throw a side eye at myself.

This slip up was enough to show me that the inevitable had happened. I'd developed feelings despite my clear-cut sex only relationship. This turning point had happened slower than in my past situationships, so I'd convinced myself that I was doing well. I had told myself that I was navigating like an expert in the easily murky waters of sex with no strings attached. I'd stocked up my ship with lies to feed my relationship starved crew like "he is too selfish to date" and "he looks at you funny when you sing along to Dreamgirls" and my favorite line "you don't need a ball and chain right now while climbing that career ladder" yet here I was- watching the storm on the horizon - listening to the thunder roar, knowing that the I can't turn back and that the only way was to get past this storm, was to go through it. Jenifer Lewis, Mama to Black Hollywood, confidently playing the fairy godmother in my mind hits the storm sirens and yells, "Honey - You gotta sit in your own feelings – all hands-on deck"

This feels like the hundredth time I've been through this. It's almost like instead of asking why I catch feelings; I should just ask myself "When?"

I wasn't expecting him to be excited at the prospect of me being pregnant – God knows I also wasn't excited at the thought of having a baby – but I knew I would make a wonderful mother. Was he doubting that? Why did it feel like every man I had been with, doubted this? They called me stubborn, did they not realize that that very same stubborn behavior would raise a child who knows their worth and can stand up to the world? They told me I wasn't nurturing enough - bringing up the feeling I felt at gatherings when I didn't feel the desire to pick up every baby on the premises or smile at every photo of a baby my coworkers shoved in my face. How can I prove to the world my ability to be a good mother without having children? And why do I need to prove that?

The clouds are beginning to turn grey. The thunder is getting louder. I am now in the heart of the storm.

"What if I did get pregnant? Why am I sleeping with a man who wouldn't be willing to deal with the consequences of sex? Was he just scared I was trapping him?"

I wanted him to trust that I was not the type of woman who would get pregnant and trap an unsuspecting man. But why did I care what he thought? Why was I so bothered by what he said about me. Lightning and thunder strike at the same time. I didn't care what that man thought... I was scared about what getting pregnant before marriage would say about me. Especially to a man whose main concern was which brand of morning after pill I'd take rather than the fact that letting him come in me was allowing him into a place that lead to me feeling vulnerable.

Lightning just struck my main sail. The storm is now in control. "Head for Safety" Fairy Godmother yells, "The storm is ready to chew this Situationship out"

My vulnerability needs to be my weapon to yield. It's not a weapon for no man to use against me. It's not society's opportunity to make me feel immoral. It's mine to use, to remind myself that I am worthy. I am beautiful.

We sail over troubled water to come out of the storm stronger. Do not to regret setting sail, we sail these oceans to find riches. And sometimes we are those riches. I've made many mistakes trying to find my sexual freedom... no voyage is regretted.

So many times, by friends and confidants, people tell you that sex only relationships will hurt your feelings – they're not wrong, and they aren't completely right. There have been fun ones where I walk away unscathed and some where I walk away hurt, but I refuse to let that be what stops me from exercising my sexual freedom, as and how I choose to.

Untitled

[Rita Mbonika]

we are also sexual beings

Why did you stand over my body looking like you were a lost pirate?

Babe, I am not an enchanted treasure

Magical yes but not the harmful kind

You seemed surprised to see a woman allow herself pleasure

We are sexual beings

 As in every wanted touch feels like thunder lightning striking our eager bodies

You need not be lost

Just come closer and listen to the rhythms of my body

 Neck thrown back means "yes do that"

Biting the lip means you are a turn on

It's a teamwork of two making this dream work

So don't be selfish and grab your mic to sing a solo song when we have signed a deal to be in this band together for life.

I want the voice with the eyes, the hand with the breathing on my neck the soft bites and grunts yes when a sound escapes my body

Like aaaaaaah

I want your grunt response

The tighter grip

The kiss & bite, the spank & sweat, the heat as we finish this marathon

We too are sexual beings

We Are Also Sexual Beings

[Munira Maria Makerow]

Afri-Femme

[Ruth Kanu]

HER PLACE IN THE WORLD

sub-theme

TO WOMEN AND GIRLS EVERYWHERE
(and to everyone else)
[Cláudia Cassoma]

I write to you with a brimming heart, although I doubt I'll be able to empty it all out in these few lines, I still would like to try. This is not a letter where I attempt to suppose your thoughts, theorize your feelings, nor do I desire to define your entire life merely because I too have a vagina. No! I do recognize and respect our differences. I am aware this is just one voice. This is simply a beginning.

For too long we've been fed all sorts of life ideals. They told us that our worth is in the way we decide to adorn our bodies; as in what we "choose" to do with it. So some of us, trusting there aren't other ways, decide to "utilize" what has long been called powerful-weapon not realizing that we're closing deals with merely a different breed of tyrants. Our entire lives we have render ourselves valuable, desirable, and most of all, useful, based solely on the size of our dresses. We have reduced our plates' weight in an attempt to feel better about ourselves when confronted by the reflection staring back at us in the mirror. We let ourselves be defined in relation to others and not as complete beings on our own. We let ourselves be defined! We dismissed from our minds the beautiful fact that we can be whatever floats our boat. We absorb the misleading concept that there's only one truth we all have to live by for the sole reason of not being born with a pointy organ of copulation. And when we fail to live up to those unrealistic expectations, we begin to hate ourselves.

I know I have hated myself before. I've hated myself for all reasons imaginable and even those that aren't. The first time I hated myself was when I understood that I was a girl. Not because I wanted to be something else, rather because I fully grasped the anguish of it all. I don't blame anybody. And those that I could perhaps rightfully blame didn't know any better, so I understand. I understand why I took the blame for simply defending myself against that testosterone-filled teenager which was only doing things he learned made him human. I understand why I made myself blind when in the presence of boys, and covered myself up so that they didn't feel the urge to sin. I hated myself for accepting such things as my truths for as long as I did, but I understand. I understand why she insisted on telling me that I would be a better woman for it and for teaching me to look at the short-skirt-bearing-bodies as products of the devil. When I understood what I wanted to be, I already hated myself too much. This was only because it hit me that by being care-full I was automatically the "flower-kind." Not even the good kind: the kind that could be both docile and poisonous; the kind that could live through both winter and spring; the kind that could serve for both valentine's day and funerals; the kind that could ultimately be absolute within its many variations.

Some of us have also heard that reproducing is the essence of our life cycle, and we shall all aspire to it. We have been told that we are nothing more than biology. Please understand: I only wish this wasn't the definition. On the other hand, distastefully, some of you have been robbed of your chemistry. Some early in life, others a bit later; eventually, you were all made senseless. Let me repeat, I do not wish to speculate on how you feel about your own mother and grandmother's heritage. With that in mind, I'd like you to know that nothing would make me happier than hearing from you; than having you as a gateway to an understanding. I've heard things that were made your truth, but rather than presume let me ask you: Is this what you wanted? Is this what came from the peace of your own thoughts? Is this actually your truth?—If yes, I apologize for sounding too moralistic. But, if not, please know you'll forever have my ready-ears and open-mind.

They've put us in categories like we are products to sell; and blindly, we have accepted all of it. Furthermore, because our trusted sources were equally taught limiting lessons, despite their wearing efforts, they'd never able to pass on anything too contrasting.

When one has successfully robbed a human the ability to think and to question, they have, by all odds, ended a life. I'm glad we started thinking just in time.

This letter is to you. You, that is still lost in the many conflicting ideals perhaps unhealthy and sometimes slaying that the world puts upon us. You, that is still trying to figure out what to be on your own while all of those things are being imposed. You, that is living a life of hatred towards your own self. You, that desires to stop. I said in the beginning, this is not a selfish endeavor to suppose your thoughts, theorize your feelings, or to define your life. Without being deceptive, I am absolutely eager to know that you are all-right. I am eager to know that you have found your voice, your very own beginning.

This is to women and girls everywhere, and for everyone else. To those who have rose to a different truth; one that entails leveled self-esteem, self-confidence, self-reliance, self-fulfillment, and a high dose of equality.

This letter is to you, momma. It is my way of thanking you for always offering yourself as an example; for showing me how strength looks like and what we are able to do once we believe. I appreciate you!

This is to you too, baby sister, Nassoma. It's my attempt to obviate all possible reasons for you to ever hate yourself like I once did, though we must still share this world and experience some of the same things.

I no longer hope, I fight.

Untitled

Veronique Moore

Her place in the world.

Objects, a mere definition.

Body sizes a label of beauty

Religion a home of abuse and oppression.

Society a dress not for all sizes

Standards unrealistic to all

A woman, a thing treated like an object.

Do not raise your voice even when the emotions rage, it's not ladylike.

Respect men, unfortunately, it's not your duty to protect yourself from the hungry and lustful

Feminism and independence will curve you

unmarried and despised by society

Be decent but they will rip you apart if they desire to

Keep your legs closed but he can unzip his pants whenever he pleases

Woman have no sexual freedom

A truth never preached woman have a place in this world

A voice that never conveys women are more than just objects

A book never read a woman is more than just standards

Opportunities never given woman can change the world

Because they are the world.

Her Place

[Rutendo.S. Maturure]

[Eugenia Shaw]

Finding Anchor

Standing at the water's edge, looking out at this calm beautiful scene, I know I have done the right thing. I have left my old world behind, to pursue fulfilment, and possibly gain some enlightenment. As I think of what I've left behind, my heart races, my palms sweat and all my fears come rushing back. The pain I have left behind and my own heartache are too much to bear. I walk towards the water...

I get to the edge. The cool water hits my toes and flows over my feet. The chill shocks me. I take a step back, and then realise I am running away again. So I take two steps forward and stand my ground.

Now is the perfect time to practise being in the moment. I close my eyes and sense my environment. The breeze is cool but damp. It smells fresh, clean. The water is almost cold, due to the time of day. It's just 6am and the sun is only casting its first rays of light across the sky. There is no heat in them, only beautiful colour streaking across the sky. The water flows across my feet. I can feel the soft mud of the river bed squelch between my toes. It brings back childhood memories. As the water ebbs and flows over my feet, the wind gently kisses my exposed skin and catches my gauze-like dress. I surrender to their harmony and let my fears and anxiety flow away with them, leaving only hopefulness and determination.

The sound of a bird squawking shatters my reprieve. I open my eyes, the sun is a little warmer, the daylight a little brighter.

"How long have I been standing here?"

I turn and make my way to my room, the room that will be home, for some time now.

Time to get ready for my new job as a music teacher, in the international school, in Brunei. I find my best, formal looking, linen outfit, for my first day. After showering and putting on some light make-up, I undo my two strand twists and style my afro curls. Sandals on, I head out the door. The ten minute walk helps to prepare me for what's ahead and take in my surroundings. The school is well kept, and the staffroom is the best I have seen so far, even including the private schools in Hawaii!

After the tour and introductions, the headmistress shows me to my class, and shaking my hand says, "Welcome to the team Miss Geba. You are going to fit right in."
I take it all in, and know that she is right. A fresh start. A second chance. My healing is sure. In the process of searching for a new focus, I now realise, "All that matters is, what I think and believe, as my belief will drive my achievement."
Now, I concentrate on giving the best to my students.

[f.gabdon]
Diluted

2,
Sometimes,
there is more English in me
than I can stand;

some days I cannot find
all of my mother tongue
and I cringe,

how polluted my mouth
has become,
how diluted my identity.

[we betray our mother tongues,
for the languages
of nations
that will never
fully accept us.

We let the strangeness
infest our mouths
until we forget
how to accommodate
our original tongues]

- Diluted

[Abigail Adigun]

dear night sky who never held my hand

can you hear the desperate prayers that race against my mother's
tears and dance with the soul of my grandfather,
three lines scarred into each cheek to remind him of a lost tribe?
what made you despise me so much that you ripped away
my kin who I never met, but you
got to hear their whispers of hope in the tear stained grass?
did you know I share their names, I share their lives?
why is it that anytime I try to peer into your,
unfocused, searching orbs, I see her?

the woman I once was, and the woman I never got to be.

[Sepopo]

I, am

Female!
What are the names that have been given to you?
The mother? The nurturer?
The assistant or secretary?
A whore, a slut?
How are you viewed?
With respect and pride?
Ignorance and disdain?
How hard you work; how little you receive.
Your body is not your own – then why is it 'your?'
Seems that they've made you theirs,
how dare they.
Females should no—   no.
She is n—   no.
Why did she w—   no.
I, the female, am my own before others
I own me – my body, my intellect, my pride, my success,
my Worth.
I am.
My sex is my sex – it is the body I inhabit – I am not embodied by it.
I accomplish. I fail. I struggle. I remain.
That is I – that is not my sex.
I AM.

I will not blame the biological clock
Which led to the "waste" of my eggs
Or the bushes and exile scuffles
Maybe, the mob rape and the mock that ensued

The war and genocide in my land?
Certainly! These I will blame
For they took the joy out of the hatching
The hacking of babies closed it off

The fizzled cockerels in my land destroyed me!
They inserted thorns and gun muzzles
They took bates on whose turn it was
Now they sing on how liberated I am!

Yet!! Am blamed for the wastage of my years
Nobody sees effects of the roosters
One after another they bring "Marek's disease" among my people

I will not go broody until the blood stops flowing in my land
I refuse brooding for mass graves
Let the biological clock tick on and on to the last egg
Twenty-five years after the genocide
I stare at the last egg that has survived

"To brood or not to brood"
Suddenly!! It is no longer the concern on my mind
As the next chick falls from the now familiar disease
I wait not for the last egg to drop but the last breath to cease

Since you failed to stop the vicious cycle of hatred in my land
Yet you fueled revenge covered in so many words
I will not blame the biological clock
I will not blame the tray I kept my eggs in
I will blame YOU for my death

I will not blame the biological clock

[Harriet Mimi Uwineza]

[Kundai Muringi]
Disambiguation

Black is what I was given
Black is what I will give
Black is my screaming
Black is my silence
Black is only what you see
Black is what you don't see
Black is what you are tired of hearing
Black is what you have not heard
Black left me in a crowd
Black is why I'm alone
Black is my anger within
Black is my soul's peace
Black is why you are afraid
Black is why I'm afraid
Black is my shallowness
Black is my depth
Black is what I'm telling you
Black is not what you tell me
Black is not what you think it is
Black is the unknown
Black is my life
Black is my death.

[Khanysa Mabyeka]

A Quem Pertencem As Minhas Mamas?

Depois dos meus partos, o meu relacionamento com as minhas mamas mudou de formas inesperadas. Consequentemente, também mudou a forma como as vejo, como as sinto e como as desfruto. Mas também, a forma como a minha família nuclear (e as vezes a sociedade) se relaciona com as minhas mamas é nova e me dá a sensação as vezes de que as minhas mamas já não me pertencem e passaram a ser colectivas.

"A bebé está a chorar, dá-lhe lá a mama dela"

As expressões que usamos estão carregadíssimas de valor e, algumas das expressões que se usam com relação às mulheres que têm crianças parecem converter-nos em instrumentos. Veículos para gerar, parir e nutrir as crianças. Algumas expressões só as ouvi pela primeira vez depois de ter tido a minha filha. Nas primeiras vezes que me disseram 'a bebé está a chorar, dá-lhe a mama dela!', senti-me confusa. Abri a minha camisa para dar-lhe de mamar, sentindo-me um pouco perdida ao tentar decifrar a frase que acabava de ouvir. A final as mamas não eram minhas? Quando é que as tinha perdido? Só umas semanas depois é que consegui reagir e cada vez que alguém repetia aquela frase eu comecei a dizer 'desculpe mas estas mamas são minhas, e eu permito que a minha bebé as utiliza para chegar ao leite que ela precisa'. E claro, recebia de volta olhares tão confusos como os meus quando descobri que a sociedade tentava roubar-me as mamas.

Sinto que preciso lembrar a sociedade que as minhas mamas são minhas. Eu escolhi amamentar (poderia legitimamente ter escolhido diferente) mas as mamas continuam sendo minhas. Eu empresto as minhas mamas às minhas crianças para elas poderem chegar ao leite que o meu corpo produz para elas. Eu poderia também ter optado por bombear o leite e alimentar-lhes através do biberão. Mas gosto do contacto físico e da conexão que estabelecemos no processo de amamentar – não lhes empresto a minha mama de forma incondicional não, eu também sinto prazer nesse acto, é uma troca. E, quando já não era necessário para a minha filha nem prazenteiro para mim, iniciei a desmamar-lhe e continuei a amamentar apenas ao meu filho, que era mais pequeno.

Essa dança não acaba, as pessoas - familiares, amig@s, colegas de trabalho, têm sempre algo a dizer em relação às minhas mamas. Normalmente para imporem a visão delas de como eu as deveria utilizar. Ouvi coisas como:

✓ Não é para parares de amamentar agora

✓ Pelo menos amamenta durante 1 ano, é bom para o bebé

✓ Ainda estás a amamentar, não chega?

✓ Como consegues amamentar uma criança que já tem dentes?

✓ Não devias amamentar ao mesmo tempo duas crianças que não são gémeas, não é bom para as crianças ou porque a mais velha vai acabar o leite do mais novo ou ainda, porque vai estragar o leite

✓ Essa criança já é grande, ainda precisa de mama?

✓ Se amamentares por muito tempo as tuas mamas vão cair

Senhoras e senhores, permitam-me lembrar-vos uma vez mais que as minhas mamas são minhas e, não me dêem recomendações não solicitadas sobre elas, por favor!

Tocar....beijar....maminha

Mesmo quando não é amamentando, as minhas mamas parecem ter uma função calmante e hipnotizante. A minha filha, a Siyanda já não mama mas quando está cansada, gosta de adormecer a tocar os meus mamilos. Algumas vezes os meus mamilos parecem ser a droga que ela precisa para fechar os olhos e inclusive se põem agressiva quando não consegue chegar à eles, porque tenho uma roupa que não lhe facilita o acesso ou porque haja qualquer coisa à bloquear o acesso às mamas. O meu filho, o Dhambo ainda mama e também gosta de tocar e acariciar o mamilo que se encontra livre enquanto ele mama. Muitas vezes tenho que gerir as brigas entre ambas porque as mãozinhas delas cruzam-se na mama que não está na boca do Dhambo. Essas brigas as vezes são tão intensas que provocam faísca e acabamos precisando de uns minutos para todo mundo se acalmar.

As minhas crianças sentem uma atração tanta pelas minhas mamas que já não posso andar nua pela casa. E não é porque elas agora abanam mais do que abanavam antes, mas porque as minhas crianças literalmente me assediam. Quando a Siyanda vê as mamas expostas fica agitada – uma mistura de felicidade e nervosismo. As vezes repete gritando 'maminha, maminha', noutras vezes pede para tocar 'um bocadinho', indicando o tamanho esticando os dedos indicador e polegar. Mas quase sempre pede para beijar as mamas, 'mamã, beijo maminha; beijo mamã!' e persegue-me pela casa.

Quando me apetece, deixo ela beijar algum ponto da mama o que normalmente resultam em gritos de excitação ou em gargalhadas. O melhor prémio para ela é beijar os mamilos e tenta de vez em quando, quando acha que estou distraída chupar um mamilo. Está claro que se dependesse dela, ela ainda estaria a mamar.

Quando o Dhambo vê as mamas, ele sorri amplamente e os olhos dele brilham, segue-me fazendo um som como se estivesse a aquecer o motor de uma mota. Praticamente não me posso sentar, se não ele ataca logo as mamas. Parece ser que de momento, sobretudo se estiver com as minhas crianças, não poderei voltar a fazer top-less nas praias.

O toque no sexo

Na relação íntima com o meu namorado, o papel das minhas mamas também mudou. Os seios, incluindo os mamilos sempre foram áreas erógenas para mim, sempre desfrutei de carícias nessa área no geral e durante o sexo. Mas, no primeiro ano depois do nascimento da Siyanda essa área se converteu em zona altamente proibida. As minhas mamas e mamilos tinham ficado tão sensíveis (fisicamente e mentalmente) que os dedos do meu namorado não podiam chegar perto nem para afugentar um mosquito. Qualquer toque dele nos seios, irritava-me bastante. Depois do nascimento da Siyanda, fiquei com umas mamas gigantes, brilhantes, atraentes e o meu namorado que como a filha e o filho se sentia hipnotizado por elas, queria tocar, chupar, beijar e... teve que se contentar com algumas poucas ocasiões em que se calhar eu estava suficientemente relaxada e lhe deixava chegar perto das mamas. Nós nunca conversamos profundamente sobre o que terá acontecido e, com o tempo essa irritação foi passando e voltei a ter vontade de desfrutar das carícias às mamas.

Mas nessa altura, surgiu outra situação. Não sei se por preconceitos relacionados com o sexo, me parecia muito estranho 'utilizar' as mamas para ter prazer sexual e umas horas depois amamentar com as mesmas mamas. As mãos durante o sexo movem-se livremente e, me preocupava também que acabassem lá fluidos que depois fossem parar na boca d@s bebés. Então, durante um tempo, mesmo desejando o toque, eu não nos permiti desfrutar desse prazer.

Ainda me pergunto porquê. Será que no meu subconsciente eu via o sexo como algo sujo? O tema dos fluidos não deveria ser um problema porque poderia lavar as mamas antes de amamentar. Porque será que me dava impressão? E qual era o problema se o meu namorado chupasse os meus mamilos e depois as crianças mamassem? As vezes eles e elas partilham talheres, beijam-se na boca, transferem comida da boca de uns para outros/as. Qual seria a diferença?

Na verdade, esta é uma das áreas que tenho menos resolvida. Ainda não estou totalmente confortável com as minhas mamas no que concerne ao prazer sexual. Penso que ainda devo eliminar alguns preconceitos que rondam no meu subconsciente.

E por fim...

A maneira como actualmente me relaciono com e vejo as minhas mamas, e ao mesmo tempo as expectativas que a minha família e sociedade têm das minhas mamas, tem sido um descobrimento interessante, as vezes produzindo simplesmente curiosidade e noutras alguma frustração. E ainda nem estamos a conversar sobre as expectativas em relação à estética! O que está claro para mim, e se calhar algumas de vocês se identifiquem com a minha experiência, é que se não fico atenta, as minhas mamas podem facilmente pertencer à todo mundo menos a mim. E, que para recuperar e/ou manter a propriedade delas, necessito passar por um processo de reflexão e de aumento do meu auto-conhecimento e da minha consciência. Creio que preciso ainda superar crenças limitadoras sobre coisas como a função das mamas, ou o desfrute do sexo e da maternidade sem limites.

Traz o segredo da vida
Em sua humilde entranha
Menina, Mulher Africana

Em cena é coadjuvante, a fulana
Mas não desiste, força tamanha
E no meio a tanta lágrima, é uma querida

Ela não quer ser mais
Quer simplesmente ser
Para que possamos ser iguais
Mas sem deixar de ser, mulher

Deixar de ser caça, olhar no caçador
Perdoar, e esquecer toda dor
Para que a Menina, Mulher Africana
Se deite no rio e acorde humana

Soneto Da Menina, Mulher Africana

[Lúcia Morais]

Untitled

[Munira Maria Makerow]

[Patricia Musebah]

Call me zena femme .AM A WOMAN.

A fierce force fueled with fusions of futuristic goals.
I am preposessing ,beautiful ,alluring and yes I am strong .
Indoni yamanzi ,ngirozi ,an angel .You can feel my
presence but you may not see me ,society has rendered you lack of
sight ,the cloth of culture and beliefs blindfolds your eyes.
I am here ,my vibrant moves and echo of my voice of change will
boom across your loud federation of noisy norms and "expectations
of a woman."

I am golden .Dear father do not auction me off to the rich
men that drink scotch stronger than them .I am not an alleviation of
poverty ,I am a limited edition published by a creator glazed with
precise accordance to detail. Read between the lines in my palms and
you will understand I can carry the weight of a home.

I hear you say I am menstruating and won't make it to the
march .I loose negative energy in my blood five days in twenty eight
and I am here .My sanitation is as important as the World peace
meeting ,sit down and discuss it! The pulse of my veins radiates
feminism ,I have engulfed gender based violence and breathed out
flames of activism .Talk about me ,I am a woman I am here!

I am running out of time ,the clock of the world strikes stop
before I hand over this button stick.They will change the law and
shut me out like the books of archaic odysseys, But like pages of
history I will be reborn and remembered.

Does my voice belittle yours? My beauty terrorizes your
peace? My eyes pierce your soul ,does my intelligence menace yours??

My dress is vulgur?Will you let me know what it is about me that threatens the world.

My figure may be too thick,too small,too jelly or too thin but here z my womb. A five star hotel to a kicking fetus, state of the art accommodation to life, It's a nine month lease marked with meticulous touch ,take it I give to you .

I am a cousin to mother earth ,we hold the keys to the array of perplexities in the civic world yet ignored and wasted .I am In shackles of religion ,chained by society.

Lift up your countenance and see how parts of the continent have hacked my horizon ,they have agreed to deprive me of an education and blur my abilities. Iam illiterate ,irrelevant and absolute in the chambers of leadership .Set me free and luminate these brains ,see ..be careful it's a mosaic of intelligence with a halo too bright it may blind you .

I am a dome of coloured glass, a reflection of sophistication and beam of hope .Im phenomenal ndakakosha .

I am not crying ,my eyes are salty.its a leak in the technical aspects of my vulnerable body .streams of saline emotions down my blushed cheeks to drown a disgusting opinion about me .These mood swings are not an art I have mastered .I simply adopt the act of swinging from mother- to daughter _to daughter in law -to sister all in one episode of " perfect woman" in the cinema of an African home .

I am here ,I bear news ,someone sealed my fate declared me a punching bag in the rings of our kitchen.

I wear a thick mask to work . Look beyond this foundation cream ,here lies scars of my untold story of the shambles I call marriage . Look beyond this mascara ,here lies the film of tears from a horrific night when an uncle told me it was ok he was simply showing me how to be a woman .look under this burgundy lipstick ,here is the full lips of a self spoken woman !

I am a female miracle ,I cook ,I clean ,I nurture all at once, But above all I dream ,Take these rare stones ,a product of my dreams ,sharpen them and lay a foundation ,the anchor of development ..Let them know .a female did it ..So call me Kostba Zena .A PRECIOUS WOMAN .

[Veronique Moore]
A Healing Break

Stinging eyes,
Ringing ears,

I'll let the world adsorb my tears.

Voice shaking with hands quaking
I'll resist the urge of my body breaking.

Take a breath,
One,
Two,
Three,

Never will this world put a stop to me

[Liko]

The Struggle Of Women

Women in society are fighting for respect just different oppressions
Men sit down and tell us what we should and expect a standing
ovation
I'm tired of the "a women should be" narrative I'm running out of
patience
I don't have to prove myself because I'm the queen of the nation
I bear the children and every month I have to deal with painful
menstruation
But every time I walk these streets, I have to deal with a whole lot of
discrimination
Why go through all these trials and tribulations
Just to show these men that you are not part of the "shameless"
Because best believe they'll still regard you as nothing but the same
mess

I'm trying to stay afloat

From these oppressive standards and norms

Disobey them and be ready to be called a whore

Man, I feel so sorry for my little sisters sitting at home

Sometimes I just sit back pray to God and hope

That one day, they don't ask me what is it that they did wrong

Because I don't want to have to say, you were born a woman that's just how these things go

I don't want to have to say get with the program and stop with your damn ego

Some of these men will just never consider us as equals

I don't have it in me anymore to fight with the devil's demons

Please respect me as a woman or be gone

Don't tell me that my womanhood is attained when my hymen is broken

Because I live in a society where I'm treated lesser of a human, just because I was born a woman

[Ana Mafalda Gonçalves Dias]
Eu Fico Onde Quiser

Fizeram-me acreditar que meu lugar era na cozinha
Enrolada a um avental conversando com as panelas
Fizeram-me a acreditar que a minha voz não teria eco
Que eu falaria, mas ninguém escutaria.
Mediam os meus sonhos com a palma da mão
Cortavam-me as assas sempre que sonhasse alto
Enfeitava-me de rosas e ensinavam-me a sorrir,
Ensinavam-me a estar linda e cheirosa e pronta para servir
Mesmo que eu não quisesse!
Quando agredida ensinavam-me suportar
A me calar e obedecer, que era preciso ser sempre forte
Mas não me ensinaram, podia ficar onde eu quisesse
Que era bravura, fortaleza e nem o escuro me camuflaria
Que poderia ter o mundo em minhas mãos
Que ficaria na cozinha, no escritório até presidência
Não me ensinaram que não podia me calar perante aos abusos
Isso Nunca me ensinavam
Estavam preocupados em inventar leis
Mas hoje me divorcio de todas as leis e de todas teorias
O mundo me espera
E eu fico onde eu quiser.

Haverá o dia
Em que eu serei alegria
Uma bela melodia

Não o som do batuque aflito
Que tenta ser ouvido em mais um grito
De liberdade, o verdadeiro mito

Até lá uma secular luta
Liberdade sexual sem ser puta
Provar que não serve só para o fogão
Enquanto por ter um utéro, recebe um não

Acredito sim, nesse dia
Em que não serei cor
Ou um ser inferior
Ao som da barimba serei poesia

Soneto In Melodia

[Lúcia Morais]

[Patricia Musebah]
I Am Me

I am not the color of my hair ,I am not the inches of my weave .. I am a precious woman ..I am me ..A star like no other

I am not my bra size .I am not the width of my hips ,..I am a stunning woman ..I am me ..A star like no other

I am not the shade of my skin, i am not the shape of my breasts.. I am a n extra ordinary woman ..I am me ,a star like no other

I am not the weight of my sexy body ..i am not the size of my belly .I am a phenomenal woman ..i am me a star like no other

I am God's handwriting,I am sassy , beautiful as i am ,i am a reflection of my soul's energy
I am phenomenal ,a limited edition ,a rose busking in the summer sun

I am full of life ..from the roots of my crown all the way to the sole of my heels

From the smooth ,sweet caramel curl of my lips ,all the way to the hidden clues of resilience in my spine
From the jewels in my eyes to the fruits in the orchard of my womb ...I am me ..a star like no other
I do not need validation to rock this look ,today im in this dress tomorrow i am in that yellow suit

Every color of my closet sings back up in the choir of my mood .my lipstick shade may lift my spirit
But it will not define me for I am me ..a star like no other

In my sandals,heels and sneakers i walk on gold.
My identity is not found in the names you call me like skinny? fat ? ,slender ? ..yellow bone?
Waive from sticking these tags on me
I could be , ,Panashe ,Ruvimbo, Nella ,Queen or Rudo .. ..Try those
I raise my head up high ...lifting this countenance to erase that gloom off my face ..i am bathed in honor.

When you see me behind a beautiful mask of make up .. do not judge me ..i have million reasons to .. non of which attract provocative insinuations ..I am me ..a star like no other

My body is a bar code of the holy sacrament of woman hood .. a pool of diversity ..
My kind radiates variety ..I come in different shapes ,shade and size .

An inception of diamonds in the rough '.I am flawlessly imperfect .. A beautiful chaos because i am me ..no other me .. i am phenomenal ..a star like no other

In a galaxy of many gems .... call me by own name .. ME
...#the voice of one woman for many

[Stella Oduro]
Am I Worth It, Mama?

I once asked mama if I am worth it?

Because just like mama all of my beauty has be misconstrued and contoured to look foreign

Just like mama, I am no longer perceived as the beginning of all things beautiful

Rather I am broken

You see, she welcomed them when they entered her

Rather than being happy and return her warm embrace with love,

They took and took everything that made mama valuable from her

They left mama in ruins in her demise so, they thought I asked mama if I am worth it?

As she lowers her eyes A smile formed on her face

Her high cheek bones rise up as her eyes flick with the warmth of the sun And she asks whose child are you?

Aren't you the child of a Mother who has endured thousands of insults and bigotry?

Have survive countless of ridicules And continues to be seen as nothing but war torn, impoverished, and uneducated

They consider my silence and my humility as my undoing my child My child

They came for my secrets

Only to take away all that they thought made me precious

Then they said I am a deep forest that can only be tamed

So, I asked mama why didn't you fight?

She asked, how can a mother fight her child?

They left me in their journey of discovery

Only to return to me as strangers in their mothers' land
So, you asked me, are you worth it?
You, my child, is one of a kind
Your skin absorbs the rays of the sun
Your hair defies gravity
When you speak my love, they listen
You are a child of mama
The one filled with all the rare minerals of the world
I have clothed you with gold and crowned you with diamonds
You are worth it because I have adorned you with the best things on
earth
My precious asset is you not the gems they took
Because you and your descendants will
Embody my strength
Speak my truth
Ratify my story
You are the light and path to the truth hidden beneath all of the
facade I was forced to embody You asked if you are worthy?
You Are Worth It My Child.
Every bit of it.

[Hazvineyi Zinyowa]

My African Story

I'm African!

I have me some African blood flowing in my bones! Guess that explains my strength both physically and emotionally, my ability to spring back up from what ever knocks me down after all my ancestors and their ancestors lived through slave trade and colonialism and still came out strong. Guess that's what it means to be born of royalty.

I was born in Africa! Guess I have that to blame for my insatiable love for African Cuisine and by that, I mean my mother's cooking. I mean Africa is so damn attractive and looks scrumptious, the white colonialist just had to have a taste! I'm that dope huh!

Africa was born in me! Guess that explains my adventurous, spontaneity and love for all that's daring and deadly. I'm rich both in spirit, culture, body and soul. And no! this is not about monetary wealth, I'm rich in my community relations, the connection I feel with the communities I come from. I embrace the spirit of humanism, that brings tears to my eyes every time I see my fellow melanin kings and queens being treated as less of a human being. I acknowledge the importance and significance of communism, what the Tanzanians called 'ujamaa', what the South Africans termed 'ubuntu'. That philosophy keeps me in check and is the basis of human respect and in my point of view that is the African version of human rights! Debatable I know but allow me to have this win after all this is My African Story.

I have this brown, sparkly, soft, chocolate layer of beauty, most people call in melanin but for me that is just beauty! Guess that explains why I glow in the sun, why it looks like the sun kissed me, imagine being kissed by the sun, hot as it is, it still finds me hotter!! Yeah melanin!

I have hair that turns curly just by a spritz of water! Guess that is just one of the perks of being born into royalty.
Being African is beauty personified. Beauty is melanin. Beauty is African.

Being born African comes with strength, perseverance, intelligence, beauty, attractiveness and personally I think AFRICANS GET THINGS DONE!!

I`m African with an African native language name. I'm an African child, call me Melanin Queen.I`m African and my Zimbabwean family calls me Hazvineyi and I`m black and I`m proud!!!

[f.gabdon]
What I know of war

What I know of war
is written on my mother's body.
I run my fingers over
the skin of her legs -
like secrets in Braille,
the wounds,
they speak to me.

- What I know of war

Being feminist is not defined by how much of a man I can be
Being feminist is the level of pride I take in being a woman,
Without having to spell out significance
Uncage me,
I belong with the birds in the sky
Don't hold my tongue or tie me down
Allow me to grow
Allow me to glow
Allow me to sing songs that ease my heart
I want to reach for things far beyond.

Firm-Inist

[Thandokuhle Sibanda]

[Joselyne The Poetess]

Pretty

"Pretty hurts" Beyonce once said
My Mama used to say that am pretty
She called me the goddess of beauty
She said I was sweeter than honey
My mind was that I have already won it
I was shawty in the house!

Looking back in the mirror
I saw the scars
A dark face with rashes
I knew that I looked like trash
I had to put a rush
For the sake of getting my crush!

Tell me, what's the difference between me and them?
We breathe the same air
We eat the same food
We drink the same water
We walk the same roads
Weren't we even born the same way?

But the word never stopped judging!
They are skinny, you are fat
They are tall, you are short
They are brown, you are black
They are rich, you are poor
They are sexy, you are vulgar

But the funniest thing is, they can be anything
But will never be your future
They can have all the wishes you adore
But can never determine your abilities
Not even your multifunctionality
Not determining your identity! Never!

The next day you look in the mirror
See the shining queen with a plan
A rising beauty no one can never harm
A future mother of the nation who can rise
A warrior who can win irrespective of the ban
A woman who deserves a real man!

She cried all night
Praying for the light to shine
Hoping for the day to come
wishing for the birds to fry
Waiting for someone to reveal
Until she couldn't wait any longer!
She took her life for it!

Those who saw her interpreted happiness
Willing to see her smile every day
Thinking she lived the best in all
Little did they know the sorrow
The anger she kept in herself
A brave heart torn into pieces
Waiting was hard! She took her life for it!

They called her the queen of beauty
A naturally created idyllic princess
A girl who deserved everything
Even if she would have nothing
Their eyes were too blinded to see
Their hearts were unable to feel
All her pain! She took her life for it!

She lives, has lived and will always live
She is a lady, a sister or maybe a mother
She is standing still-alone somewhere
People will never see or hear her
But we rise to strengthen the weakened
To be the voice of the inaudible ones
She will never think of taking her life for it!

She Took Her Life For It

[Joselyne The Poetess]

[Unique Bunny]
She is a Girl

I can't believe my body is sheltering a life
There is so much I want to say after knowing that she is a girl.
Not only my eyes will be full of tears,
but my heart will be full of Joy.
I want to look her in the eyes with so much innocence,
And whisper words that will keep her calm

I want her to understand her worth and value
I want her to understand how much she is appreciated
I want her to feel, love, and care for her body
I want her to own her body and never let a body define her
I want her to grow up eating with no guilty

Working on her body the way her mind wants
 not the society
I want her to be the boss of her body
 not the man outside
I want her to have a choice on her body
not her girlfriends, media, culture, religion, not even me.

I will whisper you are strong, determined, courageous, exuberant,
More often in the morning and in the goodbye's night.
I will embrace her beauty and celebrate her soul

She will grow believing in her energy than her beauty
She will grow to value her character than her thighs
She will grow to look with the soul lens than appearance lens
She will grow fighting for her small sisters and brother's life
She will stand firm in the world that forces her to lose her identity.

She will have her head high focused on challenging the status quo
She will have her head high untwining chains of injustice and inequality
She will have her head high working with men who were raised in patriarchy.

She will grow and embrace her beauty within her terms
not the so-called beauty Standards.
She will fight for other girls, be friends with her daughters,
and encourage her fellow girls' coworkers
She will be friends with a girl that they share man crush
She will value men and understand their emotions
She will live God's way

If she is a girl, she will be the light!

[Ladunni Peace]

Let Her.

My ears are bored
And it is heart shattering
For mouths to say her place is in his kitchen only
Don't you think it's mean to utter such?
Her place is in the kitchen
Yes! But not only in the kitchen

To state the place of a woman is simply an exciting case
Because she fills several special spaces
Her place is in her wisdom
She saves your farthing
Her place is deep rooted in the heart
She fills it with joy
Her place is in the mouth muscle
She flexes it with love to put a smile on your face
And makes you forget your sorrow
Her place is in the fertility of her womb
She birth giant kings and emperors
Her place is in her strength and courage
She never give up despite dilema

She is a darling daughter
She is a soothing sister
She is a marvelous mother
The heiress of her own home
The queen of her State

The empress of her country
Just like the river goddess
So should she be worshipped
Like a winning warrior so should she be praised
Her emotions is not a pet to toy with
Neither is she a slave to be suppressed
Her consent could be sought
Never should she be forced

But just like the panic of growing older grasps her
So does the fear of her place been taken
And the outcome of her vacant place too
Whenever she takes in
She gives a loud whisper to the Supreme
"That my seed will not be treated like me"

How long will he who does not fit in continue to take the place of
she who stands out?
She wets her pillow with silent cry
When will she take her rightful place?
When will she be crowned the queen that she is?
When will heads acknowledge it's her place ?
When will she be known and seen as the royal one that she is?
When will she be clothed in purple?
She desires to know
In the world she has her place
Let her show her face
Give her the chance
Let her fill up the space.

Untitled

[Rita Mbonika]

Sky may be the limit for some
But God guided me to my real home

No more fight against my scars
Through my healing process
I touched more than a million stars

And i want nothing to interrupt my thoughts
Patience was my guidance all along
So there's still a lot to be done.

Untitled

[Sephora Antaya]

When I was little, I used to hide behind my parents and use them as a shield. Looking back now, they were my first forms of personified identity. My mom was my first identification of beauty because whenever she smiled and laughed at my crazy dance moves, my heart would swell up and I knew that meant love. At times, I would dance just so that I could see my mom smile and laugh because to me it was the most wonderful sight ever. My father was my first identification of what African was, or rather, what it meant to be a strong African-American citizen. You see, I am what most people would refer to as first generation. My parents were born in Nigeria and came to America to give my siblings and I a fighting chance at survival. For this reason, when I was born in America, I was born a citizen, but I would forever have African identity markers ingrained in my DNA that the American national anthem could never wash away.

For instance, my lovely mother gifted me with her unique gap, which in my culture is a symbol of beauty. However, growing up in America my gap was used against me, and I would get relentlessly villainized for the same things that they praised me for back in my homeland. Similarly, my parents' beautiful accent that would crescendo down a flight of stairs when I was caught misbehaving would also get ingrained in my mind. I would later find this out in school when my English teacher would make a remark about my incorrect pronunciation. To her surprise, she could not believe that I was born in America because of my "accent". Still, the gaze at my internal battles were much more pleasant than the ones that centered around my external battles.

These included, unwanted advances from older men who for some reason identified my body as older than what it was. Or my male counterparts in school that loved to make remarks about my lips or my behind, without knowing the traumatic history of African women that have constantly dealt with objectification of all sorts by the hands of foreigners invading their countries. These comments were much more unpleasant to deal with, but what has ultimately shaped my identity the most as an African woman. For instance, the same insults that people would try to throw at me to lower my self-confidence, would ultimately be used to remind me who I was as an African woman, and to never forget where I come from. In the end, I had to grab unto my identity markers at a young age if I was going to survive the turbulent currents of America and find my place in the world. In the beginning, I used to hide behind my parents and wrap myself in their identity, but that is no longer the case. Now, I am proud to say that I am a Nigerian woman, and my people will always bleed green and white.

Claiming Your Identity
[Ifeoma Onwuka]

[Ruth Kanu]
African Woman

I am an African woman!
I have gone through a process
And I came out better
Gold passes through fire
And becomes lustre
Knife strikes against something hard
And it becomes sharper.

I am an African. Woman!
I have been down
Yet I have risen
I have passed through fire
Yet came out purer
Rubbed against something strong
And now sharper
I am better than before.

I am an African woman
I am bold, strong and beautiful
I climbed the highest peak
And conquered Everest
I am black and courageou
I invest in humanity
And touch lives!

[Chelsy G. Maumbe]

1st Street Ave. Vendor

A withering lily
Suffering from all manner of tired.
One, a dreadful need for sleep,
A chance to unburden the weight
of her world from her shoulders,
The snort dancing on their tiny
faces' a reminder of the
looming winter.
Another, a dire need for peace,
Some respite from playing hide
And seek with the law,
In alleyways to escape the itchy
Gas and burning fluids-
They've yet again trampled on her livelihood.

[Tshepo Moyo]
She

She
She tastes of ash.
Of burning.
Of the kind of dying that rots the soul.
She tastes of nothing.
Of void.
Of the kind of heaviness that drowns the soul.
She tastes of sour.
Of bitterness.
Of the kind of stings that paralyze a soul.
She tastes of dead dreams.
Of dead men.
Of midnight screams.
Of loneliness.
Of homelessness.
Of could have been. Should have been. Would have beens.
She tastes of fire and oceans and the bitter salt of seas. Of volcano
lava and earth openings and oceans vomiting.
She tastes of chaos.
Chaos.

When your heart is aflutter,
And your mind is a storm.

Such sweet memories of a time that has gone.
Yet, as always, we tend to hold on,
Some nights you lie and roll around
Mind stuck searching for answers that can't be found.

Glancing at the clock as hours toll by,
You can't help but wonder about the selfish "I".
You then turn to sleep with growing dread/
As you lie helpless in your bed...

A darkness is creeping, consuming your light
And you, little you, stuck in the fight.
With the patter of life strolling along by,
A stranger might notice the vice in your eye.

You then start to wonder and pick up a sigh,
Allowing yourself a few minutes to just lie.
Look out and see a time waiting to be
Life goes on regardless of you or little me...

Life Goes On

[Veronique Moore]

[Nokukhanya Mtshali]

Dear Diary

I hopelessly spill this ink and soil your insides
With the wishful thinking that it might be read by my daughter and
her daughter
Not only read but presented to scholars
To be used to strategize and broker a treaty of peace in this war

I dreamt I was sitting at the round table with Chimamanda Ngozie
Adichie, Kimberly Crenshaw, Queen Ana Nzinga, Katherine
Johnson, Queen Nandi, Bessie Coleman, Willa Brown, the warrior
women of Ingcugce and Dahomey, Yaa Asentewaa and Lilian Ngoyi
Sipping on age old propaganda disguised as the tales of Christmas
past, present and future
Existing not in the hypothetical nor reality of the world
Lamenting on the chance we were never given
Birthed to become a star in The Colosseum where your opponent is
your sister
Fighting endless battles long staged as bedtime stories
War stories of the atrocities Ursula and Maleficent reigned on
unwitting princesses
Camp fire tales starring evil stepsisters and stepmothers
Willing to do and be anything to earn the prized dignity only a man
could supposedly bestow
Our tears the colour of blood
Our hands and nails soiled from the endless graves dug for the deaths
of the women who never stood a chance in a fight rigged to be lost

I told them of the dream I had some nights ago
I was decked in my Sunday best
Smelling like the 4 O'Clock bloom
Carrying conversations with the bourgeoisie
We were headed to watch the play The Women of the World
A lull full of anticipation filled the room
The lights went out
The curtains opened and the play began
What unfolded in front of me felt like the re-enacting of Queen and
Slim
Only this time the characters were high school Prom Queen and
King
Heather and Gregory running away to protect their illegitimate seed
that threatened to taint the Oxford scholarship daughter and
football star son reputation

Act one was the introduction of our struggles morphed into omitted
truths to hide the stains that tainted the picture perfect sisterhood
Act two was the silencing of our voices with the silent lie that the
voice of one is the voice of the many
Act three were the puffs of smoke they exhaled as they inhaled our
struggles rolled into neat joints of addictive misplaced sympathy

Thankfully the curtains had to close for intermission
My eyes couldn't take any more of the rape and plunder
I went back-stage where the true form of the play lay
The imposters became the oppressors
'Cinch your waist, the smaller the better'
'If it doesn't hurt then it isn't pretty'

'Become the background, speak when spoken to'
'Represent him always, his reputation is in your hands'
'Cut the unruly hair, we're sophisticated women'
'Always cover up, we don't want him to be tempted'
'Lighten your skin pigment, the lighter the brighter'
'I speak for all of us but make sure that I look good while I do that'
The story lay in the eyes of the props and backstage crew
The morale had been long murdered
The funeral a silent affair with the dead individual becoming their own cortege and preacher
The curtains opened again
But I couldn't go back – wouldn't move even if I wanted to
My feet were cemented on the floor as I witnessed the flame flickering among them

Fighting for the same thing, they still bound themselves in cliques
Generations of indoctrinated segregation illusions them
No one ever took the time to explain 'Divide and Conquer' in order to take them out of their misery
In the shadows I listened:
"How is it that Becky with the good hair is the definition of the woman we're fighting for, yet she runs the world through hedge funds and centuries old inheritance?
How is she the woman we're fighting for when she's never been married off to pay debts she didn't even know existed?
How is she the woman we're fighting for when she has never went to bed empty because her siblings' stomachs growled louder than a lion's roar?

How is she the woman we're fighting for when she's never heard "To Be Young, Gifted and Black" whilst quarter to passing out, drowning in sorrows nursing soles of feet broken in by high heels, working nightshifts as a janitor simply because the chance to become a mathematician never came?

How is she the woman we're fighting for when she doesn't need to fight for dignity she's never lost, only forgotten for the simple reason of being made to feel less of a human?

How is she the woman we're fighting for when her voice is acknowledged without the validation and presence of a man?

How is she the woman we're fighting for when she's never held her child whilst the child took their last breath; the funeral a closed casket affair because the body is lathered up in bullets and bruises?

How is she the woman we fight for when her hands know no calluses, skin knows no burn from the sun, back not broken from the kisses of a whip?

How is she the woman we're fighting for when she knows no language barrier or ethnic discrimination?

How is she the woman we're fighting for when poverty is the bedtime story she's told because it is a fairytale?"

She stands alone
Tormented by the dilemma she faces
Unbeknownst of the audience she now attracted
Her thoughts are the sound of a nail being dragged on a board:
"Do I still run the world when I'm forced to vow 'Till death do me part' with the man who's already pronounced me dead?
Desecrated my temple in the name of being led into temptation?
Bear fruits of life for him in a cemetery?"

The lamentations of their souls find shelter in my heart
The questions they ask in the shadows are the beacons of light to the
next generation born with their sight blinded by ignorance:
"Do we still run the world when men become the beginning of our
lives?
Do we still run the world when stretch marks and cellulite become
contagious diseases?
Do we still run the world when the independence of the individual
is the tears of a sister?
Do we still run the world when your heritage is the red-tapes we
create to snuff out self-esteem?"
The curtain closed and then I woke
The silence heard around the table was the same one I heard trying
to shake off the dream

"I hear Earth crying at night you know", one of the women said,
"She mourns the death of her daughters
The howling wind carrying the cries of the thousand and one women
Burned at pyres made from Earth herself
Tied around Earth and whipped till the siren call of Death was but a
sweet lullaby
Stripped bare and their blood watering the millenia old anger of
Mother"

The dream faded and reality sunk
I was back
Years went by and the dream became a thing of the past
Until you were born
It came back to be as clear as day and my faith was renewed

"There might be hope after all", I thought

As you cling to my nipple sucking the milk and life out of me with all of its experience

My dear daughter

I pray that the wisdom to never think of yourself as fragile is transferred the only way mothers know how

I pray for the nights I had spent wetting my pillow to water the seeds you'll plant in your garden

Your brother soon followed

My job became harder

I needed to become smarter

I gazed upon you as you played in the yard

And I prayed for the salvation of the unpasteurized innocence of my son- soon to be salted and shriveled up in vinegar by society's ideology of masculinity in the name of preservation

Well, I'll see you again Dear Diary.

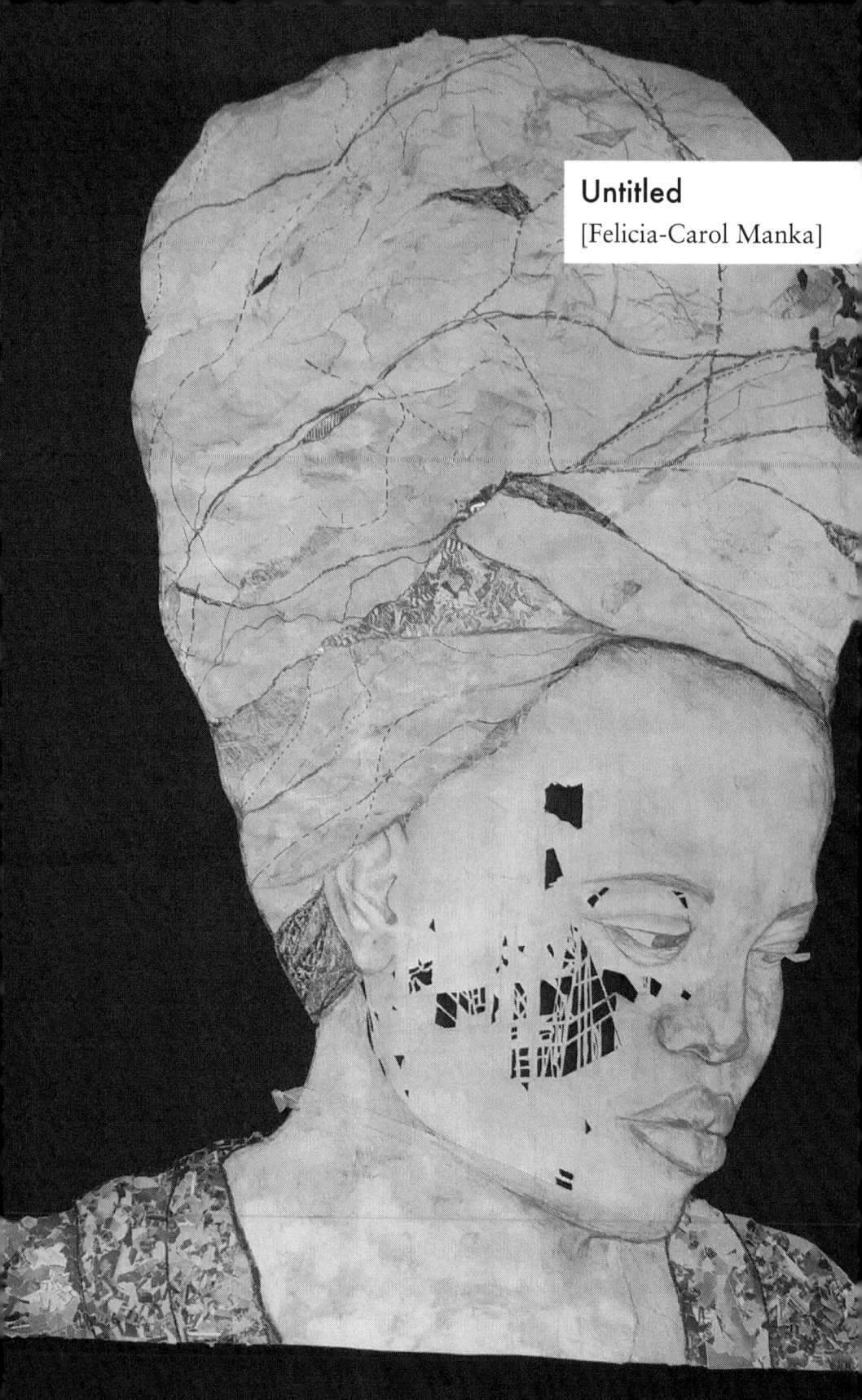

Untitled

[Felicia-Carol Manka]

[Khanysa Mabyeka]
My Motherhood Fraud

Dear mama,

I hope you are well and safe. I miss you and our time together very much.

I have been thinking about writing this letter to you for some years now. I now feel safe to tell you how I feel. Initially I felt so confused, a little angry and a pinch of disbelief. I kept asking myself what was going on, and things were also happening so fast I could not process everything as fast as they were occurring. I tried to discuss it with the people closest to me, however I could not quite articulate my thoughts and feelings and these tentative conversations never took me anywhere. And most importantly they didn't help in pushing away a growing feeling that I had been a victim of a massive fraud operation.

After some time of my awareness of the trap I had fallen in, I became madly angry, with myself - how could I not have seen it? -, with you, other members of the family, friends, community - why didn't they warn me of the pros and cons or at least tell me the truth of what lay ahead, so that even if I had decided to willingly put myself in that situation, it would be consciously. I remember this anger phase so clearly because you know I love growing plants, and this was a time no plant wanted to be near me. They preferred dying to sharing the same air with me.

I don't remember another time in my life when I cried so much. I would always be the last one at home to go to bed, I would play Simphiwe Dana's melancholic music on repeat and would allow myself to connect with my deepest sadness and just cry and cry and cry, of course, quietly. With nothing to dry my tears, I liked the feeling of whatever clothing I was wearing being soaked up with the tears until it became so uncomfortable I had to change it. Those crying sessions were kind of therapeutic, they allowed me to blame and curse everyone including myself for what had happened to me. But they also made me feel like I was slowly taking something out of the deepest me, I felt like something in me was being cleansed and one day I felt that I needed to forgive. Who? I couldn't really tell, so I started doing forgiveness prayers where I would imagine I was forgiving someone and that person was forgiving me. I forgave everyone, from myself to the plants that abandoned me.

Now I feel light and a little more conscious about what happened, I mean, I can explain it now. I still cannot talk to my close friends about it, I'm not ready for the judgement, but I think I'm closer to finally finding peace in my heart by redefining myself on my own terms.

Mama, why didn't you tell me that it wasn't true!

All my life, ever since I was a girl, I was told - through a web of stories, riddles, music, proverbs, etc., that when I became a mother I would feel complete. That it would be the best experience of my life, that I would feel the greatest joy in my life. That it was the 'natural' path of all women, that all women desired that experience. I was even told that I would be respected and valued higher in society.

Of course that was not true and I feel that I was misled into believing that motherhood defined me; by thinking that motherhood also defined what being a woman was.

Please don't misinterpret me, of course I love my children, they offer me abundant pleasant and joyful moments, they make me smile and laugh at the most stupid things, they allowed me to unveil parts of me I wasn't aware of, you know they are adorable. However the love I feel for them was optional, not natural because I am a woman or because I had them biologically. I chose to love them and to nurture our beautiful love.

Being a mother was the best thing that happened to me, but it was also the worst thing that happened to me.

The truth I wish I was told is that motherhood had nothing instinctive about it, but that it was mainly a function. Because I had the organs that allowed me to biologically have children, did not mean I had to do it. I tend to say that I chose to have and when to have my children, but today I ask myself if that is really true. Had I known then, what it really meant to be a mother in a patriarchal society, what I had to subtract from me in order to fulfil this function, maybe I would have made another choice.

This role, of being a mother, demands a lot from me as a woman. Although my husband and I share some of the caring responsibilities, the main responsibilities are still directly or indirectly pushed to me. When my husband does some of the caring work, people say I am lucky that he helps. It is actually unfortunate that he helps, he is the father of those children he should not be a helper, he should be co-responsible for taking care of them. To be able to take care of my children, be present and accompany their growth in their early years, something I was privileged to have the option to do, was also equivalent to a professional sacrifice (maybe it is temporary), limits in the kind of jobs I could do since the demands and requirements of my pre-motherhood job and aspirations do not balance well with my role as a mother. Taking care of my little humans is a full time job and nobody prepared me to have many full time jobs.

I appreciate the skills I had to develop in order to take on the role of motherhood and I really enjoy spending time with my children and bonding with them. However I don't enjoy being the main adult responsible for taking care of their material and emotional needs. And on top of that I am also expected to be an excellent professional, to look good and to be active in community issues. This means that most of the time I am the last to go to bed and the first to wake up, I do less things that give me personal pleasure and I'm not allowed to complain or risk being considered ungrateful and a bad mother.

It would actually not be a problem to be considered a bad mother, it would just mean that I am not undertaking that role as expected and maybe with the right input that could be improved. The problem is that being considered a bad mother is equal to being a bad person and specifically, a bad woman. I just don't seem to find the way out of this connection.

But being a mother is not solely who I am. And the danger of connecting maternity with the women's identity is that we remain with a single story that is told with an inclination to maintain women in a role assigned to her. And that is how women are domesticated to accept the caring work as naturally theirs. We are pushed to be guardians of a system that doesn't serve us as women. The role of motherhood has taken over my identity and I have to keep reminding myself that I am so much more than being a mother, I am spirit, I am light, I am one of God's greatest creation and this gives me the power to define in my own terms what it means to be a woman, what it means to be me. Besides, this identity is not static, in the same way that I am constantly changing, so is the way I identify myself.

Mama, I finally understood that being a mother is not who I am but what I do!

I was enough and complete before being a mother!

I promised myself that in our family, this huge lie that is told to women, would end with me. My daughter and all the other women that might come into our family after her will know the truth and will be given enough tools to make their choices knowing what they are getting into. I will teach them that motherhood can be an amazing experience and it is actually a unique experience of every woman that by choice or not goes through it. They can enjoy and grow from the physical and emotional changes that comes with it, from the relationship they decide to establish with their children, from the cuddling and the fun and beautiful experience of watching a little human grow. And I will also teach them that motherhood is a function, it is a role that is played to ensure the survival and wellbeing of other human beings. That role will most probably mean changing one's lifestyle, postponing some personal projects and aspirations, sleeping less and developing negotiating skills to ensure the father's equal involvement in the care work to ensure they are offering the best they would like to do for that child's physical and emotional development. This is mostly so because men and women are still not sharing equally the care work, the function of mothering and/or fathering.

I am happy to share with you that I now understand that I am complete as a woman independently of being a mother. Motherhood does not define who I am, particularly as an African woman. I am currently in the pleasant process of redefining what it means to be a woman, in my own terms. It is not an easy process as I have been impregnated with so many stereotypes about who I am, but it is a path worth taking so my choices in life are not by default, but reflect my true desires and vision of myself.

With love,
Your eldest daughter

I'm a breath of fresh air
Disappearing in the atmosphere.
As wise as I can be,
Unseeing my deepest fears.

Taking space freely
With no limit.
Disappearing to reappear,
Renewed with the same spirit.

Untitled

[Sephora Antaya]

[Sephora Antaya]

I Am Not.

I am not what they decide to do to me.
I am not how they see me.
I am not what they want from me.
I am not how they talk to me.

I am not something.
I am a human being.
I am not weak.
I am a divine being.

There is so much things that I am and so much that I am not. But nothing in this Life is about being someone or something, It's all about what we are made of.

I am made of strength.
I am made of love.
I am made of faith.
I am made of lust.

I am made of light.
I am made of rights
To never let anyone decide
What I should be in this Life.

[Patricia Musebah]
Masks

Look under this foundation, the black opal sealing
What's under...?
The African dark berry skin of a strong woman.
Look beyond this mascara.
What do you see?
A concealed film of tears of a broken soul
Look past this burgundy lipstick..
What do you see?
The full lips of a self-spoken woman
Look deep into these blushed cheeks.
What do you see?
Bruises of an untold story, scars of a violent past
Shambles of what was once a marriage.
Look under this Brazilian weave..
What do you see?
The raven black kinky hair of my African beauty.
Smell past this expensive Red door....
The cover to my sweaty evidence of toil.
What is there?
A dense kitchen smell, my place in your mansion.
Look past this herbivorous diet.
What do you see?
A "starved model ", a screaming soul
Loosen this corset .....
What do you see?
The criticized "fat" figure,

a rejected "plus size."

My hidden flaws, your laughing stock.

A perfect human sculpture, moulded by society

But..........

LOOK CLOSER, LOOK CLOSER!

Oh look beyond this flaking paint,

The mask I wear.

Peel it off...

What do you see?

The mother of your children, a woman of colour

The scared heart of a forgiving spirit

....JUST LOOK BEYOND THIS MASK

[Sankofa Umbi Umbi]
Ventos de Igualdade

Igualdade de direitos, mudireitos, femme direitos
Mulher intuitiva sensitiva as vezes destrutiva
Constante instintiva meio doce meio amarga
Meio plebeia meio diva
Meia verdade meia mentira
É meio ao meio é bi
Meio sonhadora meio segura
Somos metade pela igualdade

Em pleno vigésimo primeiro século
A quem que queira impor padrões
Forçar conclusões
De vida, beleza e até de existência.

Somos sementes diferentes da mesma descendência,
É preciso em friso
Respeitar esta dissemelhança, sem impor a sua crença
Ou ideologia de acordo a ciência.
Exponha, suponha porem não imponha
Divulgue pregue conjecture porem não obrigue.

Seja espírita, cristão, budista, luterano, hinduísta,
Muçulmano, ateu, persa ou espartano, afrocata...
Seja o que você quiser ser, Só viva.

Viva e deixe viver.
Viva ao feminismo para feministas;
Viva a bandeira arco-íris para a comunidade LGBTQ+.
Viva e deixe viver, justiça, igualdade e respeito.
Vivamos todos para desconstruir o preceito preconceito
BEATIFICAR, igualdade como divindade de cima para baixo,
Abaixo ao racismo, Abaixo ao machismo.
Abaixo a homofobia, Abaixo a xenofobia, Abaixo a gordo fobia.
Abaixo acima de tudo, ao terrorismo.
Povo dividido? Não! Povo manipulado? Não!
Só um povo ocupado demais
Com #hustegues de outras vidas.
Opiniões, indecisões , indiscrições
Face-manipulados, humano-parasitas,

Ham... & antes que me esqueça.
Pare de falar de quem tem os seios caídos, nunca tiveste as em bolas
em pé.

[Aisha Mohammed]
Ode To A Mixed Girl's Homeland.

The first time my soles,
hugged your brown earth.
My small lips tasting roasted fish,
I knew You were my home,
Not a place borrowed,
or rented all mine.
I hugged the smallest fragments of my father's
stories of you dearly throughout my childhood,
Those words whispered "home"

My body was moulded,
Out of the pillars that hold up your emirates,
your crocodile filled
Waters run through my veins.
This tongue speaks your words.
even if it is in tumbling,
Forced syllables,
I will try because
You embraced me that day
Even when you were a stranger to my older body,
I'm sorry.
You are only a part of me,
A part that I longed to
be with for so long.

Of origins and connections

I'm a bridge,
Mothers land moulds itself in my heart
and my blood, carries the essence
Of father's
I am the calm that
hides in the corners of
our lives too afraid to come out
I am chaos in a body
A soul fluid in it's complexity
I am dreams wrapped
around our sleep
I am the voice that echoes
"Peace"
On the streets,
music to lift us from the mud,
notes resting on our skin,
washing away fear,
washing over ignorance.
Sealing together,
mother and father,
into one.
Reckoning
Rana thrust this child into this
Place.
Naked, nipples throbbing
 crying lava out of her eyes
She danced on the threads of it's heart
when she got strong enough to walk,
teasing the fragile thing with her feet

Tip toeing nervously
On it's blood afraid to sink in.

Demons wrapped their whips around
her thighs when her body blossomed.
They ripped her legs apart,
and stared at the petals in her core
Mocking it passing it amongst themselves
they turned her into their garden,
revelling in her sweetness
whenever they could.

The demons moved into her,
swam in her head
till she could no longer
see without their tails blocking her eyesight

One day when she looked at this place
With her eyes bloodshot and her petals
Dying,
she realized
her blood was lava,
and Rana made her heart out of
Ice and Earth.

She drew her blood,
carved daggers out of it
And cut the threads,
Grabbed the heart and took a bite of it

She stopped tip toeing,
Dipped herself into its blood.
slayed the demons
hung their heads, her trophies
On her skin.

Untitled
[Felicia-Carol Manka]

[Kundai Muringi]
God of Color

Where are you god of color?
For your attention, I am pleading
My grandfather died calling you,
Now my knees are bleeding.
Was it not at your bold brown doors,
That my son was shot?
Are you behind the greying clouds?
Is it possible you forgot?
Are you the god of darkness?
Is this why we live in flames?
Maybe we didn't hear you call,
We changed our blessed names.
So beautiful is the rainbow,
Is white really a color?
It seems to have a different god,
Do you have the same power?
God of color, why do you not answer?
Is it the language that I speak?
I have carried my brother so long,
I am old, I'm getting weak.

They're so many, of us colors
Is your story also the same?
Possibly, you died for good
And will not come again.
Our hope and our salvation,
Don't you ever anger?
Or are you waiting for judgement day
To rule with a wooden hammer?
God of color, answer please,
My children think I'm a liar,
They say there's nothing to fear now,
They've always lived in fire.

[Kundai Muringi]
Cheated

Why am I standing
In your blood?
You smashed me, bashed me,
Broke me into splinters,
Never did I tell a soul
Never did I bleed.
Sunglasses, kisses,
I played along.
It was YOUR turn now
WAKE UP!
Stop playing victim
You killed me
I never bled.
I die a victim
Because you bled.

It's not the husband's feet,
Where she slaves to uplift him,
Her desires second to his,
Her dreams sacrificed for him.

It's not as the obedient daughter,
Ever willing to do her Baba's wish,
so her bride price would be high
and her worth finally displayed.

It's not as the CEO
Of the biggest companies
slaying all genders together way,
At the top butalone.

It's not only to become a Mother,
Have babes to lead the future
and correct the past
while her dreams are on hold.

It's not as a Mother,
though her babe's smile brightens her,
their innocence her source of hope,

Prove the world can be better.

She has found her place,
When her destiny is fulfilled,
When she is content and happy
and is finally at peace.

Her place in the world
Is where her dreams are fulfilled
Every single one of them.
So she can dream some more.

Her place in the world,
Is where she is free
of oppression, rape and patriarchy,
Where she can just be.

She is in her place,
When her opinions are valued,
She is allowed to be the leader,
or make her own choices.

Her place in the world,
Is where she will sit to be,
Not where the world puts her
or where you dictate.

Her place in the world

[Oluwamayowa Somoye]

[Charanee Marimuthu]

My Wallflower

At first glance you were a desert rose.
Growing against the grain of society,
standing in your power,
a strong woman - flourishing under the blazing African sun.

Your presence demanded an audience.
Your steady roots, blossoming so wild and rebelliously.
Only mother nature could create something this chaotically
beautiful, effortlessly.

But then I looked closer...
I saw that you are no desert rose.
You are a beautifully deceptive wallflower.
An enigma.
An eager observer,
hiding behind the facade of a rose.

What a beautiful, but challenging flower are you.
And I - so eager to please,
I water your ego and starve mine.

Drink up my desert rose... the wallflower in hiding.
I feed your ego to satisfy my thirst.
A thirst that can only be quenched by your enigmatic truth.
But you are a silent observer,
and I am left dehydrated.

When they ask what I think I am up to;

I hold behind the swell of my breast
grit and gut enough to drown a generation of status quo.

Untitled

[Henrietta Enam Quarshie]

[Vimbainashe Takarwa]

The Lessons She Never Meant To Teach.

Regardless of where you come from a woman are viewed as a nurturer, she is the source of all the love, joy, and assurance an individual will ever crave and from time immemorial she has done so. Change came with the culture shift that still rocks societies in this world of fake cosmetic enhancements and Viagra. The change came with a desire born of absence. The absence of contentment and gratification.

One then wonders that if a woman plays such an important role in society and is the very foundation on which it is built, what had her desire change so much? There were moments across time when certain events left an imprint. These moments were the first few cracks in a foundation that had held strong for such a long time. The seed of change was in every subconscious lesson a mother taught her children. Of great importance were the lessons to her daughters. Her life to them was a continuous class in session, she was a living lesson. Her every breathing moment left a mark on the next generation but it was and is it still is the lessons she never meant to give that mattered the most. Lessons born of her silent tears and pain have transcended time, passed down over the centuries. Her fears and desires, her dreams and aspirations, all she ever wanted and failed to attain somehow became the greatest inheritance she left behind, her legacy.

Long forgotten are the moments she laughed or smiled but they have remembered her battles with societal norms and the model of the perfect woman and the weight of expectations. The standard was to be maintained, the perfect woman was to be understanding, forgiving, submissive and above all else selfless. It is the last of these characteristics that held so much question. To be selfless is to value duty before self, a teaching society drilled into her and forgot to teach those she had a duty to. This has changed, in a modern world where a woman has chosen her duty to herself above all else. How bad could it be for women to choose themselves? Would it not be better to have a society of women empowered enough to know their place in this world and the value it deserves? It would have been okay if the change had not been born of pain, long-forgotten scars and just of ones self-evolving nature. It would have strengthened society if it had been born of anything else but a mother's pain.

One then wonders which lessons could have been so bad, how deep the pain was to threaten the very foundations of society? The answer lies in every woman's battle with societal norms, with its suppression of her will and spirit. She had to be selfless and understanding about her roles and duty to society putting these before her own. Her duties had her in the submissive role but it was not enough for society to have her submissive, no she had to be subservient as well. She had to understand her roles and where she fit in society. Understanding even the most illogical things because it was the prevailing norm. lastly, she had to be forgiving of these injustices to her, injustices that had her stuck in situations where she endured and not lived life. these were her battles before she even had to deal with her life issues before life and its trials were even factored in.

It seems like women woke up one morning and decided to be selfish but a different light can be shed to the situation. After an uncomfortable conversation with a friend of mine, he shared his views on cheating and how it affects relationships. He had observed his parent's relationship and how faithfulness or the lack of it did not affect his mother's decision to stay, she had stayed even though his mistresses were not a hidden secret. When this behaviour did not result in their marriage failing, he deduced it was tolerable and even okay to cheat. His mother's unintended lesson by staying was it was okay to cheat and it would not break a home. This holds no water at all to a woman for it's a pain she has carried and the society in which she belongs to has normalized it ignoring her pain and up until now she has let it be so. This is not the only injustice society normalised and left her suffering in turn.

Society and culture are of great importance, they give structure and preserve morals without them we are no different from the animals in the wild. The sad truth lies in the price that was paid for this great ideology to come to life. As the caretaker of these societal values and norms a woman paid and continues to pay the price for this ideology. The cost of trying to keep together a rather corrupt and extremely unfair set of values was her peace of mind. She paid with their sanity for the privileges she gave her better half. Be his peace of mind when all he has brought home is pain. Be a home when he has several of those so-called homes with other women. They taught her that marriage was sacred and yet he had the same bond with every Jackie and Jill consequently birthing resentment and bitterness in hearts that craved only love. How much bitterness is enough before she breaks? How many generations needed to pass before she realized she could have her peace of mind and the safety plus protection she had dependent on men for? This does not go to say that men are replaceable and that they serve no purpose but time has progressed and this is not the Stone Age when they were relied on for their strength and prowess. In this Modern Age where a man is defined by his ability to provide for his family and mainly the zeros in his bank account, a woman can provide for herself.

The change came when she decided she needed a place in this world that was her own and in which she was respected and appreciated. The blood and tears of her mother's fueled her, the domestic abuse and poverty changed each generation slowly. The anger from what she saw and in turn experienced changed her, it made her more protective of her spirit and she then refused to be broken. The rise of feminism came, women banded together and changed history, wanting for their daughters more than what society had given them. They united in that common goal calling to justice a list of transgression at the hands of their lovers and society. It was not a fight for gender equality but equity and respect. It was the reckoning of all those lessons our mothers never meant to teach.

It started with the small things and ended up greater, they saw how unfair life had been for their mothers and they went out and changed it. Birthing a generation of liberal women searching for a place for themselves. From property rights, education and careers, they fought to have the girl child acknowledged and valued. For her value to transcend the simple but important roles of being a mother, sister, daughter and wife. Finally, she could be a mother and a doctor, sister and designer and that was power. This was the power she needed to break the shackles that had kept her in the mould of the perfect woman. The power to shock the very foundations of culture and society, to rewrite a mother's tale and her lessons.

She grasped it, an educated woman was a concept society had not been prepared for. She could not fit in the mould so she broke it, she took centuries of passed down pain and suppression making the lessons our mothers never meant to teach not a tragedy but the core of who she would become. With that, she has said enough to the society that had bullied her into subservience. The society that had beat her down and stripped her naked making her forget the power she wielded. She took the lessons of pain and betrayal and used them as parameters of what defined her worth and how much she was willing to give. In this new world she has created for herself she is still finding her footing but while she does she has redefined norms and shocked our elders into early graves with her choices. As she learns to love herself, she raises her children not with a mask of happiness but with the same energy she feeds her soul. The reckoning had been inevitable, a mother's pains were bound to fester, the bough had to break and the modern woman had to be born empowered by self-love and determination to be a partner to man and not a servant.

Beasts Of Burden, Mixed Media On Board
[Chengetai Masalethulini]

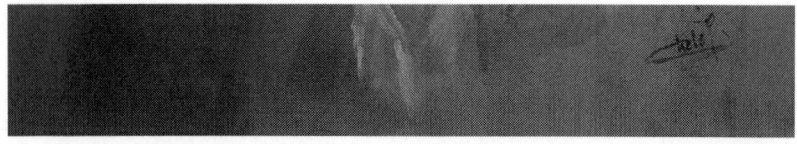

It comes in waves,

It feels like this intense feeling as if you are drowning in your skin,

The tears you want to shed but they never drop,

I suffocate again and I do not know what triggers it.

I am going mental and this is far from normal.

It is like the walls are closing on me,

I feel dead inside, how I kept it together as a child to just fail miserably as a grown-up.

It comes in waves,

Washing over me ever so gently.

It comes in waves,

This my despair.

An extension of my being,

I am part of the waves,

It is like a lover's caress,

My despair is a feeling I can hardly fight.

She comes with the waves,
 The mistress of my pain.
Clothed in memories I cannot fight back,
She washes over me completely.

She is the wave and I am part of the wave,
She is the ghost that haunts my mind,
She taints my joy at every turn.
She steals my sanity and I let her.

It comes in waves,
As the tide pulls in,
What chance did my childlike mind stand?
It comes in waves and she is the waves,
She is my ocean of grief and despair.

It Comes in Waves

[Vimbainashe Takarwa]

[Elsie Bunyan]
"Scars to Your Beautiful"

Hi.
Can we talk?
Give me a minute?
:
:

You carry scars that no one ever apologized for
Burns that those closest to you inflicted
Pain and agony that you have been told to cover up

A good girl doesn't complain too much
A good girl doesn't wear "revealing" clothes
All your life you have been put in a box
All your life you have been given expectations set by someone else

Your scars show up from time to time
But no one ever apologizes for them
You carry scars that those closest to you inflicted

You carry scars your parents inflicted,
When they did not believe your story

You carry scars your church inflicted,
When they told you pray it away

You carry scars the schools inflicted
When they told you, you're not smart enough

You carry scars, they say 'you' inflicted on yourself
When you wore a short skirt
When you opened your legs wide
When you went to that party and got drunk
When you slid into his DMs
When he became your boyfriend
These scars, they say you inflicted upon yourself

Your parents inflicted those scars
The church inflicted these scars
The school inflicted these scars
They say you inflicted them yourself
You carry scars no one apologized for
These varying communities
And many more, you name them
They never apologize

You shiver at the coldness of the world
Somehow like an onion
They hate it when you try
And one by one pull apart the layers
To show your scars and your pain

I am with you.
I have scars no one has ever apologized for.
Don't worry I do not need fake empathy or sympathy
If that is all you thought about while you read this

Give me a minute? Can I be honest?

Then you are a part of the problem.

I'm tired sometimes.
These are the scars to my beautiful
But what if sometimes I just don't want any-more scars?

I carry scars no one ever apologizes for.

[Thandokuhle Sibanda]

I Can't Find My ID

Upon birth I was given my father's forename because it takes the form of a compass,
one that always points the direction towards home, towards a tribe,
where the carcasses of my ancestors lay buried in the soils that moulded them whole
it will lead me to the rhythm, the songs that summon the rains and all things spiritual
it should point towards a tribe
one in which belong
or at least should belong

This name I carry is meant to unify parts of me the world is yet to scatter
instead it's the reason I keep searching for soul and hoping it comes in a different color
home is not home if mother and father speak two different cultures
and each one of them shoving their bitter practices down spine..
so I bury myself in a mini smoke ritual,
when I'm high enough I transcend into other dimensions
where all these voices are silenced
where all these expectations are non-existent
where who i am is not determined by this heavy name I carry

[Valerie Asiimwe Amani]

A Return

Volcanic tongue wraps around your neck
Lost words fall back, swallowed
Patience is a dried promise
liberation a hungry beast
It looks like a sunken ship
The faith you have in yourself
It is never your fault
Except it is always your fault
trying to conjure forgiveness
While Stringing together
All the "I love yous"
You didn't get back,
wearing them on your feet
Like a warning on a house
"Do not come in..."
"...I don't believe in love anymore "
But maybe
You still believe in yourself
Maybe all that estranged affection.
And digested emotion can find its way back to you
The tongue can soften and
you no longer have to break yourself or
bear fire to survive
Wash your feet
Forgive yourself
you can return all

[AriButtercup]
The Day Will Come

The day will come,
And it will be our favourite season - the fall of patriarchy.
We will walk the streets paved by the women who have gone before us,
As valiant as soldiers, marching into war.
Side stepping land mines
That our voices, raised in one song, have annihilated.

The day will come,
And like children in the rain,
We will dance to rhythm of our own hearts
As shards, like pure sparkling diamonds, are showered upon us
From a thousand glass ceilings,
That our hands, raised in congruence have shattered.

The day will come,
And the earth will resonate our laughter
We will remember the names of those, whose blood flow within us like graceful rivers,
As the world becomes a sanctuary for the ones who come after us.
A world free of prejudice,
That our passion, fuelled by unyielding purpose, has created.

The day will come.
The day has come.
The day is now.

Rose

[Chengetai Masalethulini]

A Negra Que Usava Turbante De Capulana

Há milhares de anos atrás existia uma tribo no Monte Namuli onde só nasciam meninas. A maior fonte de riqueza da tribo provinha dos seus terrenos muito férteis que faziam brilhar uma produção de diferentes culturas, criando inveja nas tribos vizinhas.

Ao completarem 18 anos de idade as meninas passavam por um ritual de libertação, em que recebiam um turbante de capulana que as identificava como membro da tribo e lhes concedia o direito de escolher uma área para liderar.

Horty fazia parte das meninas que acabavam de receber o seu primeiro turbante e escolheu assumir responsabilidades na área de defesa, onde começou a treinar meninas de 15 anos de idade aspirantes a guerreiras.

Com muita disciplina e rigor Horty ensinava as futuras guerreiras a combater, exercícios de intensidade e de resistência eram brutalmente aplicados na beira do rio, as meninas eram ordenadas a escalar e descer o monte em menos de cinco minutos.

Aproximava-se a época da colheita, como de costume os seus celeiros tiveram sempre a má sorte de serem saqueados pela tribo da planície composta na sua maior parte por homens grandes de músculos bem definidos.

Na noite do dia da colheita Horty distribuiu suas meninas em todos os pontos estratégicos do monte, e quando o inimigo colocou as patas neste território fértil foram todos abatidos com excepção do filho do rei. Horty poupou a vida deste para que servisse de exemplo aos saqueadores de celeiros das outras tribos.

Não tardou muito até que a notícia espalhou-se por toda a região, todos comentavam que existia uma negra extremamente forte que usava um turbante de capulana, eliminou os guerreiros da tribo da planície.

O rei ordenou que todos os curandeiros da tribo procurassem saber quem havia lhes lançado tamanha maldição uma vez que aquilo nunca tinha acontecido antes, e se continuasse morreriam a fome.

Segundo os curandeiros a negra que usava turbante de capulana concentrava forças sobrenaturais no seu turbante, razão pela qual ela era muito forte, mas se lhe fosse tirado o seu turbante ela ficaria fraca.

Várias tribos uniram-se e enviaram os seus guerreiros para a tribo do Monte Namuli com a missão de tentar tirar o turbante de capulana da cabeça da Horty. Mais de três mil homens tentaram sem sucesso e os que tocaram no turbante foram amaldiçoados a trabalharem numa terra improdutiva pelo resto da vida.

Diz-se que até hoje naquela região os homens tentam tirar os turbantes de capulana das mulheres para lhes saquear o celeiro mas nunca conseguem.

*Capulana – tecido moçambicano com estampas coloridas usado por mulheres, homens e crianças, no dia-a-dia, em celebrações, nascimentos e velórios.

[Vuyina Mgidlana]

Questions Unanswered... A Feminist's Battle Cry

Where do I run?
When the world Degrades my kind
When they use the term
"it's a man's world"
To be unkind

Where do I hide?
When the worlds so cold on every side
When female oppression
Is the most stylish fashion
How long will it be
Until our emancipation

How do I stand tall?
When I am defined as less than
When I am so often reduced to nothing
When I am constantly told
Who to be

Where do I cry?
When patriarchy has silenced my voice
And even when I make a noise
The world around me is deaf,
 And those who see
Are mute

Oh please, I need answers

What do I do?
When my biggest sin... it seems
Is being Womxn.

[Aminat Sanni-Kamal]
Òrìṣàbùnmi

For most humans, greed was the driving force that hurtled them to the doorsteps of Ìyá Alaanu's ibùdó. However, they always left more confused than they came because Ìyá Alaanu had a way of spinning riddles upon them that their minds; shallow as they were, would never be able to solve. While seeing the future was her gift, Ìyá Alaanu's sacred duty was to protect the world from the destruction the greed of humans would bring upon it and though by virtue of this she could never tell a lie, there was no hard set rule that said she couldn't send them on a wild goose chase with convoluted versions of the truth.

It was fate that had brought Òrìṣàbùnmi to Ìyá Alaanu's ibùdó. She had been married off to her father's bosom friend as soon as blood began to flow from her body. It was a promise he'd made to his friend when they were little boys, a gift for saving his life from a ferocious snake.

After three still born sons, the midwife had finally declared her womb rotten and unfit to have children. Things only went downhill for her after that declaration. Her husband had returned her to her father; she was damaged goods and he hadn't want her infecting his household with her bad luck, his other wives had been more than happy to see her go.

Shortly after she was returned to her father's compound where she had been treated worse than a slave, a plague broke out in the village and a unanimous decision was made by the village chief and his advisors to drive Òrìṣàbùnmi out of the village, after all a woman who could not have children was a curse from the gods and her continuous presence in the village could only cause destruction. And so, Òrìṣàbùnmi had become a wanderer. For years she had moved from place to place, searching for her purpose, wanting to end her life but lacking the courage to do so.

In trance-like haze she had found herself on the doorstep of Ìyá Alaanu's ibùdó, the old woman had smiled at her and welcomed her into the shrine.

"Come in, child," Ìyá Alaanu had called to her and still in a haze, she had stepped into the foggy shrine.

After three days of drinking from Ìyá Alaanu's healing pot, Òrìṣàbùnmi had begun to feel life running through her veins, only then had she looked to see where she was. The shrine smelled dank as it was completely dark and not even the tiniest ray of sunlight was allowed to permeate the hut, the only light in the shrine was from an ever flickering oil lamp. Ìyá Alaanu was seated on a stool made out of stone, clothed in white, her head was bald and her eyes were milky white, as she was completely blind, her neck, wrists and ankles were adorned with heavy looking white beads, her hands were placed on her thighs and although she was blind, she seemed to be watching Òrìṣàbùnmi, who was staring in awe at the strange white writings on the mud walls of the ibùdó.

"What are these?" She asked, marveling at the beautiful symbols and wondering how she could see them, in the darkness of the ibùdó.

"That is the language of the deity, knowing what they mean would cause you the most excruciating pain, only those who know their purpose in life are permitted to know the language of the deity," Ìyá Alaanu had answered, her voice sounding a bit sad and groggy.

"But, I have no purpose, I'm a woman with rotten womb. Of what purpose could I be when I can have no children?" Òrìṣàbùnmi replied, her voice carrying all the pain she had borne over the years.

"Then, I must have allowed a dead girl into my shrine," Ìyá Alaanu had said testily.

"I'm not dead –" Òrìṣàbùnmi had begun to protest but she was cut off by Ìyá Alaanu.

"You must be a rotten corpse, buried deep within the earth with maggots crawling in and out of your molten flesh to have no purpose. I shouldn't have allowed you into my house. Leave now, I don't want you here, I don't want a dead girl here," Ìyá Alaanu had waved her hands, shooing Òrìṣàbùnmi out of the ibùdó.

Òrìṣàbùnmi got to her feet, surprised at Ìyá Alaanu's sudden hostility, her eyes had cut to the words on the wall, she didn't want to leave, she wanted to read the words on the wall, they were beautiful and they called to her, she wanted to become one with the words, she felt like learning to read those words, were her...purpose in life. The realization of it had hit her with so much force, that she had staggered to keep her balance.

"Leave," Ìyá Alaanu repeated, this time as she said it, she rose to her feet and it seemed like she had the full force of the wind behind her, her white eyes shone brightly, and Òrìṣàbùnmi had had to cover her eyes to prevent herself from being blinded by the white light.

"No, I'm not going anywhere," Òrìṣàbùnmi spoke but her voice shook with fear.

"Leave!" Ìyá Alaanu's voice sounded like the rumbling of thunder and any sane person would have run for their dear lives but Òrìṣàbùnmi had been tired of running; she needed a place to call her own, a purpose to keep on living.

"No, I am not going anywhere, I want to learn the language of the deity and you are going to teach it to me," Òrìṣàbùnmi said, with a lot more conviction than she had ever had in her life and it was that conviction that Ìyá Alaanu needed, everything quieted down and Ìyá Alaanu was back on her stone stool, as if she had never even lifted a finger.

"Sit," she commanded softly, and Òrìṣàbùnmi sat crossed legged before her, ready to take on a new path in life. That was when Ìyá Alaanu had told her of the seven battles she must fight for her to read the language of the deity.

The first battle had taught her independence, as she'd had to begin all her journey without any help from Ìyá Alaanu, the second battle had taught her endurance as she had to travel through a ringlet of fire, the third battle had taught her bravery as she had to battle a depraved demon in a pit of darkness. The fourth battle brought her to a village, when the men and women worshipped her body and made her body do things that she had never thought were possible, they taught her that there was no shame in her sexuality. The fifth battle had taught her kindness, she became a caregiver to the orphan children that she had found in the course of her journey, the sixth battle taught her love, it brought her into the arms of the one who truly loved her. With each battle she fought and won, a tattoo appeared on her left forearm, stark white against her dark, ivory black skin, each a sacred symbol from the walls of Ìyá Alaanu's ibùdó. This was her seventh and final battle. Over the years, she had dreaded the final battle not knowing when it would happen, doubting that she still possessed the strength it took to fight and win the battle. Now she stood on the plain field, spear in hand, the sun shining down blessedly on her, staring at her adversary who was poised for battle. Òrìṣàbùnmi eyed the woman from head to toe. From the beautiful black dreadlocks that ran down her back, to the red beads that adorned her ankles, the woman was her exact replica, albeit with an evil scowl to her face. She finally understood what the final battle was, it was a battle against her inner demons.

She grinned at her evil twin and yelled with all her might "I am worth it!" Her adversary was rattled, she had obviously not been expecting her to say that.

"I deserve everything I have, I am worthy of my life. I am a woman who has walked through fire, battled demons, I have found purpose; I have found freedom and I will not let you take it away from me." She spun her spear and poised for attack, but her adversary only smiled and dissolved into the atmosphere.

A searing pain shot through Òrìṣàbùnmi's left forearm sending her to her to knees, as a new tattoo appeared her skin, the symbols on her forearm moved and fused together, forming the word;

Obìrin

She was a deity and her womanhood was her language, it was proud, imposing and beautiful and she would speak it loudly for the whole world to hear.

Glossary
Ìyá Alaanu – Mother of Mercy
Òrìṣàbùnmi – Gift of the Deity
Ibùdó – Shrine/home
Obìrin – Woman

When I think of powerful, African women, I think of my mom. So this is for her.

[Siju Falade]
Iya Mi

My mother's first language is not my own.
Sometimes I wonder if this is the reason why
I speak in metaphors;
why I twist and capsize my tongue
until nothing but riddles come out.

So that even I,
cannot puzzle out my pieces.

~*~

"Everything will be alright," my mother says.
She extends this lifeline over her landline.
I can't help but wonder
how she expects to save me
when we are both drowning.

~*~
"You're just like your mother,"
he spits out with venom...
as if insult,
as if sin,
as if she were not made of gold,
were not one of God's most exquisite creations.

As if she were not already royalty before he added "crown" to her last name.

"Thank you."

~ * ~

"Always leave room for disappointment,
 so when it appears it won't be as painful.
After all, it is only success that has family." -- advice from my mother.

~*~

My mom has faith like a melon seed.
With it, she can move mountains and level valleys.
But most days, she grinds it up
and uses it to make egusi soup.
To feed the twisted mouths of children
who often forget that these things
demand sacrifice.

An offering like the Father's,
A love like the Son's.

I had a thorn stuck in my fro
But how could you know?
You only spoke to my Shadow.
My shadow is silent and shines like a silver...
But I am a River...

You recognized tenderness
You quenched your thirst

you showed me your hiding place
I went to work...
Did I not pluck wild lilies and dandelions out of your yard?
Did I not sing you songs to silence your midnight storms?

tell me who shortened Those long winter hours?
Who took a broom and chased away your sorrow hiding behind
shadows?

With laughter and bright spring colors... I reminded you that you
matter..(and you do matter)
tell me who brought back your walk empowered?

who told you: Heads up, but do not stumble, remember to be humble.

shoulders down, breathe darling breathe..

it won't rain forever, so for now feel the wind breeze...

Look at them Sultan, look at them...

let the stars envy the twinkle in your eyes... look at the people when you talk and speak your mind.

I did this..I (Aniga)...

Not my shadow...

Not my flesh and skeleton

And yet you still

yearn for an empty skull...

No I won't be quite

I won't Stand still

And shine like silver...

Because I am a river...

Beneath my fro underneath the thorn stuck in my afro

thorn as in the past haunting the present, thorn as in the traumas, thorn as in ~ being a woman.

underneath the thorn stuck in my afro

I am a mind to THINK...

I am mind to LISTEN.... I am mind to SPEAK to dance and sing...

I had a thorn stuck in my fro

[Munira Maria Makerow]

[Gugu Ngwenya]

African Womb : Cradle Of Mankind

From this Womb, I create,
The feet that walk this planet.
With this Womb, I affiliate,
The history carved in granite.

Who dares to enter this Universe,
That paints the melanin on the night sky
That births the Stars and disperse,
The greatness of the African Sky.

How many more live,
Cause of this life-giving tomb?
How many still give,
The honor of time's bloom?

From this deep dark, I birth You,
For you to look and kiss the Blue.

[Tshepo Moyo]
To You

i. To You.

I wish I hadn't told you secrets about myself.
Like that one about how sometimes after a really long day I run a hot
shower just so I can cry.
I should not have scribbled my weaknesses on a piece of paper, folded
it sixteen times and asked you to hold on to it for me.
You should have never heard me say "Sometimes I don't believe in
myself"
And "I believe in you" should not have comforted me.

I should not have made a home out of you.
I should not have walked into you, thrown off my shoes, taken off
my pants and bra, settled on your lap and watched a rerun of Law
and Order.
You should not have seen the woman I am on dark cold nights.
No one should ever meet me when I am not "Poet, writer and super
hero"
No one should see what I look like without a coat of arrogance.
and I shouldn't have worn your faith in me as a coat of Armour.

But the way you say "You're Beautiful" must be the same way
God said, "let there be light" and there was light.
More like a command and less like a compliment.
And the way you kiss me must be the same way
God breathed the breath of life; and man became a living soul.

So maybe I am a woman of faith.

ii. To Me

"Unto the woman he said, I will greatly multiply thy sorrow and thy conception; in sorrow thou shalt bring forth children; and thy desire shall be to thy husband, and he shall rule over thee"

How does anyone believe the miracle of birth is sorrowful?

We need a God whose pelvic bones know how to stretch for living souls.

We need the kind of God that knows how to break.

I need the kind of God that knows loss.

I need the Kind of God that knows.

I need the kind of God.

I need the kind.

I need.

I

I am a God.

The African Woman.
She's strong and confident
enough to deliberately mystify herself insouciantly
She rules by her hands and her mind
Self-sufficient within her own universe.
Buffeted by strong winds,
still standing, she is.
She draws strength from her tears.
And when she laughs,
it bounces off walls and warms the faint hearted
Unbent to the will of all men – daily,
She fights the battle of failure.
A fight her father never taught her to win
Everyone tries to dictate to her
What she can and cannot be

There are moments in between
When she feels she doesn't know what she is fighting for
Yet each morning,
she wakes up to fight harder than she did yesterday
Yes, she knows that
every long lost dream led to where she stood
She can be vulnerable and predatory
All at the same time
She is a mystery to unfold
Whether she's envied or adored?
happy or broken?
She chooses to be a piece of everything
Unaware of her God likeness.
She is everything I am

Woman

[pen.cells]

[Rusud Makrim]

A Mulher Do Camponês

Antes do cantar das andorinhas e do sol nascer,
Desperta com ele a vontade de ser mulher.
Todos entardeceres, vê em sua imagem a possibilidade de se
rejuvenescer
E, no seu leito busca forças para a sua ceia colher.

Seus pés seguem o caminho traçado
Rumo ao seu altíssimo e majestoso arado
Oração no coração,
O cantarolar do nhambaro em seus lábios
Enxada arrastando o nutrido chão.

Se não fosses tu nesse mundo mesquinho,
O que seria dos seus filhos esfomeados
Que transbordam sobre este chão de espinho.

Árvore de pau-rosa
Raiz firme e frondosa
Suas curvas acompanham o som da timbila
A volta da fogueira, a chama em seus negros olhos oscila
Se banha nas águas do Zambeze de forma desejosa
E no seu gingado mostrando a fartura de sua colheita
Deixando a Mwandlamane e invejosa.

Oh tu, mulher do camponês satisfeita!
Como podes não beijar a terra?

Esta terra que de ti faz mulher, esposa e mãe?
E de si faz a maior forma de esperança eleita.
Para seu homem, seu maior orgulho e guerra.

06-03-2020

Nhambaro – Esta dança é originária e executada entre o povo Chuabo. É uma dança de conteúdo e significados profundos, praticada numa vasta zona sul da Zambézia.
Timbila - é um instrumento musical de percussão, do tipo xilofone, tradicional dos chopes de Moçambique
Mwandlamane – Vizinha

[Dikun Elioba]

Initiation In Terekeka

Terekeka, Sudan

your long black body glistens in the night
from your tightly coiled copper hair
to the gleam of light
reflected from your tar body

your stature already masculine
before your initiation into adulthood
perhaps it is your work in the cattle camps
or the way that you slaughter meat
groomed into masculinity
grasping your shield and spear
wandering through the village
your bareness shown in every way

I was told no ot to look at you
that when someone passes by
they rush swiftly with downward pointed
eyes avoiding your gaze
while your presence becomes nothing
but blurred imagery

I disobey and I am in awe
acknowledging you from a distance-
a vision of distance
needed in order to admire
look at how even the delicate muscles
within your face is potent
as if from its sensitive place
it longs to eject its aura

[Khanysa Mabyeka]

Os Apelidos De Mulheres São Uma Utopia?

E m muitas sociedades antigas os nomes tinham um significado. As vezes representavam o que se esperava que as pessoas fossem ou alguma característica do nascimento ou da personalidade ou ainda as circunstâncias nas quais as pessoas tinham nascido. Em muitas sociedades actuais, perdeu-se o sentido explícito dos nomes e de facto, muitas pessoas não conhecem o significado dos seus nomes. Porém, implicitamente ainda prevalecem alguns significados, por exemplo, dá-se nomes de flores apenas às meninas e nomes de guerreiros apenas aos meninos.

Mas, os apelidos continuam a ter um peso importante na identidade das pessoas. Eles falam da nossa história e dão informação extra sobre a nossa origem e identidade. Os apelidos nem sempre existiram e, tão pouco existem em todas as culturas. Historicamente, eles surgiram por questões administrativas, como forma de organizar e classificar as pessoas em grupos, em função da profissão, do lugar de nascimento, do clã, de características físicas, para se poder cobrar impostos, etc. O sistema de apelidos predominante em Moçambique foi herdado da época colonial, influenciado pelos costumes existentes na maior parte das sociedades europeias daquela época, patriarcais. O que significa que o apelido que se adopta é o do pai.

Como feminista sou a favor do direito de escolha. De as mulheres e homens por exemplo, poderem escolher se mudar ou não o seu apelido ou acrescentar o apelido do/a cônjuge quando se casam. Ou, de um casal poder escolher dar às suas crianças o apelido da mãe ou do pai, ou de ambos e na ordem que escolherem.

Por vários motivos, o meu parceiro e eu decidimos registar as nossas crianças com o meu apelido. Ele próprio foi registado com o apelido da mãe (apesar de se apresentar com o apelido do pai porque é 'Africano', enquanto o da mãe é 'Português' – mas este é outro assunto) e pretendíamos continuar com essa 'tradição'. Para mim também significa desafiar algumas normas machistas como as que consideram que as crianças pertencem à família do homem e reconhecer que os meus ovários valem tanto como os testículos do meu companheiro e que por esse motivo temos total liberdade de dar-lhes qualquer um dos apelidos.

Isto faz muita confusão para algumas pessoas que não entendem sobretudo a posição do meu parceiro. Pessoas chegadas à ele lhe disseram coisas como que ele:

—não foi 'homem' ao ter aceite registar as crianças com o meu apelido e não o dele;

—não tem orgulho de ser homem ao não passar o apelido dele;

—está a humilhar os/as filhos/as e que no futuro terão problemas de identidade;

—que o apelido da mulher não garante a continuidade dele como homem, etc.

Como se registar o apelido fosse sinónimo de responsabilizar-se e cuidar das crianças. Como se o tal apelido da mulher não tivesse valor. E, é precisamente sobre esse apelido da mulher que gostaria de reflectir.

Existem apelidos de mulheres?

Recentemente li um livrinho que gostei de uma jornalista feminista chilena, Arelis Uribe, intitulado 'Qué explote todo'. É uma colectânea de artigos que ela publicou durante um período de tempo e, um dos textos expressa a frustração dela ao dar-se conta que no Chile os apelidos das mulheres sempre são de homens.

Nesse momento também senti uma certa frustração ao descobrir que em Moçambique não é diferente. Os apelidos das mulheres são de homens. Nas sociedades matrilineares no norte e centro do país, o apelido que se dá às crianças é o do tio ou irmão da mãe. O apelido define-se através da mãe, mas pertence à um homem. No sul e centro do país, onde predomina o patriarcado, o apelido adoptado é o do pai das crianças.

No caso da nossa família, nós pensávamos que estávamos a dar um apelido de mulher às nossas crianças, mas estávamos bem enganados. O meu apelido é do meu pai. O apelido da minha mãe, é do pai dela. O apelido da minha avó é do pai dela. Não consigo encontrar na história da minha família um apelido que tenha originado numa mulher. O apelido da mãe do meu companheiro também é do pai dela.

Este descobrimento deixou-me mesmo em baixo. Neste aspecto o patriarcado está tão bem enraizado que não vejo como poderíamos ter evitado continuar uma linhagem patriarcal na escolha do apelido das nossas crianças.

A minha mãe conta que os avós e as avós dela não usavam apelidos. Eles e elas usavam nomes individuais e eram conhecidos/as como 'fulano/a de tal, do clã X). Foi só quando tiveram necessidade de ir à escola, que tiveram de ser registados/as e passaram a ter apelidos porque essa era a exigência da administração colonial. Então por exemplo o meu avô que se identificava como 'Zefanias (nome próprio) do clã dos Mahozes', passou a usar Zefanias como apelido. O nome passou a ser apelido e, o mesmo passou com os irmãos (Navesse e Matandalasse). A mesma coisa não aconteceu com as irmãs do Zefanias do clã dos Mahozes porque elas não foram incentivadas à estudar e por isso nunca tiveram de ser registadas. E, mesmo casadas (não oficialmente) continuaram a utilizar os seus nomes próprios, mas as suas crianças foram registadas com os apelidos que os seus maridos haviam adoptado.

Inventemos novas regras por favor
Será que esta poderia ser uma solução para passarmos a ter apelidos de mulheres? Será que poderíamos passar a dar à cada criança um apelido que seja só seu? Será que assim as mulheres poderão também passar apelidos que não têm nada a ver com apelidos de homens?

A jornalista Chilena achava que para solucionar este problema era necessário colocar-se uma bomba e reiniciar o mundo.

Parece uma proposta radical. Mas se calhar a profundidade deste problema requer soluções radicais para se conseguir mudanças duradouras.

Segundo o Código de Registo civil Moçambicano, uma pessoa pode ter até 4 apelidos da família. O que significa que se poderia dar qualquer um dos apelidos à criança (como nós fizemos) mas, se esses apelidos foram todos passados pelas figuras masculinas de ambas famílias, continuamos a funcionar tendo os homens como referência ou centro.

Uma amiga contou-me que no costume do povo Bakongo em Angola, quando as crianças nascem, o nome da mãe passa a ser o apelido da criança. Por exemplo um senhor chamado José Cândida, será porque a mãe se chama Cândida. E, segundo esta amiga, é por este motivo que existem muitas pessoas da etnia Bakongo com apelidos que correspondem à nomes próprios portugueses de mulheres. Esta me parece um sistema interessante mas, no sistema jurídico moçambicano o nome próprio da mãe ou do pai não pode ser utilizado como apelido da criança. Apenas os apelidos das famílias da mãe e do pai.

Se calhar nos países onde é permitido mudar de nome, seria possível mudar o nome e o apelido e assim iniciar-se linhagens com origens em apelidos de mulheres. Se calhar também podia-se criar apelidos inventados que juntem os apelidos da mãe e do pai (como é permitido nos Estados Unidos da América) e também se iniciar linhagens com origens em apelidos de ambos mãe e pai.

Não sei se as minhas crianças quando forem adultas terão a mesma preocupação, mas espero que se quiserem que isso seja possível legalmente. Que possam inventar e escolher apelidos através dos quais possam começar a contar uma história diferente. Eu não estou apegada nem aos meus nomes, nem ao meu apelido, não sinto que as minhas crianças deixariam de estar vinculad@s a mim se tivessem apelidos diferentes. O apelido nem é meu mesmo!

E porquê é tão importante ter apelidos que originam em mulheres? Por uma questão de justiça, de nos conectarmos também com essa parte das nossas identidades, de dar visibilidade às mulheres que nos trouxeram ao mundo e as que nos cuidaram, porque até no nome e apelido é importante termos escolhas verdadeiras que nos libertem do protectorado patriarcal. As mulheres somos mais da metade da população de Moçambique e não temos apelidos que originam em nós. Não temos apelidos de mulheres. Não me parece justo!

Como solucionamos esta situação?

Sinto-me impotente e presa à um sistema injusto.

Gostaria mesmo de poder tocar nalgum botão que diga 'reinício'.

[Tamary Kudita]

African Victorian

Artist Statement

When creating this series, I thought about some of the European images of Africa which existed at the beginning of the nineteenth century which were based on conflicting ideologies about the inhabitants of this continent. I wanted to present a counter narrative which serves to portray that African identities are complex.

Furthermore, I wanted to make a commentary on history, its selective unfolding and illustrate that history can be narrated in many ways. My work aims to show a forgotten elegance. 'African Elegance", which is a celebration of the diversity, complexity, richness, and hybridity. I illuminate once invisible bodies by challenging the representation of minorities while undermining the authority of simplistic readings of the black body.

Stemming from my ancestral mixed race lineage, my images take on superimposed characters. I intentionally use African elements that have been super imposed filtering through a western medium. This layered symbolism of the minority illustrates an affiliation with a multifaceted identity. Both innate and superimposed variations of my work are capable of division into those which are more and those which are less obvious to the human eye. Assimilation to European culture, and also in part appropriation, is a way of coming-to-terms with and overcoming of history and the colonial experience.

African Victorian

[Tamary Kudita]

[Rumbidzai Zamukudzi]
Hierarchy Of Patriarchy

Cry my beloved country, cry.
When will we see matriarchy
When will women's voices be heard
It's a hierarchy of patriarchy everywhere
Unless you are a lucky one,
But I guarantee you
They will dim your sparky
With their snarky character.

Our country has turned parky
Anarchy is the order of the day
They call us empty darkies
Oligarchy of patriarchy is seen everywhere
When they involve us
Our views are judged as melarkey
Masculinity is overestimated
Hierarch of patriarch is over emphasized.

They oppress us indirectly
Misogyny rings in their heads
They take our perky hearts as idiocy
From the day of menarche
They labeled us defiled
Male chauvinism is overstressed
It's all a hierarchy of patriarchy.

I long for day
When woman will be given power to rule
A day when they will be equity
A day when subjugation will fall
I long to see this day before I die
When sexism will be removed from the dictionary,
Because it wouldn't have any meaning.
I long to see a hierarchy of matriarch once.

I long for that day to come
When we will not use our pudenda to earn promotion
Hierarchy of patriarchy must fall
Hierarchy of only patriarchy must vanish.

[aladywithapen]
Female I Was Born

I am the rain
With gentle drips
And heavy downpour
Too brute for a drain

I am the rain
Perfect for a bloom
Sometimes a tornado
Smiling as you gloom

I am like the sky
Pregnant with the clouds
Uncertain it will rain
Or thunder will strike

I am like the rain
The rough or the smooth
That makes or destroys;
A rain or a storm

I cry and call
To live and love
To read and write
But get denied a pen

For fear of my word
Cruel to my ancestry
Harsh to the gender
I choose to be stronger

I am a being
Beautiful with a twist
Solid as a rock
Emotional like a being

I live old like a man
With a mind of my own
Either to live and excel
Or live like in cell

Let's write in a text
When you see me next
The power that exudes
Comes from hardships I survive

The strength that dominates
Adds nothing to my weight
Takes nothing from my bright
An African Female, I was born

I am the daughter of the
Nigerian princess and the
Ghanian scholar whose
legacies have been infused in
my blood, my faith, my
lips who cradle the cries
of fallen warriors and grieving wives
who wept into the empty air,
believing their love would ignite
flames of vengeance.
my ebony skin that glared into
the heart of a drying star,
boasts the caress of an aging mother
singing her unruly babe to sleep once more,
knowing their eyes will never see
her laughter again.

I stand before you with my
pores oozing of
sweet bountiful cocoa and
maggi stirring in my eyes,
hoping for you to love me
like my heart yearns for you.
but I always seem to forget that
I can never hum your melodies of the
American dream in tune. those notes
were never mine to reach.
I speak your words, but in a different rhythm.
a rhythm only the stars on a late,
yoruba evening would sway to.

your tongue is not mine

[Abigail Adigun]

[Janice Allotey]

Don't Poison My Ivy Dreams

Dear T,
Yale was indeed my first choice college.
Why the surprise and doubt
when the only class we had together was acting?
What made you think you knew of my academic performance?
I am an A student.
My coming from Africa did not make me ignorant of Yale's competitiveness.
I did feel capable. I still do.
It is unfortunate that you could say,
"If you can apply to Yale, then I should apply to Harvard."
I didn't know what it meant then. I still don't.
And even though I was not accepted, I do not feel any less capable.
Yes, I am African. And yes, I can.

Dear J,

Cornell was no doubt your first choice college.

Granted, it wasn't mine and yet I got in.

But why the resentment and negativity?

Why would you reduce my acceptance to affirmative action
when you qualify for it too?

I was not an Athlete,

unlike you, but we were both in the National Honor Society.

Is that why you thought I was less deserving?

I didn't know why you felt that way then. I still don't.

And even though you were not accepted, I know you are capable,
as am I. I am African. And yes, yes, I can.

Sincerely,
Your fellow woman of color.

[Gugu Ngwenya]

Cultic Womanhood

I taint my sheets with the sign of life,
Red Full moon,
You greet every month.
A small hello
To remind me that I AM,
in tune with the patterns of the Earth.
Release my tide Red Moon.
Flow these glorious waters.
Tear down my walls
And paint my surroundings,
Velvety, bright and magnificent.
Birth me afresh in my femininity.
Remind me of my covenant.
The deal I sealed,
In my mother's Womb.

[Vivian Ibemere]

Until when would
you walk on thorns

I t was on a harmattan Orie day, you found your way out of your mother's womb. The trees had lost most of their leaves and were now naked as the wind thrust its branches back and forth. Papa paraded the entryway of her hut with an Mkpi which would be slaughtered to celebrate the good news. His eyes were awake like that of an owl in the dark and twitched every time Obiageli wailed in gripe. That was your mother's name; they jibed that she had come into the world to be a baby factory and eat to her full, if she did right by men.

That same day your cousin was born too. His cry was like an Ogene, deafening to the ears and travelling to the borderline of the village. You didn't bawl much, just a little sound as you broke free from the cord that cinched you to your mother. Your arrival planted a furrow on Papa's forehead and made him turn up his nose; the shape of a vulture's beak under hot breath. He marched back to the market to re-sell the goat. You didn't complete your mother's joy either. Although you were her splitting image, you still didn't meet up to expectation. You had few visitors, peeping into your bitsy face and yakking, "Another child will come," with tightened lips while your cousin had the whole village gracing his arrival with gifts.

At twilight, the aroma of roasted Mkpi infiltrated into your mother's hut. She had been sitting on the straw mat with your brittle body in her sweaty hands since your birth. She drowned in the flood of her tears from the blare of exultation that crowned her sister's-in-law teeming hut. Papa came to see you only once and shook his head disturbingly when he saw you.

"Better a deformed male child to this thing," he wounded her with his words and your mother bent her head in abashment to avoid contact with his wrathful eyes. Your mother mused herself as an unaccomplished woman, no better than a barren one. You became a burden too heavy to bear, a child whose name will never be treasured. You were a chirpy baby clutched in mourning arms, unaware of the tenets that came with your birth.

You made appellations for yourself as you sprouted into an agile girl. You left the villagers with talks so wild that it burnt their lips. You did things only boys like your cousin were meant to do. The other day, your cousin Nwaokoro had to stand guard while you climbed a tree; to aggravate the abomination, it was an Udara tree. You overlapped your grassy tinted wrapper too high that your udeaki oil smeared legs were ajar for Nwaokoro to see more than his cocoa eyes could carry, until he lost count of the Udara fruits you plucked and threw down at him. Your mother scolded you when you got home but not compared to what Papa did to you. He made you hug the sour-sop tree in the compound and bound you to it as he lashed your buttocks with a sturdy palm frond.

'You'll learn to behave like a girl," he bellowed, tearing your tender skin. To your mother's amazement, you didn't shed a drop of tears, you held the stem firmly and with shut eyes, you swallowed the pains. Papa got tired and left you in that position till the next day, when he sonorously pointed out where you belonged; below, in a place where pots burn under tongues of fire but certainly not on top, not even the top of a tree.

When you turned thirteen, your mother gave Papa a new born after innumerable attempts. His splotchy lips, vibrated as he showered your mother's tawny face with saliva, "Give me children that will stay in my compound, not the ones that are fleeting."

Your mother had raised his hackles again. You watched him slam the door and its thundering noise jerked your little sister. You noticed that your mother threw her mouth open to say something but no words came out. You wondered how long she would be heaped with curses for birthing female children. How long would she walk on the thorns decorated on her path by men?

It happened in the farm, that which will change you. You didn't know what it was, your mother had never said anything about it to you before. The fear of death also gripped you, but when death didn't come and you continued to bleed profusely, you cut out an extra piece from your palm oil stained wrapper and placed it firmly between your thighs; this made you walk like Agaba Masquerade: the one women were not allowed to see except they wanted to be flayed. The knifelike pain you felt made you whine as you clasped your waist like one in labour. You couldn't carry the harvested yams, so you left them behind and tottered home in the company of flies, they were overwhelmed by the smell you reeked. Some women observed your wobbly steps and shot you the look meant for those with leprosy. They said you were unclean and shouldn't touch anybody but you still didn't know what was happening to your body. The only person you knew with an answer was at home. Your mother's bruised arms caught you as you lurched into Papa's muddy compound, where four huts stood; the first was your mother's, everlastingly isolated. She slightly pinned her nose as the smell you vented, wafted into her nostrils.

"Mama, help me," you shrieked in your unconsciousness, your henna face drifted to coal in distress.

Your mother gave you something which had the colour of salt for your lost strength and assisted you behind the hut to clean up. She said it was your "Iheonwa Nwaanyi" and that it had taken yours a while to visit.

That windy evening, Papa saw you clenching to your stomach in front of your mother's hut and hexed you at a distant for feeling so much pain because of the untold gizzards you had stolen from your mother's pot.

"Wild girl, now you're paying back for eating the meats you weren't supposed to eat!" he looked you up and down, causing his bushy eyebrows to dance irately and strolled to sit with his brother, on whose face sat two vertical tribal marks, under the moonlight. You heard them call out Nwaokoro to taste a cup of palm wine as a son of the soil, his name wasn't fleeting. You didn't belong to that soil, this was the reason Papa didn't add 'nwa' in front of your name rather he gave you a name with a hovering question mark. Papa called you, Amurunwa... did they born a child? Mama called you Amie, to ease the chagrin that came with calling your name.

"This means your journey as a woman just started," your mother added, startling your thoughts as she slowly sat close to you under the moon. Her hands, sliding into yours; they were coarse from trying to melt the heart to their happiness, still, it remained hardened. Your head was filled with questions as you gazed into her pale eyes; colourless and lacking strength to tend to her wounds. If the journey she meant was the one she's treading on, you don't wish to take the same road. A journey void of empathy for a fellow traveler wasn't the type you plan to embark upon. A journey coated with thorns, piercing deep into your feet as a woman whereas the other traveler treads on immune feet and stabs you with insults when you groan with pain, wasn't the kind of journey you pictured. When you're ready for the journey, you plan to take the road without thorns and shackles.

Soon, news of your first blood which visited you at the age of seventeen spread like wildfire and suitors started to troop into your father's compound. Your hips seemed to have transformed overnight looking voluptuous, even Nwaokoro couldn't help but stare in wonderment. You didn't like any of the men and Papa became scared that if you're given too much freedom, you'll end up like an old model bicycle in his garage and he threatened that the next one that comes, you'll definitely be sold off to him. Your mother didn't say anything. She was only to be seen, not heard.

That night saw you in another village. You told your mother that you wanted to take a leak but had already packed your bags early that day and hid it in the empty terra-cotta pot which you flung over your shoulders and journeyed. You refused to be buried by the drought that reigned over you the day you were born. If the road to freedom isn't easy to come by, you plan to go in search of it. But first, you changed your name to Nwanyibuaku... because you know you're priceless.

[Ewuradwoa]
Born a Crime

I was born a crime
By virtue of just being black
Since day one, a target
Has always been loaded at my back
There are many struggles and pain
Of being black in America.

I was born a crime
By virtues of just being black
I am the police favorite target
Because of the color of my skin
Because of the color of my skin
They paint me as
Violent
A threat to society
A thief
Someone who always resists arrest
These are the many struggles and pain
Of being black in America.

I was born a crime
By virtue of just being black
My life has been normalized
Normalized to being a statistic
A statistic of police brutality
A hashtag of senseless killings

A 911 call for being African American

I was born a crime
And all these Karen's are fully aware
These Karen's are fully aware of their privilege
The privilege that they enjoy which I lack
So they bank on time
And more times than we are ready to admit
Frame a black man for an injustice he didn't commit

Karen is fully aware of this fact so she calls
The cops immediately
Karen makes these false accusations which
Happen more often than we think
False accusations made to the police against black people
I was born a crime
By virtue of just being black
These are struggles of being black in America

I was a born a crime
So my voice is powerless
So my cry is silent
So my pain is meaningless
So my anguish is their music
So my fear is ignored

I am dead now
Being black in America wow
It's what got me killed

I cannot breathe
I cannot breathe
My stomach hurts
My neck hurts
My everything hurts
I cannot breathe.

Dear police officer, I am dead now
Dear Karen's, I am dead now
Do you not hear me
Do you not hear the wailing cries of the dead
We are dead now
Why is your knees pressing down on my neck
Why are all 3 of you killing me
Why are all of you killing me
Is it not enough that everyday
I am powerless
Powerless in a system that says my blackness is a crime
Is it not enough that I cannot breathe
Can you not feel my pain
I could still be alive
I could still be alive
Had you checked my pulse

I am dead now
My blackness in America killed me
I cannot breathe
I cannot breathe
My everything hurts

Being born a crime
By virtues of being black
Has killed me
I simply cannot breathe.

Please do something
So my death does not just become another hashtag
So my death does not just become a series of furious posts
I am dead now
Do not kill another of my fellow black brothers.
Being born black killed me.

[Lerato Makuwa]
Boundless Matter

One of my wildest dreams includes black women not being told they're strong, are matriarchs of and for atrocities and are more commendable as housing of pain. It is a wild dream, it is a constantly prevalent forethought.

I am being honest where society has let us be vulnerable, silently, through the glide of letters - things enough to pass in prison.

Stereotypically the sound of my voice is thought too loud, but sure has more to do with the prick of the truth. Here honesty lays blatant and audacious, potentially to be buried, but conscious enough to evoke a few interrogations for constructs - baring similarity to the life of an African woman, before and after death.

The idea that the absence of strength is parallel to powerlessness is groundless and an insult to those who moved through emotion honestly and offered softness and clarity that healed a lineage, or simply made one love dearly. Trauma ignites no supernatural ability within me and the expectation is deeply rooted and unproductive to my healing. Let me pick my power.

My power need not be revolutionary but present. Presenting itself in sufficient manners that make oneself feel whole. Mistakenly it is thought to be integral that power overrides other elements, instills fear – but unmistakably, my power exists as things I'd like to remember fondly of my spirit. Less of things that control the way I am to exist.

The parts of me that are whole are decided by me, influenced by the women who exhibited their joy before me. I am no longer a part of what I am to "be".

Let me provide my choices without the thought of deviating, in question of where misogynior will place me on moral hierarchy. Morals created to fence the comforts I bring, morals present to clothe the pain he'll pick – things enough to pass prison.

Tiring upkeep of the narrative of what I am to carry "as a woman", stripping me, a black woman of my humanity, rooted in the idea of strength in a black woman, is weighted by the terror systems of patriarchy, which leak into race, class, and the rest of what aims to engage with limit. A system instructing how women are to be treated, thought of, reasonings for their murder, and other stomach knotting numbers of numbing normalcies.

Being boundless beyond these matters is something that shouldn't have happened or provided surprise. But is as we acknowledge, a gearing towards validating the existence of every woman. Validating that harm is not of way, inclusion only is simply not enough, choice is not of opinion and that joy is for us too.

For now, my existence is held together by vulnerability, spaces of kindness, every brink of honesty, every light of black woman joy, every place I am heard - all these the tenderness of African women. May they be protected, remembered, taught, acknowledged and let to outwardly glide through letters - words that remind them that they deserve to be alive and leave this earth with dignity. Before the archives.

Weary not Mother

Nguseer Gavar

On colorism. The 'I,' is not always self-referential.

[Siju Falade]
Dark

This dark...
This dark.
This crow.
This dark.
This oil spill.
This dark.
This tar baby.
This dark.
This tar baby bathed in oil.
This dark!
This midsummer night's dream...but ain't not beauty in that.
Won't ever be anybody's dream,
any man's wet dream,
anyone's dream girl.
Beyonce don't live here.
Ain't no sunshine in this skin.
Only lonely and spite and shame
And sin so black make you forget your name.
Demon's so heavy you forget to call upon Jesus's name...
Forget to ask for forgiveness.
...ain't no forgiveness here.
Only dark.

A Broken Clock Still Chimes

The last time I heard the screams sipping through the walls that demarcated my room from my neighbour's, I had goose bumps all over my skin. It was midnight and the sound travelled far, flooding my room with invisible demons. What is happening to Sekoni? I asked myself. I thought of going to rescue her from whatever was inflicting pains on her but "what if the monster overpowers me too and kills us both?" I was still thinking of what to do when I heard a loud banging on my door.

"Don't answer" a voice in my mind told me.

"But that could be Sekoni calling for rescue" another voice told me.

"You can still hear the screams coming from her room, so that cannot be Sekoni" the first voice said logically.

"But you can hear the shouts from the door" the second voice countered.

"What if I open the door and Sekoni's predator pounces on me?" I reasoned. "No, it's too risky" I convinced myself.

It was double trouble for me: firstly, Sekoni is in trouble and needs my help; secondly, I may be in danger if whoever is knocking on my door is not Sekoni. Why has whatever is plaguing her chosen today? Today that my other neighbours are not at home and we are the only ones around. I looked at my elder sister who came to visit me and wished she didn't come. What if something happens to her? Mira had always wanted to visit me in school but her job didn't let her. "Thank God I'm finally on leave" she shrieked into the phone when she called me two days ago. "I'm coming to see you in school baby" she added before I could respond. I was excited to have her around. I prepared a delicious plate of jollof rice and plantain for her. Among my siblings, we were closest. Now I don't know what will become of us if anything happens.

That night was exceptionally long. At 6 a.m., I opened my door and peeped at Sekoni's door to see if there was anything unusual but there was none. I walked out and knocked on her door.

"Sekoni!, Sekoni!," I called. No answer. I hope she's still alive.

"Sekoni!" I called louder, banging on her door. I was getting agitated. Why isn't she answering? Why is everywhere so quiet? I was panting and my head was aching. Lord, have mercy!

"Is she unconscious? Did the beast hit her? Who do I call for help? How do I break this door and get in?" These were the questions running through my mind.

"Sekoni! Sekoni!" I screamed. If she was traveling to the world beyond, she might hear me on her way and return.

I was still trying to help Shekoni when I felt a very cold palm land on my right shoulder. I froze. The beast. The predator. I am finished! O Lord! I closed my eyes to wish off the dread. The hand shook me as if to shake off the fear from me.

"Oke, wake up. I'm here"

I opened my eyes. Sekoni was staring at me.

"You were shouting my name. Sorry I didn't come on time; I was washing my clothes outside. Is everything okay? You sounded apprehensive." There was a look of concern on her face.

"What happened to you last night?" I asked, surprised at her composure.

"Last night? Nothing. We were watching a movie here before you slept off and I went to wash my clothes. Mira went to see her friend" she replied, a mocking smile playing around her mouth.

I looked at the laptop on the bed. I glanced at the clock on the wall. It was 3pm. I had slept for three hours. And dreamt.

As my head became clearer, I recalled my literary theory lecturer explaining Sigmund Freud's psychoanalytic submissions on dream analysis. This dream is a collection of fragments of the fears that gripped me whenever Sekoni's boyfriend was at it. The screams usually start from the bedroom and move to the kitchen. The utensils are instruments of war. Adam, Sekoni's boyfriend, was usually soft-spoken, but when he screamed at her, his voice roared like that of a thousand demons. What an irony. Looks can be deceiving. He looked responsible with his finely trimed beards and outlined hairline. His long sleeves and trousers were always ironed with defined creases. I thought he worked in a bank until Sekoni told me he was a barber. He sure has barbed humanity off his senses! At a glance you'd think he was a gentle man but he is not even a "g"!

I had always told Sekoni to respect herself enough to refuse such treatment.

"Sekoni, you were screaming in my dreams..." I was trying to make her see why being with Adam was not right. But as usual she gave me a look that questioned my alertness...

"I'm not even joking." I said, waving off her playful expression. "That was how you were screaming last week", I added hoping to get her attention. It worked. Her face registered pain, anger and in a swift transition, a resigned and nonchalant look.

"Oke, come off it. It's behind me now". She can't fool me.

"Are the pains also behind you now? Don't be fooled by the short respite you enjoy when Adam isn't around. Right now, your life is a mess of pains and horror punctuated by short mirages of fake happiness...

"Come on, don't make me the object of your worry. I am smiling, aren't I?

"You can't fool me. You can't fool yourself. That smile is a failed parody of true happiness..."
She held up her hand to stop me. "Oke, please! I am not having this conversation". She was making move to stand up but I held her back.

"Sekoni, you're like a sister to me. I can't watch you continue hurting like this. I am talking because I don't know what else to do. Girl, you don't deserve this". I held her hands in mine and watched her tears drop on her lap.

"He loves me. I know. He's having a bad time right now..."

"He's been having a bad time since you met him" I cut in. She sighed. "Let me go finish up my washings". She left.

I felt bad for being so hard on her. Maybe I shouldn't have pushed the conversation so far. But it was high time I did; it's in my place to help her. I thought of talking to Mira about it but I knew what her response would be. She'd say "if he doesn't treat you right, you're in the wrong place". Mira wasn't one to tolerate any form of maltreatment. When Mira returned we talked about Sekoni and how to rescue her. We were still talking when Adam retuned from work. From my room, we could him querying her the moment he walked in.

Adam was mad with Sekoni for not answering the phone when he called. She explained to him that she was charging her phone in the house while washing her clothes outside. He wouldn't listen.

"Today I wanted pounded yam and egusi as against the beans we planned to eat. But no, you wouldn't pick your calls. I don't give a rat's ear what you were doing..." Adam spat in rage. Mira and I decided to intervene because we knew blows would follow.

"Adam, I said I am sorry. I can make the pounded yam..." we entered into the kitchen in time to see Adam slapping her across the mouth so violently that blood spilled from her mouth, spraying the sink and the wall in the side of the kitchen where she stood before she landed on the floor. Blood was oozing from her mouth, staining the floor where her face lied.

In one swift move, my sister picked the frying pan from the gas cooker and landed it on Adam's head, knocking him clean out. Everything happened so fast I couldn't believe it was real. Adam was bleeding from his head where the pan hit him. Sekoni was on the floor crying. Mira was frozen in shock. I was standing but I couldn't feel myself. In a flash, everything seemed to resume movement. We took Adam and Sekoni to the hospital nearby. Sekoni had been there before so the doctors knew it was domestic violence. We paid the bills from the money we found in Adam's work bag.

It's been three months since Sekoni left Adam. Yesterday, Sekoni and I attended at a ladies' function themed on self love. "If you don't know your worth, anyone will misuse you" Sekoni whispered to me during the closing remarks. A broken clock still chimes; and it tells the time correctly. I smiled at her smiling face as she turned to focus on the speaker again. Leaving Adam was a smart choice. It's a new dawn for my friend.

[Ifunanya Juliet Ottih]

Even With My Period

I am strong, I am vibrant
But when they see me among men,
Chasing dreams, with an open face.
You hear their voices fade
With long faces, they say
She is as soft as the nesting dove.
The tiny sparrow of a woman
Whose legs are too weary
 to make a high jump.
Amidst them, she won't last for two days
Because in between her legs,
Lives the waves of pains
Rushing down like heavy rain.
With a burning gaze,
I laughed lines on their aging faces.
As I unapologetically took spaces.
Today, I can hear their muted voices

saying my name in different phases
I know that with their tongue,
They had pushed me to the path of exile,
They hindered my glory from excel
And there were nights,
I was consumed by fear.
But In one of those nights with strive,
The sweet smell of success,
told me that I am history about to happen.
So without cold feet, I moved to glory.

In generations to come,
Their daughter's name will be scribbled down
That their periods, unhindered them.

[Ladunni Peace]

Equality

Her place is her smile
Just like the sun and the moon
So is he and she
Her smile lightens the planet
Without daybreak there will be no dusk
Without dusk there will be no dawn
She has her place to take

Why treat one less than the other?
Why not give her her place
Let her face be seen
Let her fill her space
Because no one can fit in
Yes! Not even he, will fit in

She deserves a life to live
Her goals to achieve

As the rain and the sun is important to a growing plant in the garden
So is he and she important in the garden of life

Why then make her live in fear
Why do the world think she's weird?

Her place is not just in pumping and shipping of breastmilk
She is a focal symbol too
She needs her place that will be her base in this world
Where she won't be scarred off
Where intimidation and superiority walk away as she assume seat

Enough of letting her potentials waste
She's had enough of shattered dreams
Her place has been neglected
Her world is in a mess

Her world needs her
Why not surrender to her her post
Where she will pursue her passion
Where she can survive reasonably well

For how long will he that does not fit in fill up her space?
Her shoes are too big that no leg will fill the space in it
She is, that turn tears untold

To tears of gold
She is, that make the days brighter than the sun
She is, that makes life sweeter than honey
With her life is not just one flavour

So the journey is not monotonous
With her life is full of different colours
She is the center of the world
The world around her revolves
She just must be involved

She fills her place in a distinguished manner
Her place is the bright light that will make Africa find her way
through the labyrinth of the world.

[Glennise Ayuk]

On Becoming

I have always thought that plants have it easier. Laurina mango seeds will sprout into laurina mango trees. And paw-paw seeds will grow paw–paw trees. You are certain of this at planting. Humans, however have it different. Birth through living is an adventure-like journey. You inevitably have to explore, in order to discover who you are (identity) and why you're here (purpose).

To discover and embrace your identity is what constitutes the process of becoming. The process to fully identify, define and understand the substance you're made of; without which the full purpose and expression of it will be suboptimal. This piece is about that journey for me. A journey that was influenced by three different inputs: the things I came with, the things that came to me and the things I went for.

I was born a fair-skinned black African woman. My kinky hair and melanin came with my genes. I was born with my mother's resilience and my father's epic ability to write. With the pride of ancestors who willingly died by drowning over been taken as slaves; and the fortitude of the women and men who defied the treacherous, barbaric practice that colonization was. From that September day almost 26 years ago, the blood in my veins was filled with emotions and power; and they would shape my identity and purpose by simply being there.

I was born into a blended family and grew up amidst a family dynamics that left me crying why? That was something that came to me.

Just like all the things reading exposed me to, when I ardently started at 7. Most of my early story books were written by non–Africans and the novels I read in my teens were Harlequin, or set in Europe or America. My dad's was the among the first African folklore books I encountered. So yes, one thing that dawned on me with a strong impression was the scarcity of stories set in Africa; which I interpreted to either mean African settings were not story-worthy, or that we didn't have stories to tell about ourselves, or both. These are highly inaccurate, of course, but the literary input that came to me as a child delivered them as fact.

I read many history books. I'm talking of the textbooks that were used to teach African history to children in classrooms here. They often looked like this. A sketchy chapter 1 describing Africa as uncivilized; highlighting no autonomous identity, culture or pride; and then many proceeding chapters about how colonialism changed us. (Guess who wrote those books, and guess who permitted them to be taught to children? Well, that's a story for another day!). These books and many others that began African history from when Europeans "discovered" us, and how they "named", "tamed" and "constructed" us, were one of the most destructive things that happened to my growing identity as an African.

Forming an identity around being woman was not an easy task either. The patriarchy in African society (like in non – African societies as well) is sickening. The practice of genital mutilation, child marriage, child sex workers, girl child education perceived to be wasteful, women restricted from owning or inheriting property, carry-over wives, near 0% representation of women on decision-making tables, widows' rites that make you cringe, and the highly-propagated, widely-believed fallacy that a woman without a marriage or man is incomplete and unworthy of respect. Ahh! These things came to me. And they influenced my thinking of what I should be and become as a woman. What was expected. What would result in shame and what would be applauded.

These, and the objectification of women as sex symbols – their highest worth being the offer of sexual pleasure their vaginas give – is the reason society blamed (and still does) rape victims over the rapist. When an incident happens, people want to know "how was she dressed? Was she walking in a way that showed her tempting curves?" Like somehow that justifies the evil, entitlement and abhorrence of the rapist's heart.

I grew up learning also that sexual expression was filthy and taboo...for women. No talks about menstruation. Frankly, people, menstruation??? Talk less of being horny, or expressing frustration at a sexually unfulfilling marriage or relationship. Haba! Even reading, learning or asking about sex was a "God forbid!" The result of this was that many women shrunk, and then hid or tamed their sexual expression. Detrimental! (Now, there is a difference between vulgarity and the freedom to embrace/explore the sexual part of your being. I mean the latter, but you are entitled to your opinion).

There was also visual media, which like the novels showed this African 90's kid mostly the West. The white West. Cartoon princesses I came to adore had pale white skin and straight hair that looked nothing like mine. I was fed standards of beauty that hardly included the African woman I was.

So as an adult, I began to struggle. I am a beautiful woman. A very beautiful woman. When you add that to education, a creative edge, a kind, soulful spirit and a smart brain, I have heard and seen how that beauty can be magic! I turn heads when I pass by. Heads of men and women. But I struggled with accepting that I was beautiful. I often asked myself "was I beautiful because I was fair – skinned?" Because what had come to me was that "the whiter, the nicer", so here I was, feeling guilty for being beautiful as a light-skinned African woman. Even feeling ashamed sometimes. All these struggles, before I finally came home.

Let me tell you the worst part about the things that came to me. It was how as an adult global citizen, the media, literature, structured institutions and several of my personal interactions influenced me to believe that by being a woman, black and from Africa, I was at the lowest on the world's prism of honour. They propagated my race to be most inferior. Then they propagated my gender to be most inferior. Then they propagated my continent of origin to be most inferior. When you apply all these metrics, a black woman from Africa is seemingly the lowest human on the planet. Absolutely perfidious and completely untrue, but my sub-conscious accommodated it at the time. The conditioning into this thought process was subtle, believable and came through familiar faces and cultures, prized books and award–winning TV drama. It left me thinking that I was at the bottom of the world's caste, and needed to undo one or more of these aspects of my identity, if I was going to find a place in this world.

The things that came to me have also been good, of course. Through the very channels of family, literature, media, internet and societal culture. But this piece is about my struggles and challenges on my journey to discovery, and I would not sugar coat that.

The things I went for were my choices. I had been borne. I had been exposed. But I ultimately only became who I chose (both actively and passively) to be and embrace.

I have loved men. My early twenties saw me sweetly naïve, and fully but wrongfully indoctrinated about what a woman had to be. I was also a growing girl still intimidated by my childhood insecurities and possessing a raging rebellion against a lot of the things that had come to me. I wasn't even conscious of it – this rebellion – but my spirit lived it in the recklessness that a child would. So as you would imagine, I chose a man who resisted aspects of that rebellion, which irritated my "demons" and triggered them to grow.

More than once in my life, I have settled. Friendships, relationships, ambitions. There was an intimidation that arose from within, not without, that silenced me in the language and voice of all the struggles that had come for me. Some of whose remnants I still carry today.

...like my weariness about marriage. When I was 21, I came across the diary I had kept as a 9 year old. Here's what I'd written "I want to marry at 39. I know it sounds late, but I want to have time to enjoy before I suffer". Tears rolled down my eyes to see that. I hugged the book to my chest like that would somehow comfort my 9 year old self. I could sense the little girl's concession to marry because it was what was expected of her. I could feel her fear to deviate from that expected, even though she perceived it a painful path. But I could also feel her courage to dare live at least some of her life on her terms, and that made me proud.

I am not proud though, of those times I deliberately underperformed in a bid to not stand out. I feared I would be too much and people wouldn't like it. That they would reject and question my worthiness, because how dare you at the the very bottom of the prism attempt to shine this much light?

I am out of numbers recalling the times I did not seize the moment and fully express my opinion, skill, intellect or sexuality. When I didn't walk in confidence because I was afraid of being called proud; or explore my sexuality weary of being called inappropriate. When I tolerated associations longer than I should have for fear of "losing people" or self-tormented at the thought that a "no" I got came because I was black, African and woman in a pool of humans. (Frankly, even if that were ever the case, now it doesn't matter. I know I'll just walk out and build my own table). Now is about a part of the journey where being Black, African and Woman (**BAW**!) is not a weakness. It is not something I should be pitied for, or have standards lowered to accommodate me. Naaaaa. Leave your standards where they are and bring me in. Try the power of **BAW**! It's a matter of time, and then you'll be raising those standards to meet me.

Now more than ever, I know that whether by metrics of race, gender or continent of nationality, I am not inferior. My place in the world is in the spaces and rooms where all other humans are found. Now is about a never – ending journey of self – discovery. Of deliberate choices. To self – love even more fiercely. To serve, and to be at peace with myself.

"You owe it to the potential within you to not be mediocre" is something I always say. So now is also about the relentless pursuit of the things that set my soul on fire. And the relentless loving of the people who do. It is about working hard and smart and carrying zero entitlement. Embracing prayer and spirituality. Actively choosing my path, tribe and reactions; and finding in myself the purpose that enables me to find others.

Now I look in the mirror and see a goddess. And she's a **BAW**! At every mention of "goddess", I see myself, my mother and the women in my tribe. I see Arikana Chihombori–Quao, and I feel the spirit of Yaa Asantewaa.

So I can call on African girls to proudly bear that privilege of being woman and African, because I have felt the honour of that gift in my bones. Proceed to embrace this honourable identity with soul and grace, because to run away from it is to compromise your path to purpose.

I want you to remember that you are beautiful by all measures; and that is so because you say so. That the world has not seen the full spectrum of an African woman's prowess because they have not seen you. That your courage, leading and impact – whether overt or concealed – are part of your purpose, so you shouldn't deter from them. You are it, **BAW**! You are enough and you are all. Just like I am.

[Hazvineyi Zinyowa]

Herstory 25years Later

Born 2 years after the Beijing Conference that called for social equality for women in the global space, the words that characterised my childhood included but were not limited to;

"A woman does not sleep in! Is that what you will be doing at your in-law's place?

"That is not how a real woman holds a broom, apply pressure on your wrists and work diligently"

"A woman does all the chores in the house, so you have to practice by doing your brother's laundry, clean and cook for everyone"

First time I knew I was different from my older sisters was when I asked mother "who said I am going to get married anyway? "And the answer I got from that was "women who think that way end up being "whores" wrecking other people's marriages "Now fast forward 23 years later, I have had a chance to witness what 'African marriages' are all about, I have had exposure to gender studies, I have had the chance to travel to some of the remote areas in my country and I have met people my age with the same mentality my family had 23 years ago. In my group friends I am considered "the feminist", man who I have had a chance to differ debate with on matters to do with respect are so patiently waiting to see how "marriage /the person I will settle down with puts me in line. "I consider myself lucky to have been enlightened on feminism, gender equality, gender mainstreaming and I cant help but worry about young girls my age who are subjected to a life of a basic education, early marriages, a life of working hard to be good wife material, a life where the choices of their spouses overlook their own preferences, a life where a man`s infidelity is blamed on a woman`s disrespectful nature, their unhygienic tendencies and their lack of spontaneity in the bedroom.25 years later and women are still exposed to the dehumanising conditions, practices and beliefs that apparently determine what makes one 'wife material". My question is what makes men "husband material" who judges them, who rates their manhood?

I acknowledge the political progress that has been made, to have female representation within the administrative part of countries, civil society interventions have been sensitized to include women in their implementation processes but the reality in Africa today is that women are the poorest beings alive, young girls are still forced into marriages ,they are withdrawn from school and very few of those cases are brought to light. Feminism and the involvement of women in development projects has remained that 'project', It has come with a start date and end date. Feminism is so much more than that. The only way real progress will be made is when feminist beliefs and ideologies are woven into our daily lives, into our religions, our practices, our cultural beliefs even if it means rearranging and modifying those to cater for the voice of the African woman. Equality will only be achieved when fellow women stop attaching derogatory phrases to women who stand up for themselves, women who stand up for other women and have proven to the rest of the society the bitter truth that is hard to swallow for most women and that is 'there is more to life than being a good wife material'.

Its high time society realises that not every female can be boxed into the 'marriage material' box, not every female can fit into that tiny box that is not big enough to fit their dreams, aspirations and career. So much more remains to be done for feminism, a lot has to be done to ensure that men do not feel threatened, disrespected and insulted when a female stands up to them. The male populations need to be sensitized on the fact that none of their respect as human beings is tied up in their ability to push women's opinions into oblivion. Men need to provide space for the flourishing of women in the political, social, economic and cultural spheres of interaction without them feeling like their efforts are undervalued. All we ask for as upcoming feminist activists is space and support to right the wrongs that have been intentionally structured to dehumanize females the way colonialization did to the African continent. We matter! Black women lives matter in Africa! Treat us right! Encourage us! Lift us up and help us realize, recognize and acknowledge our strengths as females.

The feminism movement has to start in the mindset first, let it revolutionize the psychology of women across the continent, in the remote areas of each and every country, let it be readily available in all parts of the country, let new-born babies have that information at their fingertips. Allowing the girl child to have access to education is a good a thing but it is not enough if their male siblings are not taught to respect women, to delegate the chores and to view women as powerful capable beings. Do not let boys be boys, let boys be accountable for their actions the same way girls are held accountable and responsible at a young age.

25 years later and so much more remains to be done. A lot has to be corrected, so many gaps need to be filled, a lot of sensitization has to be done to make progress for everyone even the marginalized.25 years later and the battle has literally just begun!

[Ammywrites]
The Rapist Takes All The Blame

Mother taught,
Father did too,

Watch the companies you keep.
Never go out alone, in the dark.
Keep your legs closed for that ONE man.
That dress you wear is exposed, cover up a bit more.
No, avoid night parties.
Yes, you shouldn't go to see a man alone.

A lot they said to me right from when I could understand words.
But they never did teach that:

When she says stop, do.
Her exposed legs doesn't mean an invite to a treat.
Taking what is not yours from a lady's body is ASSAULT.
A friend who assaults, should be exposed.
It doesn't matter your closeness with such person.
-to the male child.

Fingers are pointed at the female child,
To be educated, to be blamed.
Shame on you
If you totally ignore the male.
And blame it on the state of déshabillé
As the master minder of every sexual mistake.

Being Woman

Woman. It's the title society gives me. Why? Simple reason; I was born with breasts and a vagina. At first, that was all the title meant to me. I was distinct from a man because of this. But, being woman has begun to mean much more to me than the sexual organs I possess.

Let me talk about myself a little. My name's Ursula and most people say I'm a tomboy. I rarely wear dresses, I don't own skirts and make-up actually scares me. If you want to find me, you'd have to look for the girl wearing African print shorts, a T-shirt and long sleeved shirts rolled up to the elbows, with a cap.

Now, you may be tempted to say that the way I grew up is the reason I tend to lean towards masculinity than femininity. You might be tempted to say that I may become transsexual. You may be highly tempted to say (it's already been said) that I am attracted to other women and thus dress this way so that I'm more masculine than feminine to them.

Let me disabuse you of those – at least almost all those – notions. This is not to say there's anything wrong with being trans or gay. I'm a woman, and except for once every month where I rue the day Eve ate that apple, I love being a woman. I suppose you would expect me to start gushing about all the advantages of being a woman over being a man. While I'm tempted to do this, I'll indulge later. Right now, we're talking about what being woman means to me.

At first, I felt like an impostor. I don't think that is the right word but I can't think of a better one. I wasn't a conventional girl and the people around me made sure I never forgot it. Whenever I came back from the barbershop with a new haircut, I was reminded of how "a woman's glory is her hair." Whenever I went out in shorts instead of a skirt, I was reminded of how if I wasn't feminine enough, I wouldn't attract men because they would see me as one of them.

I felt wrong. Yes, wrong. As if I was an anomaly. Why couldn't I be feminine? Why couldn't I walk in heels like my friends and spend time making myself up? Why did I not enjoy having my hair in different hairdos every other month? I felt like an accident. Perhaps, I was meant to be a boy but there were some mix ups at the assembly line when I was being put together and ended up with "extra" body parts. I began to wish I were male instead of female.

I hated the people who kept making me feel like I was not worthy of having a female body. I hated the people who made me feel like I was abusing a gift. If I had your body, I would flaunt it. I wouldn't be hiding it behind loose shirts and unflattering shorts. I hated those who judged me because I didn't fit into their idea of who a woman should be. Why can't you be feminine? Why do you walk like that? Why can't you behave like a girl? I especially hated those boys who would tell me that I was gay after I turned down their

269

advances. I'm very sure you're gay. If not, why would you say no to me? Girls are dying over me and you're here telling me no. You're gay. Even the way you dress and act shows it.

First of all, you can't tell a person's sexuality by the way they act or look. That's just nonsense. Also, it annoyed me that they thought I was gay. I have no problem with being gay. I'm not homophobic and I think a person has the right to love whomever they want, regardless of what gender the other person identifies with. What annoyed me about their thinking I was gay was that those obnoxious asses felt so entitled that the only reason they could think of for my refusal was that I was gay. As if they were perfect people and could never have any flaws that may turn a woman away. They spoke as if being gay was a blight, like it was some kind of leprosy. That really irked me.

Most of all though, I hated myself for actually believing those people and letting their words get to me. I went through a phase where every once in a while, I would doll up just so people would realise that I could be feminine if I wanted to be. I just wasn't inclined to be. I would hate very minute of it but I would do it.

The deal breaker for me was the harsh response I got each time I said I had no desire to be married. If it happened, fine, but it wasn't something I was actively seeking out. One person went as far as telling me that no matter how many degrees I got or how well I made a name for myself, I was a useless woman if I remained unmarried. That stung. It didn't sting because I believed that I was actually useless if I didn't get married. It stung because I realised, albeit a little too late, that I lived in a society where despite all the strides that were made technologically or in any other aspects, we were still deeply sexist.

My place wasn't the one I painstakingly carved for myself. My place was the nook society decided was mine, based on how well I did on its scale of femininity. Being a woman meant I had to work harder than my male counterparts for the same things. Being a woman meant I had to get married and have children else I was a waste of a woman. It meant that what was between my legs meant more to some people than what was between my ears. It meant that I had to spend the rest of my life nodding and doing as I was told, not speaking till I was spoken to and accepting that no matter how good I was at anything, I just wasn't a man.

I almost accepted all this. I very nearly decided that life would be much easier for me if I just went with the flow, you know. Just do what they expect you to do and everything would be fine. I stood at a crossroads, deciding whether or not I wanted to be cast into a predetermined mould or if I wanted to forge my own identity, society be damned.

Making a decision became very easy when I realised something that my hatred of myself had made me blind to; almost all the "conventional" women I knew weren't truly happy. They faked it, yes but deep down, they wanted more. Some even told me how they envied my difference, how they wished they could be like me. This was what made me realise that I wasn't at a crossroads at all. I was simply in a prison of my own making. I could walk out at any time.

People didn't like that I didn't fit their definition of a woman? How was that my problem? Deciding to be what they wanted me to be was letting them win, it was bowing to a deeply flawed system that was enduring because people like me decided to fall in, instead of stand out. So what if I cut my hair and thus had no "glory?" Glory didn't pay the bills. What if boys thought I was gay because I dressed like them? No sweat. It reduced the number of people I had to politely let down. And I was a waste of a woman if I didn't get married? Pfft!

The day I realised this, I attained a level of nonchalance that terrifies me sometimes. These days, I tell anyone who deigns to tell me how I'm doing womanhood wrong to go have biblical knowledge of themselves. Let me wallow in my wrongness. I like it and it benefits me.

I am a woman because I have breasts and a vagina, true. However, I am also a woman because I refuse to soften and let people tell me how to live my life. There is no right way to be a woman. There is no one definition of what a woman should be and there certainly is no right way to do womanhood. I have learnt that and I am glad I have.

Accepting myself hasn't meant that life has suddenly become easier for me. It means that this time, I am more equipped to face whatever is thrown my way because I am accepting of what I am and what I am capable of. I am choosing to forge myself each day, rather than be moulded into a soulless version of myself.

[Adedoyin Adebiyi]

Liberation

Chidinma drew her jacket tighter around her body, she was holding her paycheck as if it was the first time she was receiving one. But it might as well be the first time, how was it that she had never thought to ask how much her male colleagues in the office were making. They worked the same hours, spat out roughly the same amount of ideas in their advertising firm and yet she was being payed twenty thousand less than the rest of them.

She remembered coming home, fuming when her envelope had being accidentally switched only to realize that she was well below her junior, her junior who was payed better because his genitalia was protruding from his body. Chidinma was mad, she was livid because how was it that she had not seen this before, she thought everything was good but apparently she was wrong.

And then the look her boss had given her as she matched to his office in righteous fury had further made her mad. "It's not me, if it were left to me you would even be payed more and as you know my hands are tied,, it's the board of directors that run this show," he then shrugged apologetically, forgetting that she works in an advertising agency and could sell ice to a penguin. So she did just that, she inputted subtle messages in her new proposals. She actively twitted about workplace injustice and she garnered the help of her husband and friends to make sure that if you were in the same department you should be payed equally regardless of what was in between your legs and provided you worked hard for it.

273

There were moments when Chidinma felt like she was fighting a losing battle and going down a rabbit hole and there were moments when she got a breakthrough and then she was yanked back forcefully. Two steps forward ten steps backwards but she persisted because she was not only fighting for herself, she was fighting for women around her, before her and after her and their support gave her strength.

She knew her place in the world, she knew her place as a good daughter, sister, wife and mother but it seemed for the longest of times she thought she knew her place at work. She felt like the maid scraping the bottom of the barrel even though she had soured the grapes to make the wine. Half of the successful commercials were hers, right from a young age she had a very wacky imagination and she used it to her advantage.

So clutching the last paycheck from oyc advertising agency she swung open the glass doors to her new place of work, a comic book agency where she had free rein to let her imagination run wild and make the exact amount plus some if her projects were chosen. Being appreciated was good, doing what you love is splendid and doing what you love and getting payed well for it is liberating.

Afri-Femme Est Une Femme Africaine.

Elle est dans uneculture qui sous-estime son genre.

Elle a grandi avec l' idee que son principal travail est de trouver un homme qui va la marier et

de faire des enfants.

Sa terre natale essaye de fermer sa voix. Elle ne doit pas partager son opinion sinon elle est

consideree "DISOBEDIENT"

...

Afri-femme est cette femme dans le champs qui porte sa culture sur son dos.

Elle se leve avant tous le monde le matin, cuisine pour toute la famille, et nettoie toute la maison

Elle se couche avec des douleurs physique et se reveilles chaque matin avec un sourire sur sa

face.

Sa terre natale est precieuse. Elle est "MULTI TASKING"

...

Afri-femme est une femme forte malgres les epreuves endurees dans sa vie par la societe.

Elle s'occupe toujours des autres parfois a ses depends

Afri-femme est cette femme qui t'a permis de lire ce message. Elle t'a soutenu, t'a epaule et t' a

nourri.

Elle est forte mais "UNAPPRECIATED"

[Sonia Jona (Sonita castanha)]
Raras Relíquias

Hoje tenho 44, mas quando era mais nova, vivia ainda com os meus país, no seio das famílias, os rapazes eram super protegidos.

Pode ser que se viva assim até então, mas não seria difcil de medir pois, devido aos indeces elevados de pobreza, não é dificil para qualquer familia, ter um empregado doméstico.

Há domésticos para todos os níveis e bolsos. Há escravos.

Eles viviam pela casa aos gritos, a dar ordens às irmãs, às mães, às avós que os protegiam e permitiam tudo e mais alguma coisa. E então, os que eram rapazes únicos, em algumas casas, quase que andavam de ombros levantados como de reis se tratassem. Quando eles falassem,todos ficavam em silêncio.

276

Alguns chamavam pelas mães e pelas irmãs sem modos, fossem as irmãs mais movas ou mais velhas. Era como uma relação entre o chefe o subordinado (diga-se, uma má relação) Ou de Brão para escrava.

—Mãee, já preparaste o matabicho?
—Mana, eu estou com fome!
—Avóoo, eu estou com pressa, eu, eu eu....

Parecia o vovô a falar com a vovó, lá no campo de onde vieramos nossos pais, a vovó estava sempre ali, quase que de sentinela, pronta para servir o marido, ele nem se podia mexer, esse sim, era um verdadeiro rei, e sabia ler e escrever, teve tempo e disponibilidade para aprender...

Às vezes não era o único filho, eram dois, três e alguém tinha que os suportar, cuidar deles.

E na hora da catequese ou da escola:

—Mãe, já limpaste a casa de banho, queremos tomar banho, é que está quase na hora de ir...., logo a seguir, um grito lá do quarto para cozinha o outro filho

—Mamãaa, já se pode almoçar?...Vou me levantar, já podes vir varrer o quarto....

O Ivo, meu único irmão, nunca teve essas regalias, graças a Deus, somos frutos de uma democrata e vivíamos num regime socialista, tudo igual para todos. Porque com a mamã, não havia "cunha" nem vantagens para ninguém, apesar de ela as vezes tratar o papá como rei, não muito rei, mas rei. Porque apesar de tudo ela era independente, tinha uma vida, amigos, liberdade de ir e vir, pelo menos parecia!...

Fazia petiscos para ele e para os amigos altas horas da noite... Guardava as pernas e as miudezas da galinha pra ele. Mas pronto, o papá também ajudava. Ajudava a manter a casa arranjada, pintava as paredes, trocava as redes, arranjava as maçanetas, as torneiras e nunca lhe foi permitido dormir sem tomar banho, nem que viesse demasiado alegre.

—Vai tomar banho... Vai tomar banho, eram as palavras de ordem da mamã.
Não é normal o homem Moçambicano fazer as obras de casa, é tudo encomendado a tereciros. Nisso o pápa era especial. Talves ele merecesse mesmo as miudezas e pernas da galinha.
Com o Ivo já não era assim.

—Vou sair para o mercado, e vocês, ficam a dividir as tarefas ao meio, um varre fora, o outro dentro, um lava a louça de uma refeição e outro de outa, um limpa a casa de banho o outro rega o Jardim, mas antes, vão comprar pão para o matabicho – dizia a minha mãe.
No início ela preparava o matabicho e depois saía, alguns dias era salada de alface, com sardinha, ou salada com carapau desfeito, ou salada com "badjia" (um croquete de feijão) quentinha, ovos fritos com salada de alface, com bastante limão, hum..., tínhamos um vasto menu a medida da situação.
Lá ia o Ivo para padaria, eu ficava a ferver a água para o chá e punha a mesa. Lembro-me, como se fosse ontem, do Ivo a chegar na

cozinha, com o saco de pão na mão, de onde o tirava e punha no cesto.

Éramos, cinco na casa, e nestes momentos, sei que o papá tinha saído para o trabalho, era Director, naquele tempo, era raro para um negro.

Não me consigo lembrar onde estava o outro membro da família. Era eu e o meu irmão. A mamã ia para o Xipamanine, para o mercado fazer compras nas lojas dos Indianos, para arranjar comida para a família, e produtos para revender, porque na altura, faltava tudo.

O ivo ia lavar as mãos, voltava para cozinha, pegava no prato dele, servido por mim, conforme a ementa do matabicho, já vinha com a régua de 30 cm na mão, calculava o centro do pão, marcava com a ponta da faca e depois dividia-o ao meio. Talvez seja por isso que ele hoje seja arquitecto...

Às vezes penso também que a minha mania do perfeccionismo possa vir dai. Tudo igual, tudo certinho, porque até a roupa que vinha da RDA, que a mamã comprava na cooperativa, para mim ou para os meus irmãos era um para cada um e era igual a dos nossos vizinhos da mesma faxa etária que a nossa.

Ao lado da minha casa vivia o Raúl, a vida dele também não era "moleza" mas ele gostava. Lavava, passava, cozinhava, fazia muito bem chamussas, mas bastava andarmos uns metros para a frente e a realidade era outra.

A sociedade não educou os nossos rapazes a fazerem trabalhos domésticos, não os repreendeu e nem os preparou para vida. Um rapaz Moçambicano diferente é uma relíquia, penso cinquenta vezes para ter que me casar com eles.

As meninas tinham que comer de boca fechada, sentar-se de perna fechada, lavar as mãos antes de comer, fazer depilação, lavar e trançar muito bem o cabelo, levantar-se para dar lugar aos homens, fazer a cama, aprender a cozinhar, lavar a louça, tomar conta dos irmãos, varrer, apanhar as cuecas do irmão, cozinhar para o irmã, cuidar, controlar o período menstrual, não se mostrar aos homens, não brincar com eles principalmente nesses dias. Muita confusão.

Mas entretanto, os meninos como o Ivo e como Raúl hoje, também se escondem por trás da conjuntura, já não sabem fazer nada.

—Homens não prestam, dizem as mulheres daqui, o tempo todo.

Mas ainda assim, dentro da educação que receberam em casa, contrariada com a que recebem do mundo através da televisão filmes, terem estudado mais nos dias de hoje as mulheres, casam-se e vivem com este tipo de homem.

Tomam conta deles o tempo todo e depois ganham mérito, de boa ou de má, esposa, numa altura destas em que somos todos Engenheiros, Pilotos, Ministros. Eles continuam sentados a comanadar o remote control, ver futebol a gritar, a criticar e a avaliar as mulheres...

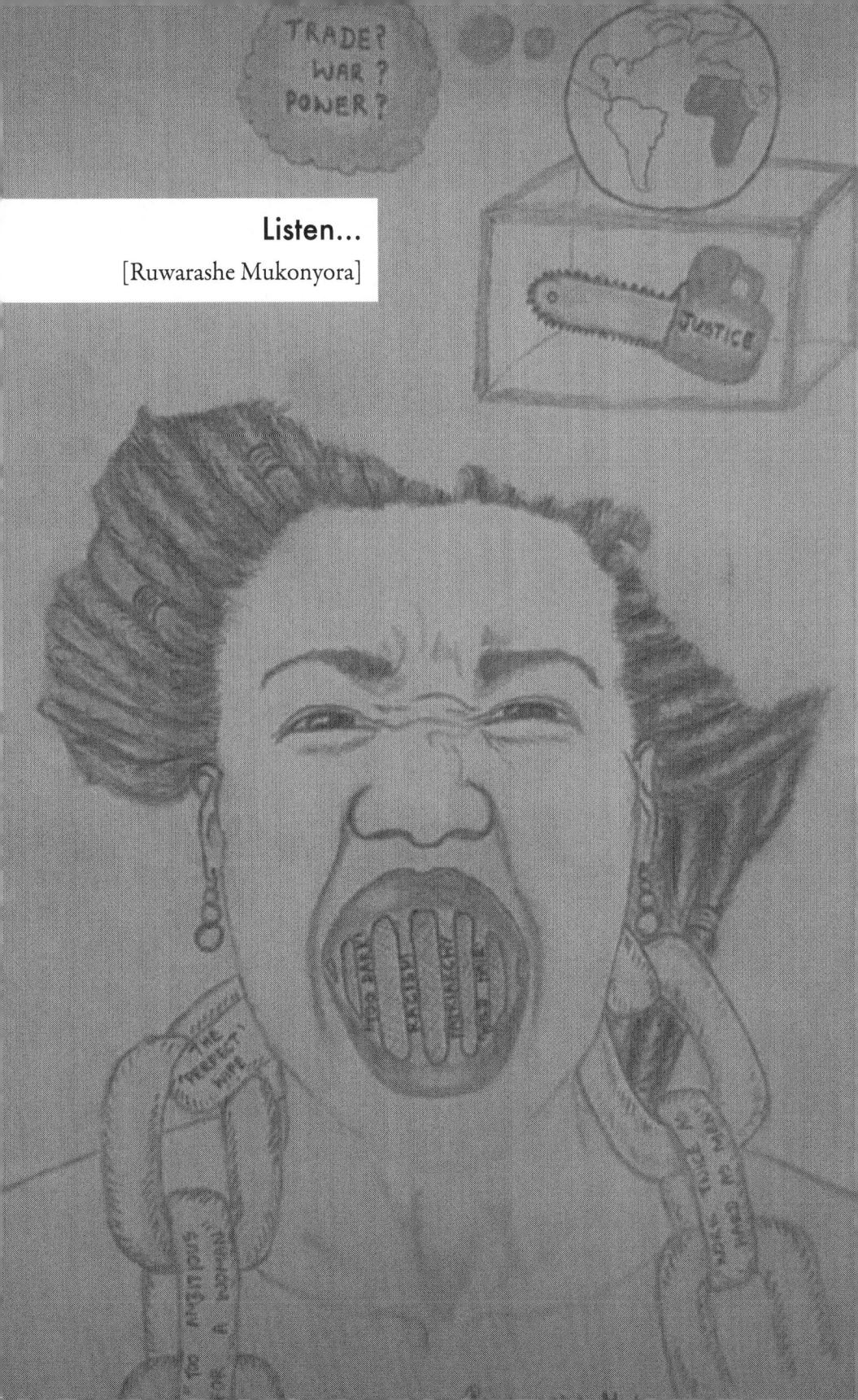

Listen...

[Ruwarashe Mukonyora]

[Joselyne The Poetess]
Gender Equity Issues During Pandemics

A Clear Insight of Gender in Ebola and COVID-19 Outbreaks: The Susceptibility Normalized

"We are in this together", is a popular phrase used by leaders and news reporters during the Covid-19 lockdown, and one that is rarely conceptualized. In the past few years, the world has faced a socio-economic and political crisis as a result of the outbreak of pandemics; the Ebola virus which first affected West Africa, and the current on-going Coronavirus also known as Covid-19. Many questions have been raised about the explosion of these diseases and how they affected and are still affecting the global society. Gender is among the most heavily affected areas of the global society. However, the world has failed to realize the vulnerability of women within such outbreaks despite the awareness of gender issues. Recognizing the vulnerability of women in pandemics should be a basis for formulating policies that address the gender imbalances embodied in the different socio-cultural and economic systems of countries. This essay evaluates the vulnerability and probability of women being infected by the Ebola and Covid-19 viruses, and the lessons the world should learn from their experience. The discussion draws examples from a global perspective, with a focus on the Democratic Republic of Congo (D.R.C), United States of America (U.S.A), Rwanda, West, and Central Africa.

Women's primary role in some societies has been marked as a risk factor in the spread of the Ebola outbreak (UN, 2014). This deadly virus that was named "a care-givers disease" in 2015 by Dr.

Paul Farmer, Chief Strategist and Co-founder of Partners In Health, was reported to be a zoonosis that has spread through West and Central Africa and killed more than 25,000 people (BBC, 2016). The spread of the disease was associated with the ways people lived and their contextual circumstances. In D.R.C, as in most African countries, the primary health care providers both at home and in hospitals are women (Menéndez et al., 2015). In fact, because of historically-reported mistrust in some leaders (Richardson et al., 2019), most sick people first consulted mothers within their communities for treatment before going to hospitals to seek more formal treatment and care. This has put many women at risk of being infected because they lacked the necessary "stuff, staff, space and system", which are the materials, skilled personnel, and well-organized health system needed to fight against Ebola (Farmer, 2015). However, a clearer solution should be taken to relieve women from the risk they face as primary caregivers.

The complex socio-cultural rules that normalized women staying home giving them a primary duty of caregiving while men worked as heads of families left some African people blinded and inconsiderate. Wouldn't it have been easy to fight against the spread of the pandemic if the negative gendered paradigms had been solved before?

Later in 2020 (Onyango, 2020), the vulnerability of women to these infections was said to be associated with sexual agency and domestic violence. After gender factors came to researchers' attention, findings showed that the Ebola virus survived in male semen for some months, which put women at risk of getting infected during sexual intercourse (Davies & Bennett, 2016). In fact, women's power is limited when it comes to sexual reproductive rights in most African cultures. This posed risks for more women to be infected by their survived husbands because there were risks that in some cases, there might be limited consent for sexual activity. The number of women infected by the virus kept increasing, more so than the infection rate for men. In West Africa, there were 8,703 cases of women and 8,333 cases of men by November 4, 2015 (Davies & Bennett, 2016). An increase in the number of cases in women could have also been associated with domestic violence. Notwithstanding the effects of domestic violence, society keeps normalizing this socially constructed violence which poses more risks to more women now and in the future. The question that should be asked is how much longer will women put up with being taken advantage of?

Despite the worsening of the Ebola virus with unrecognized gender effects, the world hasn't learned its lesson yet. Most of the mistakes made as a result of the proven gender inequities during the Ebola outbreak are still playing out in the Covid-19 situation. In Rwanda, though the government has tried to make strides in reducing existing income imbalance(GOV.RW, 2019), income inequality between men and women has left women struggling since most of them do less paying and casual jobs. This quantifies the global percentage of 76.2% of the unpaid work being done by women (Twahirwa , 2020). Staying at home is a good strategy and major recommendation in Covid-19 prevention but vulnerability occurs when the only way of survival comes from jobs that necessitate working out of the home. In fact, in the USA, research showed that the rate of unemployment during the Covid-19 had an increase of 0.9 in women and 0.7 in men (Henriques, 2020). This shows the existing imbalances of how jobs typically prescribed for women are sometimes considered less valuable than those occupied by men. Therefore, society should be sensitive to the fact that women's limitations due to socially constructed roles especially in Africa plays a role in hampering their employment.

Rwanda's journey to battle gender-imbalance is continuously moving forward. The existing gender imbalances manifested in job provision and accessibility should be put into consideration to build strong health systems. Men in Western Europe were found to be more prone to the physical ramifications of dying from Covid-19 due to their weak immune system as a result of their lifestyles such as high alcohol and cigarette consumption compared to women.

However, there is a lack of enough clear evidence to back up the difference in proneness based on gender (Henriques, 2020). Nonetheless, women tend to suffer the social and economic consequences of quarantine more as a result of limited access to a fixed income. Paying no heed to these facts poses more risks to women mainly during pandemics. A lesson the world should learn is that neither men nor women should be victims of their gender when fighting against health issues.

Reported cases of domestic violence have increased in Rwanda during the Covid-19 outbreak (Iliza, 2020). The "stay at home" policy has put spouses with violent partners at risk of being either sexually, physically, or mentally assaulted. Andrews Kananga, a Rwandan lawyer, and executive director at Legal Aid Rwanda has confirmed the receipt of more cases during the quarantine. These cases were mainly from teen mothers obliged to live with husbands who impregnated them and couples whose divorce cases had not yet been resolved before the Covid-19 outbreak (Iliza, 2020). Domestic violence doesn't discriminate, a victim can either be male or female. However, a large percentage of reported cases, mainly sexual violence, were perpetrated against women. This shows how unresolved sociocultural issues can expose and exacerbate inequities during a pandemic.

Given all the challenges women faced as a result of gender roles, what should be done? The global society should recognize the key role that women play, not as a way of repressing their roles but as a basis for formulating policies against the sociocultural violence embodied in these roles. There needs to be a reflection on these gender roles as we fight against the pandemic.

Equity and gender-centered institutions should raise awareness based on the data available on gender inequities. Normalization manifested in these imbalances makes the battle harder. Fighting against Ebola would have been easier in West and Central Africa if structural violence resulting from culturally gendered roles had been resolved. By reflecting on this, policymakers need to see that despite ongoing conversations and actions to try to level the imbalances, gender imbalances still exist and not only hamper efforts to fight against pandemics but also countries' developments.

Additionally, we need to shift our conversations from 'how far the pandemics have spread' to 'why the pandemics have spread'. Taking a closer look at why the Ebola and Covid-19 pandemics have spread, there was a big contribution of the structural violence that was already taking place before the outbreaks. A good way to go is to think big and solve the issues before they cause more problems.

The gender-related vulnerability will never end unless there is a friendly ecosystem across every sector, professional, contextual environment, and at national, regional, and community level for women. Women have been among the high prone groups in the Ebola outbreak because of the socio-cultural responsibilities they have in African society. The world needs to learn from the Ebola outbreak lessons to prevent vulnerability in the current Covid-19 pandemic. During these hard times of quarantine, governments should not only put into consideration the general poor population but also consider teen and single mothers without a reliable source of income who are struggling. There is a need for specificity because we cannot ignore that the more we generalize, the more vulnerability increases. It is this specificity that will enable health providers to look at particular reasons why women are disadvantaged. In addition, institutions in charge need to continue to fight against structural violence embodied in socio-cultural organizations manifested in job provisions, and other areas. Ebola and Covid-19 pandemics have exposed the existing economic and sociocultural gendered imbalances. It is time to create new policies, and for each and every one of us to commit to our own personal gender equity agenda, to eradicate these issues before they affect future endeavors.

References:

BBC, . (2016, January 14). Ebola: Mapping the outbreak. BBC News. https://www.bbc.com/news/world-africa-28755033

Davies, S. E., & Bennett, B. (2016). A gendered human rights analysis of Ebola and Zika: Locating gender in global health emergencies. International Affairs, 92(5), 1041–1060. https://doi.org/10.1111/1468-2346.12704

Farmer, P. (2015, May 20). The Caregivers' Disease. London Review of Books, 37(10). https://www.lrb.co.uk/the-paper/v37/n10/paul-farmer/the-caregivers-disease

Henriques, M. (2020, April 13). Why Covid-19 is different for men and women. https://www.bbc.com/future/article/20200409-why-covid-19-is-different-for-men-and-women

Iliza, A. (2020, April 17). Domestic violence rises during COVID-19 lockdown. The New Times |Rwanda. https://www.newtimes.co.rw/news/domestic-violence-rises-during-covid-19-lockdown

Twahirwa, A. (2020, April 8). The Gender Dimensions of the COVID-19 Pandemic Outbreak. news/the-gender-dimensions-of-the-covid-19-pandemic

UN, (2014, September 2). Ebola outbreak takes its toll on women. UN Women.

https://www.unwomen.org/en/news/stories/2014/9/ebola-outbreak-takes-its-toll-on-women

Menéndez, C., Lucas, A., Munguambe, K., & Langer, A. (2015). Ebola crisis: The unequal
impact on women and children's health. The Lancet Global Health, 371. https://doi.org/10.1016/S2214-109X(15)70009-4

Onyango, M. A. (2020). Sexual and gender-based violence during COVID-19: Lessons from

Ebola. The Conversation. Retrieved July 1, 2020, from http://theconversation.com/sexual-and-gender-based-violence-during-covid-19-lessons-from-ebola-137541

Richardson, E., McGinnis, T., & Frankfurter, R. (2019, November 11). Ebola and the narrative of mistrust—Democratic Republic of the Congo. ReliefWeb. https://reliefweb.int/report/democratic-republic-congo/ebola-and-narrative-mistrust

GOV.RW, State of Gender Equality in Rwanda.pdf. (2019). Retrieved July 1, 2020, from http://gmo.gov.rw/fileadmin/user_upload/Researches%20and%20Assessments/State%20of%20Gender%20Equality%20in%20Rwanda.pdf

You hit me with a whip
I will go to a G.P and get medicated
You steal my money
I will work that 9 to 5
Trying to get it back

Physical pain is far less detrimental
Physical pain can be domesticated or even healed
You might be left with a scar
To remind you of it
But it will be healed

Wounded trust is psychological pain
Psychological pain is psychological scars
Psychological pain is deeply entrenched
And takes time to unravel

Wounded trust makes it difficult to form new relationships
Relationships of any kind

I have never been in a romantic relationship
Only sexual ones
I want to be loved
I yearn to be loved
And vice versa
But I do not have the vigor
To withstand treachery and deceit

My mind is too tarnished
My heart is too apprehensive
Wounded trust is leaving me incomprehensible

Tarnished Mental View
[Sinenhlanhla MlilowokuNqoba MaPhezabantu]

Dreadlocks Extended

"Amandlovu, are they permanent?"

There it was... he said amandlovu. Whenever my dad used his shona pet name for me, I knew the question was one that he had grappled with before asking.

Alarm bells went off in my head. I knew the question was addressing something deeper than just the fact that I had dreadlocks in my hair. I knew I had to tread lightly with my answer- So naturally, I answered with a question, "You don't like my hair, baba?"

"Hmmpf" he sighed.

Just like he did, I used the shona name for father as a weapon in our conversations. To remind him that I was not some overaged rebel teenager, some 'rovha' who had moved into his home to live rent free after getting an irrelevant degree in an expensive foreign school. I used shona to remind him that I was his daughter, forever seeking his love and approval.

Since moving back to Zimbabwe from Atlanta, I often found myself doing what I called "Prodigal daughter defense moves – PDDM (not a cool acronym but still PDDM was a way to remind my parents that I did not have an evil Americanized carefree character that acted out of sheer whim or worse a spirit that made calculated moves without regard of how they would make them feel but that my actions were merely an attempt to find my place in a world that didn't fit me.

It's my 4th dreadlock anniversary. My hair is shoulder length now, hangs like a cute bob and ties into an actual ponytail! I want to remember every compliment my hair has ever gotten - compliments that inevitably lead to questions – questions about my lock journey from girls thinking about the big chop or the irreversible decision of permanent dreadlocks. "How short were they when you got them?" "How much did it cost to maintain them?" "How often do you go to the hair salon" Do you miss your hair" They use my answers as a yardstick, measuring them against every tale they've heard of moisturizers, routines, brands that helped, homemade recipes and regimens- without realizing that every hair journey is incomparable and unique. It's like they'd never heard the hit jam "I am not my hair, I am not my skin, I am not your expectations"

They never ask me about the most important part of the hair journey. The part I'm longing to share.

The most important part isn't the present, where I get compliments from my elderly judgmental black aunties, or where my friends call me "Rasta" because I'm the only one with dreads in their phone book, or even how the men in the street stopped calling me "sister, pssst sister" in a lecherous voice but now respectfully say "Empress" when I enter the bus.

It's not the beginning of the journey where I sat in the salon chair with my hairdresser cheering me on, only for him to work his magic and turn my gorgeous afro puff curls into mangy little worms that even had to braided with yarn because they didn't compliment my long face.

The most important moment in the lock journey for me, is the before, the why.

"Yes, baba, it's permanent. I was struggling with fixing my hair. I'm tired of adding big hoop earings everyday to make my afro hair look lively, fun, acceptable. I just wanted something easy. Something that says – this is you – before I open my eyes to everyone who wonders why I have an accent I wasn't born with."

"So who are you?" He asked and I realized it was the first time he had ever asked me that.

"hmmmpf are you like all rastas? A reggae artist, a weed addict, a person who doesn't bath" He continued listing every stereotype I knew him, my aunts and uncles would be thinking about.

He hadn't even waited for my answer.

"No baba, I'm a person willing to admit I don't know who I am"

"That's not an answer amandlovu."

"Urgh it's just so weird being home dude" I cried to my friend on the phone. On yet another long distance call.

"Did you think it would be normal?"

"I just didn't think" I lied.

In truth, I had agonized over this and every decision. Permanent dreadlocks had felt like the last step in the metamorphosis. I thought I'd come out looking like a butterfly. Instead I just had wiggly worm things on my head.

The lines from the book I was reading "Ghana must go" kept ringing in my ear. "Think about it. Barring Rastafarians, what kind of black girl grows locks. Black girls who go to predominantly white colleges, that's who. Dreadlocks are black-white girl hair. A Black Power solution to a Bluest Eye Problem: the desire to have long, swinging, ponytail hair"

Damn, truth – ish. Yet another opinion that fit didn't fit.

The truth – My dreadlocks were a reaction to feeling different in my own home country. So different that I was resolute to look different too.

After all, dreadlocks were still a masculine look in Zimbabwe. They were a sign of rebellion to my parents, but I could still hide behind them being a part of the "black is beautiful movement" This was another part of me trying to make sure I was just different enough. Funny, I wanted to remind people to treat me like I had never left Zimbabwe, by reminding them that I had left.
I wish I had accepted the answer I gave my own father. That I was the person willing to admit I don't always know who I am.

I am the prodigal daughter of Africa, not sure why she left or why she came back. not sure who she is, or who she isn't.

I am the prodigal daughter, wishing her return was a blessing strong enough to ignore the curse that made her leave in the first place.

It's my fourth dreadlock anniversary and and I'm ready to be a different person. To try find another version of myself, as if I've never heard the hit song "I am not my hair"

Baba, can I go to your barber for a haircut tomorrow?"

"But Amandlovu, ah your hair is so beautiful."

I smile, "Nevermind Baba"

[Onyeka Nwabunnia]

The Gathering

All the women inside of me are tired.

They are exhausted, fighting a battle with my internal demons, while giving me the strength to challenge the world. These women, Nigerian and Liberian, whisper gospels of revolution and freedom that shape my movements. They are the forces that ground me, like angels with wings they spread their arms to comfort me in the darkness.

All the women inside of me are tired.

My entire life I have swallowed pain, forcing a smile on my face. Like the African women I call home, I have learned the tradition of enduring, of living in silence, and of finding peace only when my body finds sleep. When the world tries to shame me for being a Black woman, I remember that the stories I embody are revolutionary.

All the women inside of me are tired.

And I am breaking.

They warn me. I remember the first time I saw him. I was all butterflies and feverish cheeks, fumbling over words. I wanted him to see me even though I couldn't see myself. The women inside me knew that he was too much undealt trauma for a woman who is all broken pieces with sharp edges. But when you are broken pieces, you learn to give love to men who will scatter your pieces like ashes; men who will use your body as an escape. When he turned his back, the women inside me guarded my spirit and warmed me with love. With them, I started the process of collecting and putting back together.

All the women inside of me are tired.
And I am still breaking.

My anxiety has taken peak form. As the world around me seems to crumble, I cannot sleep. I am haunted by the burdens of a country driven by hate and marked in the blood of dead Black women and men. At 2 AM, my mind is too preoccupied with stories of the forgotten, so I scroll through twitter. Before I know it, I am crying, curled up, knees close to my chest. I am sobbing. I am shocked to see the tears. We do not cry. There is still too much fight left. But I can't control it; the tears are flowing, and I am breathing as if oxygen is escaping me. The walls in my room seem to be getting closer together. I am falling. But where are the women inside of me? It feels as if they have turned their backs on me.

All the women inside of me are tired.
And we are falling together.

In the shadows I see a gathering of faces. They are seated around a small table, laughing. As I try to get closer, I notice these faces are familiar. The women inside of me are meeting. My grandmother's hand lays gently on her mother's thigh. My paternal grandmother is holding my cousin, her granddaughter. They are sharing stories about the world. Without moving, they sense my presence and usher me over. Seated amongst them, I know the women inside of me are tired, but they have never left.

[Mahafuza Abdulrahman]

My Africa

Africa ! Africa
My Africa
A proud land of our forefathers Africa my jewel
Your recipes of courage has been pass from generation to generation
A continent carved out of glory
A land blessed with fertile soil on which the world grow A land
known for their hospitality
A land known for our skillful potter
We survived by unity and love for one another A land blessed with
many talents
The land that's solid like the baobab tree that always flourish We
map our future from your stories
The land where my heart resides and will always be
A land blessed with different language like swahili, amharic,
oromo,zulu,hausa,shona
The africa that is at the heart of different people, language who we
all call this land our home

A land blessed with great heroes and leaders like Ellen Johnson
sirleaf, jomo kenyatta, Nelson
Mandela, Thomas sankara, kofi Annan
We're black in the outside but white in the inside
For Africa to them is just a continent but to me is my identity and
my home
From the depth of my heart comes the blossom of greatness
To them we're slaves but that's their view
My blackness is my strength
My Africa will rise from the shackles of adversity
My Africa will rise from the ashes of distorted history 1 speak for
myself, you and the Africa
We're blessed with great poets like Kwame Dawes, jack cope
Have you heard of Alhanislam,shefeerh, soulunraveled, teen Tag
together we all are Africans The world is like a picture and we the
Africans are the frame that holds it
Dear Africa your love unite us
This is my home

There is a niche I belong
A place with flowers and gold
I step into it slowly and fearfully
Like a thief breaking into a house
That noise of my door is like a crack in my brain

I'm afraid someone will tell me, "you don't belong there!"
That niche of mine,
Niche of decision as regards career, ambition
Family, love, and what I am
My restriction as regards life

I worry because I know a maker made me
He tells me I have talent
But they say I can't use it
I dare not speak

There is a world in our world
That still have darkness of ideas
Despite the global age growing far and wide
There is a world that sees woman as inferior and less

My talents wait and knock for expression
I hide her and won't let her go
She screams and make my ear bleed of wax
It ain't going to get better, would it?

I can model just within those room
But not in a world of flashes and recognition
What do you know?
They tell me continuously
Your body ain't fit
It's not perfect for it - bad fat lies everywhere

My eyes are red
My head is hot
The ear wax increase now it's blood
A force pushes me to man my niche
It keeps telling me that:
You've a place dear

Now I want to go out and use it
The talents my maker made are for use and world benefit
Not to keep them
Lemme explore my world
And retouch the beauty of this world!

Her Place In The World
[Mojisola Esther]

STORIES THE WORLD WOULDN'T BELIEVE

sub-theme

Coincidência Fatal

Minjurda era uma menina de 10 anos de idade, sonhadora incurável passava o dia a imaginar o seu futuro, cada dia numa profissão diferente. Filha de pais separados Minjurda era a mais de nova de um total de três irmãos onde dois primeiros eram rapazes. Depois da separação do seus pais a mãe casou-se novamente e começou a viver com o seu padrasto um homem jovem, muito antiquado e sem filhos.

Como toda sonhadora ela tinha sempre novidades para contar a família e sempre escolhia as horas das refeições para exibir a última versão dos seus desejos.

—Mãe eu ainda quero ser Engenheira mecânica, Medica cirurgiã, Educadora de infância, Gestora de empresa, mas hoje eu descobri algo que também gostaria de ser e minha professora disse que eu poderia ser.—A mãe sorriu e disse.

Oh filha és tão sonhadora, que podes ser tudo o que quiseres, mas me conta o que descobriste que eu estou curiosa. – Disse a mãe com um sorriso que roubava o seu rosto.

—Eu sempre gostei de ler histórias, e gosto muito de escrever as minhas próprias histórias, descobri que quero ser escritora e quero ter uma editora de livros.

—Sim filha tu podes ser uma escritora e ter sua própria editora. - Disse a mãe com um ar de orgulho da filha.

Quando inesperadamente ouviu-se um estrondoso grito.

—Paraaa. Para de alimentar essas ideias absurdas na cabeça da sua filha mulher, quem disse que ela será tudo isso. Olha menina pare de sonhar no impossível deixe isso para seus irmãos, eles sim podem ser o que quiserem ser, onde já se viu uma mulher ser engenheira mecânica, gerir empresas, educar e tratar da saúde de uma pessoa? Você não tem capacidades querida isso é coisa de homens. Perdi a fome. – Disse o padrasto da Minjurda com a cara toda amarrotada de nervos, chiou desde da sala até a varanda onde sentou-se num banco feito de madeira de coqueiro.

Um silêncio confuso engoliu a sala. Minjurda não se intimidou com o comportamento do padrasto perante os seus sonhos, em todas as refeições ela não poupava letras para construir palavras e frases sobre como ela se imaginava nas tais profissões. Esse evento era tão recorrente que o padrasto percebeu o potencial da sua enteada, com medo do que a menina pudesse se tornar este decidiu que a menina tinha de parar de estudar.

—Olha querida ultimamente vejo-te muito cansada. Com os miúdos na escola não tens quem te ajude com as tarefas de casa e não só precisas de um tempo só para ti, para bordares novos panos da mesa. - Disse o padrasto da Minjurda com uma amabilidade falsa.

—Obrigada esposo mas eu aguento, além do mais as tarefas de casa me distraem.

—Não querida, eu não gosto de te ver tão cansada. A partir de hoje a Minjurda já não vai mais a escola, ficará em casa para ajudar-te com as tarefas, ela irá limpar o chão, cozinhar, lavar a roupa e passá-la a ferro.

—O quê? Não. Me alegra que a Minjurda vá para a escola, ela é muito inteligente e isso faz ela feliz.

—Já está decidido, a sua filha não voltará para a escola e prontos, esta casa é minha e eu sustento todo mundo aqui, dou de comer e de beber a ti e aos seus filhos olha só, filhos quem nem sequer são meus. Enquanto o pai deles está lá a usufruir dos apetitosos prazeres da vida, eu aqui a alimentar e a aturar estes pobres famintos. Se não estiveres de acordo arrume suas coisas e saia desta casa com os seus três sanguessugas. – Disse o padrasto da Minjurda com uma cruel arrogância.

Com coração aleijado a mãe da Minjurda aceitou que a sua filha parasse de estudar, uma vez que ela era desempregada não tinha como alugar uma casa naquela cidade, para que não prejudicasse o estudo dos outros dois filhos, esta foi obrigada a aceitar a situação, sofrendo a cada lágrima que brincava de escorrega nos olhos da sua filha.

Minjurda ficou um ano sem estudar, mas não parava de ler os seus livros da escola. Passados um ano, a mãe decidiu separar-se do padrasto e foram todos viver na casa dos seus pais, na cidade vizinha onde Minjurda deu continuidade os seus estudos e se formou.

Passaram-se 18 anos até que ela e sua família voltaram para a cidade onde moravam antigamente, pois era uma cidade maior havia muita chance da Minjurda ter uma carreira brilhante. Durante os 18 anos o seu ex padrasto abriu uma empresa de frotas de camiões que levavam produtos de uma cidade para outra, voltou a casar-se com uma outra mulher muito mais nova que a mãe da Minjurda onde tiveram uma filha.

A vida ia bem até que o seu negócio começou a andar para trás, os camiões começaram a avariar um por um, o ex padrasto da Minjurda decidiu solicitar uma reparação da sua frota na oficina mais prestigiada da cidade mas o orçamento para reparação era muito alto, com poucas encomendas de entregas de produtos a sua situação financeira era de lamentar, os problemas de saúde entraram em acção, o coração começou a sentir os batimentos da conta bancária negativa.

Surgiu-lhe a ideia de pedir um empréstimo no maior banco da cidade, mas não foi possível pois os bens que tinha não cobriram o valor do empréstimo caso estes fossem penhorados, para piorar a sua filha de 5 anos foi expulsa do jardim-de-infância por mau comportamento, chamou sua educadora de preta, pobre, cara de Chimpanzé.

Com todos esses assuntos acumulados na sua vida, o sangue recusou-se a circular pelo seu corpo, só aceitava sob pressão e acabou sobrando para o rim esquerdo que imediatamente zangou-se com o coração e demitiu-se do cargo abandonando as suas funções, exigindo a sua retirada com máxima urgência.

Já no hospital foi submetido a cirurgia de retirada de um rim, a cirurgia correu muito bem. Ao acordar o ex padrasto depara-se com a médica que lhe atendeu observando os seus pontos.

—Desculpa a senhorita tem uma cara que me é muito familiar, não sei porque. Talvez esteja a fazer confusão. - Disse o ex padrasto tentando puxar pela cabeça com que se parecia aquela mulher.

—O senhor não esta a fazer confusão sou a Minjurda a menina que tiraste da escola para poder fazer os tarefas domesticas. – Afirmou Minjurda

—O que fazes aqui vestida de bata branca? Trabalhas numa padaria e vieste fornecer pão ao hospital? — Interrogou o ex padrasto.

—Não, eu sou médica cirurgiã, e sim fui eu quem operou o senhor. Pelo que vejo o senhor esta reagir bem ao procedimento submetido. — Respondeu Minjurda sem perder a pose.

—AHMMM!!!... — O ex padrasto ficou de boca aberta como se a articulação temporo-mandibular tivesse encravado.

—Sim. A propósito o documento de reparação dos seus camiões passou pelas minhas mãos, para além de sócia da oficina eu sou engenheira mecânica, e se tivesses dinheiro para bancar a reparação com certeza sua frota seria salva por mim. E o empréstimo no banco também recebi o seu pedido de empréstimo, formei-me em Gestão de empresas e actualmente sou a nova gerente do banco não podia admitir que o banco penhorasse bens sem valor algum, porque cá entre nós o senhor não soube gerir muito bem os seus lucros.

Ahm e ainda sobre a sua filha de cinco anos de idade, eu como dona do jardim-de-infância assinei o documento de expulsão da sua filha, não poderia admitir racismo e má educação dentro do meu estabelecimento, é muito chocante ver uma criança negra que não gosta de pessoas negras.

—AHMMM!!!... — A articulação temporo-mandibular voltou a encravar.

—Sim, enquanto fazia engenharia fazia também medicina ao mesmo tempo, foi duro não tinha tempo para nada, terminei a engenharia, comecei a fazer educação de infância dois anos depois terminei a medicina e concorri para fazer residência médica em cirurgia, dois anos depois terminei a educação de infância e entrei para faculdade de gestão onde me formei finalmente em gestão de empresas.

Enfim não tive vida normal nesses anos todos, mas o sucesso que tenho hoje é mesmo gratificante realizei todos os meus sonhos. Como eu sei que o senhor ficou sem dinheiro e sinto muito por isso, para alimentar a sua família eu lhe ofereço um emprego na minha editora de livros, temos um sector com falta de pessoal, o senhor vai gostar acredito que lhe fará muito bem trabalhar na cozinha. — O ex padrasto começou a suar de desespero e de seguida começou a gritar.

—Socorro, socorro essa mulher quer me matar. - Uma multidão de vários profissionais de saúde acumulou-se na sala, quando de repente o ex padrasto da Minjurda parou de gritar e uma forte dor se espalhou sobre seu peito, aí os sinais vitais começaram a oscilar, a Minjurda alertou os colegas.

—Está tendo um enfarte, esta tendo um enfarte. — Rapidamente os enfermeiros equiparam as suas mãos com luvas de látex, eis que o sinais vitais desapareceram do monitor deixando o piiiiiiiiiiii consumir a sala.

—Vamos reanimar, vamos reanimar. Eu quero esse homem vivo para ver de perto como uma mulher é capaz de se tornar no que ela quiser, e assumir lugares importantes na sociedade. — Ordenou a engenheira e doctora Minjurda sem hesitar.

I am Fierce

[Nguseer Gavar]

[Munira Maria Makerow]
Untitled

There is an ache deep inside my heart a deep-rooted pain I can't seem
to reach the end of it or the root to it so I may yank it out.
It has ties with unheard cries of a child
Uninvited pains from grownups laying on us.
This ache deep inside my soul has made war my father and refuge my
mother.
It's a black hole deep inside my soul
If this pain could speak it would sound like loud echos coming from
empty indoors parking lot.
It's like fearing for your life, walking fast with keys in your hand,
looking over your shoulder wondering if a robber is watching you.

And you wish it's your gold they are after and not the treasure you carry beneath your waist.

For it is not something they can take without forcing your soul and peace out of your own body as they force their way into your body

But they can't live inside your body so they eventually leave

Evacuating a vessel behind

now

A war starts within you.

You become alien to yourself hating yourself...

Now your soul can't adapt to live with your shattered self-image.

It's like they didn't just compel peace out of your essence they also injected a toxin within you.

Self-hatred is a disastrous kind of war. For where does one find rest when their own mind replays awful memories?

Was it something I had done? Did I speak too softly? Was I rude? Did I sit wrongly or did he mistake my laughter for an invitation to invade my space? Was it something I ate? What did I do? What about me said "it is fine to go ahead and take whatever you like? Discard the cries and the horror in my eyes"

A deep rooted ache...

A war took my father and made us refugees but now I am on the run from myself looking for a place to lose my head a bit without somebody trying to make me their bed willy nilly...

This ache you see is deep beyond my reach

Like an empty well, a black hole that sucks up joy and life purpose...

Why me? Why. Me?

"Get over it, let by go be bygone..." But I have learned that the only way to live with the past is by taking a walk through it. And making peace with it.

****

Rape does not attack the body only. It attacks the soul and the mind. Like I said they force your peace and sense of worth out of you when they push themselves in you.

But there is no escaping me. Or the memories...I carry myself where ever I go... There is nothing else to do but make peace with myself. I have tried to go... Like they did... Step outside my vessel and leave it behind... Cuts on my wrist thoughts of ways to sleep and never wake up.

I have Prayed for better body to host my soul. cuts on my wrist,or pinching myself hard to feel anything else, but... The thought of going to sleep and never wake up... All that just to evacuate my body. A deep-rooted ache... They start a war in you but only you can make peace with your soul. Teach Yourself how to live with You. how to love yourself.

How to love yourself. With all the cracks and burn marks in you. You carry yourself, with love, Simply because you are worthy.

We are valuable. Nothing can ever make us be less worthy. The war is ongoing. But now we know how to live with it. And for the record, there is nothing I had done there was nothing you had done. We didn't ask for it.

This ache is deep-rooted, but now I have managed to make a room for it. I build a room for it in my soul, I let me cry, grief get furious then calm down. It is part of me. But it will never be me. Hear me? I said my deep-rooted ache is part of me. But I am not it.

Meu cabelo duro e crespo
É a herança deixada pelos meus ancestrais
Ele é denso como o sangue que escorre em minhas veias
O meu cabelo é a coroa que jamais me será tirada
É a raiz que brotou nas plantações de café e algodão
Que por muito tempo permaneceu preso a um pano branco
Hoje ele se libertou.
Quebrou as correntes da escravidão
Não me venha dizer que ele é ruim
Não me faças sentir vergonha por tê-lo
É a minha coroa
É minha resistência
E ninguém vai-me tirar
Podes comparar-me com as savanas e chimpanzés
Não adianta. Vou assumi-lo
Não vou permitir que apagues esse legado
Que lá no tempo me foi negado
De ser quem eu sou,
De assumir as minhas raízes

Essa é minha coroa
E ninguém vai-me tirar.

A Coroa Que Jamais Me Será Tirada

[Ana Mafalda Gonçalves Dias]

[Eugenia Shaw]

The Custard People

" Dinner's ready" mom called. "Please come to the table guys."

"What are we having" called out Johnny.

"Well I know there's ice cream", said Katie with a big smile.

"We're having a light dinner guys, seeing as we've had a big heavy lunch" mom replied. "Johnny can you please go and get your grandmother from her bedroom. Thank you lovely".

Johnny walks down the corridor to the guest room and shouts out

"Grandma, dinner is ready, and we are having ice cream for dinner!"

As mom finishes setting the table, she hears the shuffling of her mother's feet as she approaches the kitchen diner. Together she and the children sat at the table.

"Where is the ice cream" Katie wines.

"Mom, you said we were going to have ice cream" Johnny accuses.

"We are having ice cream guys, however, you have to finish all of your dinner before you can have any ice cream. So make sure you finish all your dinner if you want to have ice cream."

"Ok, can I please have only one slice of bread and a small piece of cheese mom", Katie implores.

Mom smiles and says, "I'll give you just enough dinner my sweet, and if you finish it, you can have as much ice cream as you want."

Katie's eyes widen with anticipation.

Mom smiles, as her heart melts looking into her daughter's eyes, "All the ice cream you can eat", mom says with enthusiasm, "just imagine! And we also have apple crumble and custard to go with the ice cream.

"Ooo..." Katie shrieks with excitement, as she claps her hands.

Grandma pipes up and says "This all sounds very exciting and all this talk of the food is making me feel very hungry. Can we please say grace and start eating."

"Yes yes yes, come on everyone". mom says.

Grace was said and all hands dived into the food. Not one complaint or a voice was heard as everyone demolished their dinner with dessert on their minds. Even grandma was eating without any complaints. In no time at all dinner was done and Johnny asked if he could help clear away the table and get the dessert bowls out. Mom smiled and accepted the offer.

Suddenly she started, everyone looked over at her, and then sat back with a sigh of relief, smiled and said, "I thought the oven was still on" she said.

Katie shrieked "I'll get the Ice cream!"

"Erm... should you not be asking, young lady?" mom asked.

"Mommy, can I please get the ice cream?"

"Of course you can my sweet" mom said with a smile.

Mom got up and got the apple crumble out of the oven. Johnny brought the custard over from the kitchen counter. Grandma asked if anyone wanted hot custard verses cold custard.

There was a resounding yes for hot custard. So grandma emptied the custard to a microwaveable bowl and popped it in the microwave and sat back down at the table. As the dishing of ice cream and apple crumble commenced, chitter chatter and excitement ensued and the kitchen was filled with laughter and warmth. As the discussions of which ice cream tasted best raged, and who wanted more crumble and less fruit, and more fruit and less crumble, everyone forgot about the custard in the microwave. Mom was accused of taking too much crumble, it was her favourite bit, she disliked cooked fruit. It was really and actually quite true, mom did take more crumbles. Her excuse, "The kids have more fruit to have." was said with a mischievous smile.

Johnny and grandma did the duty of sharing it out evenly between him, grandma and Katie. As the sharing was nearly done, mom remembered the custard in the microwave looked over at the microwave in an attempt to go and get the custard but froze in her seat. Grandma looking over at mom realised something was wrong and reached out to mom over the table and asked, "Is everything alright?" The kids hearing grandma looked over at mom to hear her response. But seeing her eyes wide stretched and still unresponsive to their questions, everyone followed her gaze. They too froze in their actions. Their eyes must be deceiving them, for the sight they beheld was not anything that they would ever, ever have dreamed, thought of or imagined. For climbing out of the microwave and unto the floor using the baskets in the shelving unit, upon which the microwave stood, as a ladder was the custard-people! They were talking to each other! There was a leader, he was on the ground already, with 7 others and was directing the last 5 custard-people down the ladder. Everyone at the dinner table was speechless. The leader suddenly realising that they were being watched turned to address the dinner table.

He cleared his throat with a little cough and said "Dear Madame, I am so sorry for the delay. We have been trying to get to you as quickly as possible, before the heat runs out of us. It is best not to reheat us, as that makes us a bit jellified and not very nice to eat, which is why there is an urgent need for us to be in your bowls as soon as possible. Upon seeing you all were beautifully occupied with each other, I did not want to disturb such family fun, but slip quickly and quietly into your bowls." Johnny was the first to recover his voice and blurted out "Where did you come from?"

"We are the custard that you emptied out of the carton into the bowl to be heated."

"What do you mean, the custard turned into people?" Johnny asked incredulously.

"We haven't turned into people; we just took this form as it is the best form for us to use to get the job done quickly."

"Mommy, I don't want custard anymore," Katie said with tears in her eyes.

"It's ok honey, they're not dangerous."

"Can I keep them?" Johnny asked.

"No you cannot!" mom said.

Grandma still hadn't spoken a word.

Whilst all this exchange was taking place, the last five custard-people on their makeshift ladder had joined the rest of the group and they had now formed three rows of three, one row of two, leaving the leader at the front of the group in front of the two-man row. The leader looked back, seeing everyone was there, turned and said

"Right... Madame, we are ready for your bowls."

"Just hold on there a minute, you have been on the floor! We don't eat food off the floor."

"Right you are Madame, but we have not touched the floor or anything for that matter. We are able to hold onto things and walk using the energy that is created by the heat in us and the energy that every matter gives off. We hover just above any and everything."

"That is all fair and... oops... are you alright?"

The leader's head had dipped into his body like the headless horseman.

"We are losing heat, and quickly too, as we are now on the floor where it is coldest. We need to get into your bowls quickly, because once we lose all our heat, we will splat on the floor, as we will have no more heat energy within us, for us to use to hover. Madame, please hurry. Bring your bowls down to us and we will climb in."

Mom still in her shocked state instructed everyone to take their bowls to the custard-people. As they did this mom asked, "Does this mean that you die when you enter our bowls?"

We were never alive, to begin with, we just have energy. You would not be 'killing' us. In fact, you would be helping us to accomplish our mission."

"Ok... if you say so."

"I do say so. Hurry now, before we splat."

As everyone took their bowls to the ground, the leader divided the group into four groups of three, and sent them off to each bowl. Even grandma was on the floor with her bowl. The leader and his group went to mom's bowl. As they each climbed in, they melted onto the apple crumble in each bowl. The leader saluted mom as he melted away. They all picked up their bowl and gingerly, almost reverently carried their bowls back to the table. They all looked at mom, mom looked back at each of them and then looked into her bowl. They all started into their bowls for what seemed the longest. Finally, mom lifted her head and said "I don't know what to do, do we eat this or do we not eat this?"

[Lúcia Morais]
Um Poema

Eu queria escrever um poema na brincadeira
Mas as bonecas não representam a minha bandeira
E cresço assim um pouco sem sentido
Onde um poema não seria sentido

Eu queria escrever um poema emoção
Mas há troça na minha coroa latão
Chamam meu cabelo de esfregão
Eu sou só uma menina, doi, doi tanto
Até minhas lágrimas molharem o poema em pranto

Eu queria escrever um poema em mim
Mas todo mês a sujidade ruim
E fico impura para escrever
Até meu poema desaparecer

Eu queria escrever um poema bonito
Mas na minha lingua africana é esquisito
Ex escrava e mulher querer pensar
E meu poema se suicida ao se analisar

Eu queria escrever um poema
Mas ser ouvida ou se calar, é nosso dilema
A lavagem cerebral é feita
E meu poema da janela espreita

Eu queria escrever um poema a minha maneira
Mas mesmo sem querer cedo fui mãe solteira
E se quero um pai para essa criança
Até meu poema me olha de esgueira

Eu queria muito escrever um poema
Mas meu marido diz que sou um problema
E do nada começa a me bater
Até meu poema morrer

Eu queria um poema escrever
Mas por ser mulher
Não me foi permitido aprender
Minha luta agora é para aprender a ler
Um dia o irei escrever

[Harriet Mimi Uwineza]

Exile

Yes! The famous place where all my people go to die
Where they go to die or to sell their souls to the devil
Yes, no one has returned from there sane.
That place is where the devil resides

I want you to prove me wrong
For those who spent there a decade did not come back with humanity
Those who are living there, slaughter men and women in forests
I have no hope for those who will exile later on too
Unless exile styles up

Is it the place that transforms my people?
Or, do my people have demons inside that thrive in exile
There is also another possibility I don't want to consider
That what makes them heartless resides at home
That the solution is also back home

Considering that I saw some of them the other day
They were not carrying any machetes
They sat and discussed in peace
When they returned home
Their noses became their perimeter walls

Maybe it the tiny size of our home
Or the lack of resources maybe?

Which is why we always have to find a reason of exclusion
Criminalizing the other to feed our own
Why are you looking at me like that?

Untitled

[Munira Maria Makerow]

[Rusud Makrim]

A Mulher Morta-Viva

Há muito tempo, na costa do Índico, Ilha de Moçambique as pessoas eram negras e brancas, as machambas eram feitas de negro e do branco, a terra era negra e branca, enfim... tudo era descolorido.

Havia uma senhora viúva e muito pobre que cuidava de sua filha donzela negra e branca e lhe preparava comidas menos negras e mais brancas, passava dias limpando chão em negro e na maior parte dos dias em branco.

Um belo dia a senhora adoeceu e foi ter com a sua patroa negra e branca que por acaso era esposa do rei, para que lhe ajudasse, esta que tinha inveja da beleza da mulher então perguntou:

—E porque a devo ajudar? O que ganho eu com isso?

Ela em sua dor, tirou sua capulana e entregou a mulher, disse-lhe:

—Esta veste a tornará mais bela e mais poderosa se cantar para ela.

A mulher espantada não acreditou, porém mandou chamar seus curandeiros para tratar a mulher.

Esta ficou desfalecida por cinco dias e quatro noites. Neste período, a rainha cantou para a veste e o pano não se alterou, mandou então todas mulheres da sua corte cantar e nada aconteceu. Se sentiu traída e mandou matar a mulher e a enterrar.

Enquanto ela dormia, ouvia-se a veste chamando seu nome, por vários dias se sentiu amedrontada e mandou chamar seu feiticeiro, que lhe aconselhou:

—Deves levar até a casa da mulher andando em marcha ré, cantando a música dos mortos.

Enquanto a rainha seguia as instruções o manto mudava de cor, forma e não era nada preto ou branco, tinha tons e cores berrantes. Quando lá chegou, encontrou a mulher sentada e a cumprimentou espantada:

—Mas tu estavas morta!

—Não se mata o que nunca esteve vivo, este manto agora pertence a minha donzela que o usará para carregar seus falecidos, seus filhos e ser dona de casa. Quebraste o trato quando te revelaste de coração preto.

A donzela usou o pano colorido até virar mulher. A rainha na sua pesada consciência mandou fazer panos e ofereceu a todas mulheres para que usassem nos funerais e cerimónias aos antepassados cantando a música dos mortos como forma de se desculpar e recordar da mulher que transformou o negro e branco dando vida ao colorido. Deste então as mulheres africanas usam a capulana coloridas como sinónimo de respeito pela mulher morta-viva.

14-05-2020

[Rumbidzai Zamukudzi]

Haunted

As I stood with my attenuated body on top of a pinnacle, probably 100 meters long, ready to join her, I had been tormented enough since the day she left the world. I closed my eyes ready to spring, I was hearing her voice calling my name, cheering me like I was in a game, maybe I had joined a death race. Just when I was raising my right feet I had another voice, no it wasn't Nathalie, it felt like I was in one of the loudest clubs, two voices continued piercing my ears.

I didn't know what to do. I closed my ears, I wanted this to be over, I had endured enough I just springend off the building, as I prayed going down I thought the fight was over but no the devil still wanted to play with my soul. I bounced on a net, it felt like I was on a trampoline, it was so painful. My langy body kept on being tossed up and down the trampoline. I woke up in an emergency room.

How did I get here, that was the first question which popped out of my mind. I saw my mom laying on another bed beside me. She looked so peaceful I tried not to wake her up so I just laid hopeless on my bed. Within some minutes she was up. " Tiffany you are up, am I seeing properly or I'm dreaming". I never wanted to talk to her. I had deserted my family since the day they couldn't protect Nathalie. They should have fought for her, where were they the day she took her life. They should have protected her from the very day they declared being her parents.

I remember it vividly like it was yesterday when Nathalie took her life. It kept on flashing in my mind everyday, I always see her chunk remnants. She had thrown herself from her room, we were staying in an apartment which was on the 15th floor. She had tried several times to take her life with no success. I had warned my parents about it but they never took me seriously. It was too late to believe me, she was gone. I decided to move and study in South Africa. I never wanted to see my parents. They had failed me in a way no one could accept. They had failed me and Nathalie.

Like it was not enough going through the pain of morning my sister suicidal thoughts started crossing my mind. I always would think what If I take my life and join Nathalie. Nothing in the world make sense without her. I had lived with her for 15 years, she had become my best friend and my human diary. I trusted her with everything . I began to see her in my dreams, she kept on telling me how peaceful it was where she was. She always would ask me to join her. I would wake up sweating and having a feeling that it was real.

That was the turnaround of my life. I never knew peace from then. Every night I had to see Nathalie in my dreams. Sometimes forcing me to take my life. I moved to South Africa. I thought our house was being haunted and there was no any reason to stay as my parents never spent much time home. As I arrived in a foreign country I felt much peaceful. Though I had no scary dreams but not a day would pass without shedding a tear for my sister.

Life lost its meaning to me. I never had a friend at all. I was staying alone and loved it. I lost appetite and wouldn't take care of myself. I found it hard even to wash my body. I started bit by bit to lose interest in attending lectures. I would spend the whole day in my bed and I would switch off my phone. After a week I started having weird dreams again, it was always Nathalie asking me to join her. I kept on having the same dream and I would wake up everyday laying in the hall way and sometimes on my door step whilst I would know well I slept on my bed the previous night.

I became a call of concern, my lecturers started to complain and my parents would be called because of my attitude towards studies. I started to lose weight. I was not much of a big built person so when I started losing weight my body became so skinny that anyone could count my bones. I started to hate myself. I thought to end all the suffering I had to avoid sleeping. I was scared and tired of seeing my late sister in my dreams. The idea worked for the first two days but then it became worse when I would see her during the day while my eyes were wide open.

Nathalie would come and ask me to join her. I would here her voice calling my name. Asking me to just jump off the balcony. People thought I was losing it. My parents took me to several psychologists and many neurological doctors but it never helped. I endured the suffering till I couldn't anymore. I tried so many times to take my life without success. I wanted to just end my life. I was tired, my life never had a meaning. I was always staying indoors. My parents on some point took me home. In their presence I wouldn't see anything but as soon as I was alone Nathalie would appear in my eyes. I would hear her singing for me my favouirite song. She would play with me my favouirite games. A day came when I really wanted to join her. She started calling me outside the house. She went straight to the church building. She started climbing the stairs slowly as I followed her, when we reached the top she just disappeared and I saw her calling me from the bottom of the building. I jumped off but I didn't die. I had to stay on comma for 3 months and I woke up. I was given my life back. I lived a new life once again. I had a chance to give my life to Christ and I started afresh.

[Harriet Mimi Uwineza]
Springboard

Don't look at me like that
Accusing me of being heartless
Of using blood and bones of the innocents to boost my cause
I will say this for your sensitive heart" I did it all for my people"
I sacrificed my exile perks to save you

But hey!
When you discover that I do not give a rat's behind about you
Don't remind me of the dignity I put aside decades ago
For when a divine descendant hit rock bottom
A shrewd and merciless mortal came out of that pit

I will sing of sacrifices I made to liberate you
I will milk any opportunity "for my people"
Since you still think dignity is part of my DNA
I will make you believe there is divinity left in me
Hopefully, the mourning in your heart will crowd your judgment
forever

And if you dare wake up to my true nature
I will remind you of how I rescued you from death's gates
Then I rise from your ashes like a heartless sphinx
Soaring high on praises of Mr. White, Smith, Francois and brothers
of Albert and Wilhelm
Legitimized by the blood and bones of a multitude

I'm a bridge,
Mothers land moulds itself in my heart
and my blood, carries the essence
Of father's.
I am the calm that
hides in the corners of
our lives too afraid to come out
I am chaos in a body
A soul fluid in it's complexity
I am dreams wrapped
around our sleep
I am the voice that echoes
"Peace"
On the streets,
music to lift us from the mud,
notes resting on our skin,
washing away fear,
washing over ignorance.
Sealing together,
mother and father,
into one.

Of Origins And Connections

[Aisha Mohammed]

[Aributtercup]
You Should Have Just Kept Quiet

"You should have kept quiet, this could ruin his life.
Can't you consider that he now has a wife?
He's moved on from it and i think you should too
You know it's just one of those things boys do.

You should have kept quiet, you're not the first one
Women have been molested since before you were born
You must have enticed him with the clothes you wore
You shouldn't go around town dressed like a whore.

You should have kept quiet and hidden your shame.
Now you just look desperate for someone to blame
No one is ever going to believe your jargon
You're just jumping on the 'me too' bandwagon."

[Dikun Elioba]

Naked

You have seen me at my lowest hour
timid with shame masked on my face
did I try to turn to you
in trouble you
when my body felt like it was
at war with itself?
The measurement of nostalgia
reawakens
I used to wake up to your presence
when the ray of a new sun dawns
I have to get my body back
through the length of my fingers and the memory of my eyes.
We used to be together somehow between a circumstance of meeting
and through windows of desire.
Sometimes I feel like my body no longer belongs to me anymore.

Some have showed me the pain others have gave them
while others have showed me how they have learned how to forget.
What hands have covered me?
Who summoned another to
trespass my skin to touch
me like an unknown whisper?
How do I receive my body back?
Even in the cold distance
I try to find the owner of the key
who decided to discover a chamber
of yes
without permission.

[Ammywrites]

A Tale No One Cared To Hear

..Never believed.
Uncle Deji..
The very fair angel that bought me chocolates at every visit.
The angel who clutched a bible at every holiday spent here.
The soul winner,
When he sings, he drew a breathe from my tender chest.
Heard him talk?
Uncle Deji was truly an angel.

Then I grew, just with a little pump on my chest.
Uncle Deji..
Became the devil,
That took the form of an angel.
They said the devil comes,
To steal, kill and destroy.
He did steal my innocence,
Killed my dreams

And destroyed my EGO.

For every wreck he did, I got a milky way.

And then I grew again, a little pump to my broken courage.

Uncle Deji..

He had told me never to tell anyone.

But I did,

And all I got,

Was a scorn,

And Laughter.

'What is she saying?'

They asked me.

My courage was broken again.

Still, I grew.

And I spoke up again,

This time, Mum dragged me to a corner.

'Do not say this anymore to a soul!'

'Trash those words and be silent!'

She dragged me by the ear.

I could see the devil's harsh laughter.

After all he had told me.

It saddens me that I'm still growing,

And I can't speak up again.

Not once I tried, twice I did.

A soul never believed.

If during my childhood, no one trusted my words,

Who now will at adulthood??

[Michel'le Donnelly]

A Great Love Affair Gone Wrong

It started off as your typical love story; girl meets the love of her life, falls madly and whole-heartedly in love and becomes so consumed by her desperation to be with said love, that she's blinded to anything that could stand in their way of being together. If you haven't already guessed it, I am said girl and the love of my life? Well, let's just say they're kind of a big deal.

From the first moment I walked out of the tube stop into the hustle and bustle and pit of hell that is Oxford Circus, I knew that London was the city I wanted to explore my twenties with. I've always considered myself a nomad. I'm South African, when I was 15 I immigrated to Australia and by the time I completed high school, I decided that I would be studying in the UK. Although my university was in Kent, it was only a 40-minute train journey into the wonder that is London, which I tried to visit at least every second weekend.

Our love affair began innocently enough. I'd take the train in on a Saturday morning, arrive at St. Pancreas International and hop on the Central Line to Liverpool Street. I'd start my day with a morning coffee and a bite at The Breakfast Club before slowly making my way through Brick Lane, browsing the best in vintage attire. I'd walk on through to Shoreditch, and start making my way onto Holborn and Covenant Garden. By the afternoon, I'd be strolling past all the matinee attendees in the West End before taking a moment to stare at my favourite building, Westminster Palace. I'd spend the last hours of my day on London Bridge gazing out onto the Thames, watching as the boats gracefully rode upon its muggy waters. Then, time was up and I'd be back on a train to Kent.

It wasn't anything serious at first. Sometimes I'd let a whole month pass by before heading to see London again. But the more I visited, the harder it got for me to get on that train back to uni. I remember this one time, I just lingered in a toilet stall at the train station and almost missing the last train out. I didn't even care that I would have had to wait 6 hours for the next one.

The day I realised just how deeply and madly in love I was with London, was also my last day with her. It was too late at that point. I had had three years to sort out a plan so we could stay together but seeing as I thought it would just be a brief affair, I made no such plans. How was I to know that this was to be a love for life? I was shocked by the sadness I felt when I left. I mean, I was a traveller, someone who couldn't be tied down. And yet I found myself struggling to see my life without London in it.

After a year of "finding myself" in Sydney, South Africa and Cambodia, I could no longer deny my fate. I decided I had to go back. This time I was going to study a Masters in Human Rights at University College London (UCL) and I'd be spending every waking minute with the holder of my heart.

I arrived at Heathrow Airport in June 2014. I was all set for life with the Netflix to my chill, London. As far as I was concerned, there was nothing that could stand in the way of us being together now. Of course, there was the minor issue of visas but I had already figured that all out. Plus this was my destiny; nothing goes wrong when destiny is involved.

Oh, how wrong I was.

The week before I was set to begin my induction week at university, I still had not received my visa. I managed to contact the UK Visa and Immigration Office. (Just a side note about the UK Home Office – it is one of the most difficult places to get in touch with, they don't have a physical address and between us, I've not convinced it even exits!) but yes I managed to get in contact and was assured that the decision on my visa was still pending and that there was nothing wrong with my application. I could begin uni with no stress, but more importantly, my relationship with London was safe.

With my worries about my visa put at ease, I embarked on my next adventure, as a loved up masters student. UCL was amazing and I was far too blinded by love to watch the other shoe drop.

After 12 days of being a "loved up masters student", an admissions officer called me in. She told me that she had spoken to a colleague at the Home Office and was informed that my visa was going to be denied. I remember everything kind of just going silent at that moment. I felt so numb and had nothing to say. She kindly touched my shoulder and offered me two options:

1) Withdraw my current application, fly home and make a new application and be back by final enrolment. (Uhm, I don't think she realized that final enrolment was in 2 days and I lived on the other side of the fucking world!)

Or

2) Defer my degree to the next year.

And just like that, I watched as my destiny faded away.

After consulting with my department head, I decided it would be best to defer my placement. So I withdrew my visa application and started making preparations to head home.

As if being denied my visa wasn't enough to deal with, when I requested for my passports to be returned, I was told that the visa office no longer had them. Instead, I would now have to deal directly with 'Voluntary Departures and Immigration'. According to customs, my leave to remain in the UK expired back in 2013 and since I was there illegally, I would have to go to the airport immediately and be put on the first flight out.

I was absolutely devastated. I really had no idea how this had happened. I mean, I just wanted to be with my bae, the Michael to my Janet, the Aunt Viv to my Uncle Phil - instead, I found myself an illegal immigrant in a very suspicious country without any documentation to prove my identity! Is this what the Greeks meant when they said love is insanity?

I certainly felt insane as I spent days making panicked phone calls to immigration and keeping the blinds to my flat shut in case immigration officers were waiting outside. I spent most of this time replaying events over and over in my head.

How could I allow this to happen? Ever since I could remember, I've always planned ahead. I planned to work really hard at school and get into a great university. I planned to spend a year volunteering abroad after graduating, and I planned to study again and receive my Masters. Yet there I sat, with nothing. I'd read books and watched films about how falling in love ruined peoples lives - but I could not believe it had happened to me.

I listened to Aaliyah's "The One I Gave My Heart To" on, repeat for hours. I'm kind of a drama queen as it is, so throw in a broken heart and an immigration scandal and I became unhinged. What was I going to tell all my friends and family back home? Would I ever get my Masters? How could I face moving back in with my parents and starting from scratch all over again? I didn't even know who I was anymore.

And as for London? Well, Aaliyah's lyrics really rang true. "How could the one I gave my heart to, break my heart so bad? How could the one who made me happy, make me so sad?" As I said, I'm a drama queen. I just needed a white pants suit and some rain on cue and I could've recreated that entire music video.

And so, after what felt like an eternity, I got my passports back. I booked a flight home that same day, without even saying goodbye to my housemate. I didn't want any chance for London to twist my arm and change my mind. We were over. For good.

Oh, how wrong I was.

It's six years later. I am a recent Masters graduate, I'm no longer a planner and in the midst of this global pandemic, all I can think of is how can I be reunited with my greatest love?

In the words of Maya Angelou: "Love recognizes no barriers. It jumps hurdles, leaps fences, penetrates walls to arrive at its destination full of hope."

And as crazy as it sounds, I'm full of hope and ready to leap.

Maintaining Memories
[Tamary Kudita]

My great great great grandfather was a white Anglo Boer war Commissioner who fell in love with a black plantation worker named Rosy, who worked for him at that time. Because of the political climate in the Orange Free State they had to separate, but before parting ways they had six children. Two of them were classified as black (Sophie and Namasi) two of them were classified as coloured (Martha and Lindy) and the other two were classified as white (Peter and Ben).

My great great grandfather, Peter, grew up to become a Boer soldier. He would occasionally sneak food to his siblings at night but when he was caught he was chased away to a black urban area with his wife. Years later they had a son named Harry, who married a black woman. This cycle of inter racial union in my family history is the driving force behind this project, which is based on my family album (both real and imagined).

My work makes visible what might otherwise would have remained obscure.

[Yvette Lisa Ndlovu]

A Debt Repaid

On the day uncle is to fetch me away, my mother allows me to bath with two buckets of water. She only ever does this on Christmas morning so I know today must be special. She also gives me matombo, the three small scrubbing stones prayed for by Madzibaba Tawanda himself, the most powerful prophet among the Mapostori in our village. Instead of using the green bar soap which is rough on the skin, she gives me geisha which is a fragranced pink soap that foams as soon as it hits the water. She says uncle bought the geisha soap.

After the bath, I speed outside to do my daily ritual of watching girls leaving their homesteads for school. They have on the Grade 7 uniform. Shirts of the cleanest white and pleated green skirts that blow dust in their wake as they sway with the swing of the girls' hips. I always look at their shoes. How is it that even with the dusty roads, schoolchildren still manage to walk with shoes as shiny and black as their faces oiled with too much Vaseline. I've always longed to know what those school shoes that never catch dust feel like around the feet and how heavy on the back those bags must be that carry all those books filled with knowledge. I can't ask them. I can only lower my gaze each time they point at me bent over with a mutsvairo, sweeping the ground outside our hut. Today, however, I hold my chin up high at the absence of dust-free shiny shoes on my feet. I am going to live with uncle in the big city and use geisha soap everyday.

When uncle arrives he comes with groceries and raucous laughter. My parents have on their cleanest white Mapostori robes. They look like a madzibaba. The white against their smiling faces, blackened from sitting in the sun during the day and around the fire at night, brightened our home.

When you see my uncle, you wouldn't think he is the richest man in our village. His thin frame is held up by a belted trousers that balloons at the hips, mismatched neon shirts, and pointy leather cowboy shoes. He is more likely dismiss him as one of those door-to-door salesmen that tried to sell you magic cooking water that brings back lost lovers. But uncle is not a salesman. He owns all the Zupco buses that run from our village to the nearest big town, Bulawayo. Father says I am to live with uncle in the big town from now on.

I tried to look at our home through Uncle's eyes. The firewood in the middle, the steaming pot of beans on the fire, the plates laid out against the mudbrick wall, and the mats where we slept. I wonder what Uncle's house was like in the big city.

"Your debt is paid," uncle said to my father as he sat down on the only stool in the room.

Head bent, my father thanks uncle for his generosity as he sits down on the mat next to my mother. I sit behind them.

"You don't have to pay back any of the money you borrowed from me," uncle said.

My father sings uncle's praises.

"Don't thank me. Thank your daughter." uncle says peering behind my parents for a glimpse of me. "I might even send her to school. Musikana akanaka so, such a pretty girl."

"Ah kana, kwete Mudhara, not at all," my mother chimes in, her head falling back in laughter at the thought. Her white headwrap falls off as she laughs and she scrambles to pick it up and covers her head in embarrassment.

"Don't spoil her like that," she said after fixing the white cloth back on her head. "The only thing she is good for is housework."

"You are too kind," my father says, shifting in his white robe that flowed up to his feet. "But I hear your wife has quite the temper."

"She will come around eventually," came the response.

They praise uncle's kindness some more until the sun sets. When it is time to leave, uncle extends his hand to me and says,

"Huya mukadzi wangu." Come, my wife.

As I take his hand and walk out of my parent's home and into his Range Rover, I realize I do not know much about uncle. What I do know is that uncle only started coming to our home about a year ago when I turned 11 and that uncle is not really my uncle.

[Adedoyin Adebiyi]
Taste The Freedom.

Ibironke stood, arms raised high above her head, chest heaving and panting heavily, the knife in her hand gripped tightly as she contemplated giving the final blow. Abiodun was terrified, had already pissed himself and was saying nonsensical things below her, everything he was uttering was not registering but as she slowly came down from her high, his words seemed to flow back into her.

"Do You promise to leave me alone?" She asked without lowering her hand, she knew at this point he would say whatever just to get away from her but he was well and truly scared. Ibironke could care less but it was done. He would do whatever she asked for the first time in her life, this selfish, self centered, absorbed man that she had been married too when she was barely a woman at the age of eighteen.

For a long time she stood, towering above him watching herself take deep breaths through his wide blown pupils, memories of their fights, his beatings flashing through her mind like a fast forwarded video. Times where their roles were reversed and she was beaten black and blue for speaking up.

"You bastard!" She snarled bringing the knife down for a moment before raising it back up, if she wanted to kill him she wanted it to be slow, he did not deserve any death that was swift and fast, what he deserved was to be sliced open while the vultures feasted on his insides.

"You beat me, you beat me till I have no womb, no child to call home, to make this pain worthwhile and you now want to kill me?" She roared above him and he flinched, trapped on the bed with cuffs on his wrist connected to the bedposts. Her tummy would never rise again with the sign of life because just like everything in her life, he had beat it out, her submission, her free spirit, her happiness, her joy and even her sadness he had beat it numb. But he failed to beat one thing out and that was her anger.

Ibironke had been fighting for a divorce for a year now, when she saw her life flash before her eyes the last time he hit her, a ruptured spleen the doctor had said, 'a disobedient consequence and a simple lovers spat,' her stepmother had said before dismissing the matter and that's when she realized that she would die like a chicken, never to be remembered or heard from again. So she filed for a divorce and ran away for a while. With little money to her name and nobody to run to because he had beat the spirit of friendship out of her, it took only a week for him to find her and drag her back to the fortress of doom. Sometimes it seemed as if she had lived for a hundred years, always so bitter and pessimistic but she was only twenty eight, not even up to three decades and her eyes had seen more than it should see.

"You will sign it, and you will get lost or else I will kill you. I have friends now in high places and the government is by my side. Abiodun I wish you harm, I-I." And she choked on her words, tears desperately trying to part from her eyes as she thought up the worst of curses on his head. He deserved it, a bleak end for all the suffering she had been through at the hands of this monster.

She climbed off the bed, swinging her legs to the side to retrieve the Divorce papers and shoving the papers in his face. "This document says I am not longer yours, it says I want nothing to do with you. I don't want your name anymore, your money-in fact I want nothing to do with you from now on till forever." She picked up the pen that had rolled to the floor during their brief tussle and contemplated stabbing him in the eyes, or at least an eye and shame coursed through her, she was a Christian and God would not approve her blinding him, but then God wanted her enemies to suffer so for good measure she stabbed his palm instead and got satisfaction from hearing him yelp out in pain.

"Sign this now," she said putting the pen in his other palm and shoving the paper under it with the knife pressed close to his jugular should he think of any funny business. Shaking furiously with fear on the wet bed he signed it, all the while cursing about his palm, enraged she snatched the pen from his hand and stabbed his right thigh and he fainted.

"Come in Cynthia," she called out to her lawyer, friend and confidant.

"Ah ibironke this is too much," she said stepping into the room and scrunching up her nose at the smell. "Is he dead and what is that smell?" She waved in front of her nose to dispel the odour.

"He fainted after I stabbed his thigh, here are the divorce papers," she shoved it to Cynthia with a triumphant smile on her face, "and the smell is pee, he can dish out beatings but can't take it," she said with a smile.

"Finally," Cynthia said mirroring her smile, "and then I will file a restraining order and you must visit a therapist, I'm so proud of you," she said gripping her arm and dragging her from the bed and to a chair by the far side of the room. She collapsed into it, all the while shivering as the adrenaline left her body. It was not advised to become close to a client but she just couldn't help herself, here was a woman who was powerful and strong and great but had being caged for over ten years in a marriage that had reduced her to nothing but a shell. Here was a woman who had taken it upon herself to win her freedom come what may and even though the incident that had happened in this room was illegal and must not be heard of she had agreed to it because she knew she would not be able to attend ibironke's funeral.

"How are you feeling?" She asked, kneeling beside her with a bottle of water she removed from her bag.

"Ugh, take it away from me, I might barf," she declined.

"How are you feeling right now?" She repeated the question and ibironke smiled, a smile so bright and free, like someone reborn.

"Do you know that the taste of freedom is the sweetest thing ever? I can do anything I want, I can go back to school to finish the course I started, I can start a business, I can even become a lawyer just like you," and she rambled on and on about endless possibilities she could never have hope to have before and Cynthia just let her ramble on and on, tears streaming down her cheeks as she stared off into space. She gave her a brief cursory glance and satisfied that there was enough bruises to present to the court on her domestic violence case she pulled her towards the door and away from the horrible stench emitting from the passed out Abiodun on the master bed.

Ibironke smiled at the lawyer who held the divorce certificate in her hands, she may have gotten her freedom violently but that was the language of the unheard and she didn't regret it, because now she knew her place in the world, in her life and the prospect of being in charge of herself once more was worth it.

[Vivian Ibemere]

Under The Umbrella Of Blee

Every night, I scowl in a mirror at my pale self in an itsy-bitsy body with a price tag hovering over my body parts; from the bleached golden strands of hair on my head down to my dainty feet and I would snivel myself to sleep, praying with piety that God takes me out of this hell but then, I remembered how grave robbers dug out the decaying body of Arithi because she had my type of skin and had died in her sleep. She was buried in the morning and at night her bones were stolen. Even in death, I would still be unwhole. This made me fear both life and death.

In the morning, I would sing like a nightingale that had never felt the wetness of tears on its face. When I sing, my brothers would hold their hearts with fear, the pitch of my voice would burst my pinkish lips and cause blood to gush out of my crystalline face.

"You're disturbing the neighbourhood," Mama would caution, catapulting a liss smile at me. I would smile back with squinty eyes but I gave no care about the people in the neighbourhood for the scars they inflicted on me and the pain they made Mama pass through.

Mama was accused of having an extra-marital affairs with a white man the day she birthed me. Her mother had counselled her to dump me in a ditch or suffocate me preferably, to end the suffering I was going to put Mama through, but she won't heed. Grandma flung her hands over her head and left my mother to bear her burden. Papa too, ran away from the burden with accusing lips, he faulted Mama of infidelity and bringing in bad omen into his household. Papa left with Tumo, my mother's first son, whom I never got to know.

Mama was soft and at the same time, strong as an ox, her beefy hands have fought numerous battles for my sake. Since the day I started to share the same sun with the world, Mama had been my warrior. I have survived this long, because of the kicks she unleashed on the pompous ushers for making me sit behind the church, claiming that I was impure; the slaps she struck on the bony cheeks of the children that called me a ghost because I only wanted to know what it felt like to skip a rope; the sturdy chairs and tables she broke on the heads of freety men that had tried to rape me with claims that they'd be cured of their viruses; the reverberating knock she landed on Uncle's head the day he laughed at my dream to become a Singer; the punches she whammed on the jaws of ignorant teachers in school who punished me under the sun, and the thief who came to amputate my arms and legs with a machete but didn't go back alive. For these, I intend to disturb those who had denied me a placid life without dulling my blades.

Like her name, Editha, she was always prosperous in war...my war. Countless times when I thought of bending to the wind of the society and end my pains, Mama's brawny image gave me strength to push on and stand equal like all of God's creations. I am hunted like a bush meat, always on my toes and ready to take off from ghost hunters who haunt my type.

One night in February, two days after my tenth birthday, some hunters sniffed me down to my village and into our house. Mama was still awake and heard the stealthy sounds behind the fences. She sent my brothers to go outside and confirm her suspicions. Darweshi, the holy one and Erevu, the clever one, weren't like me; they had honey-coloured skins, brown eyes, black hairs, black eyebrows, black eyelashes which were different from my pale golden coloured own, and large brick red lips. The only thing white on them, were their teeth which coruscated at night. Whenever we had moonlight stories with Mama, I get drunk in the whiteness that emit from their mouths as they talk or answer Mama's questions. Unlike my yellowy set of teeth which Mama says, 'Shines like a sunflower', just to soothe my nerves.

We ran to Grandma's house, escaping through the second gate of our house, when my brothers confirmed Mama's suspicion. Grandma's face wrinkled with a frown when she espied my colour before that of Mama and my brothers in the dark. Mama pleaded with her mother to let us spend the night in her house.

"That's the kind of visitors you'll get when you're carrying a half-done child around the village," her mother riposted. Mama wanted to get apoplectic but with-strained herself to prevent her mother from rejecting her plea.

"I can only take the boys. Find a place for you and the ghost," grandma vomited and dragged my brothers into her house before shutting the door at Mama's speechless face. Any mother would have committed filicide at the cold treatment they received from people of same bloodline because of the colour of their child's skin but Mama stayed strong for me, she saw beyond my complexion.

Mama died fighting for me on the bridge between the farm and the market. Before then, the market women with eyes popping out of their sockets, hurled their pointy discriminatory fingers at me, crying out at the top of their voices, "See, it's a Mbolimbwelu."

Mama had fired them a face with boiling eyes and retorted in Sukuma language. "Show me the one you created. If not, don't call my child a white goat," she released a deafening hiss, making some of the women to cover their ears and others laughed their lungs out.

On our way home, the sun shone its wicked face at me. Aside the sun, the people were my worst enemy, they made me feel less than a human being and more like a thing for sacrifice. I inhumed my head in Mama's wrapper which she hung over her broad shoulders, saving enough hem to protect my skin from the scorching sun when we were interrupted by the sounds of swift feet. It was Abasi and Mwamba, clinging to rocky sticks, equating the looks on their faces: unfeeling. Mama read their faces and quickly gave me the whole wrapper to cover my fifteen year old self, so as to aid my vision and avoid more freckles from sprouting on my cheeks and nose. Then, she thrutched me aside and brought down the weighty basket from her head to gather enough strength to wage war on those who have sworn to see her daughter dead.

"What is it?" Mama asked flinging her hands in the air and bringing them down to tie her short wrapper firmly on her voluptuous waist.

The gawky looking men perused me with preyful eyes. They smelled of fermented local drinks, which I nosed from a distance and prayed Mama would be able to stomach their stenches. In a flash,

Abasi, the community leader's son, broke the stick on Mama's stocky leg and like a tigress, she pounced on him, biting deep into his ear and spat a bloody flesh out of her mouth. He whined in pain as more blood plashed down his neck. The other, a stubble faced man, ran into Mama with full force, taking her off balance. She fell with her head to the ground, soiling her newly braided hair. This made me run toward her, but she stopped me in a feeble voice, "Run straight home and don't look back."

"Mama, please come home." It was election period, when men unleashed the evil in their hearts for my kind but Mama always took the blow for me.

As I ran home in sweaty palms, achy heart and thoughtful head, I resolved that I won't let superstitions pin my existence. The society won't define my existence. Mama's bruised dark sheen face as she struggled for my white life was all I saw on the muddy road that carried my feet, now sore in hot race. The thud that came with her fall on the bridge sent steaming tears to my eyes and left my path blurry.

During Mama's burial, those familiar faces came to sympathize. Most of them possessed pitch-black skins, some brown. I stood close to my brothers in my pale skin, gaping at Mama's lifeless body and gnashing my teeth in anger for the loss they'd brought upon us. Grandma came too, she shot a hateful eye at me that read "Finally, you've killed my only daughter. Let's see how you'll survive now!" What they didn't know was that a new person...a rebellious being in me had been resurrected and I was ready to soar in my skin regardless of what the society say. True to my name, Zahra, I'll shine and blossom like the sunflower.

[Mahafuza Abdulrahman]
She's The Root

Sitting on a worn out stool on a beauteous evening
Enjoying the chilly breeze
Reminiscing through the fondest memories Of my childhood, as the sun falls
I remember the little me
When my little world was around my toys, everything was fair
When my universe was full Of rainbows   heart and soul painted With bright colors With a beautiful imagination and delightfu ike the sun rays ooking cute likea bunny
Living in a quiet beautiful neighborhood a range style home
I remember the scent Of cinnamon
I remember the river and how we dance to the sound Of it rushing
Oh' remember the Story Of a phenomenal woman Who created her own planet where she could fit she listens to her needs and desires
She celebrate her body rhythm and value it as an exquisite gift
She's the blue Of light before time draws
She kneels in prayers to keep her soul
She gives the best in What she does
She wears confidence and grace
She walks sure footedly
She's a life giver
A phantom Of delight
Discipline is a gown she wears
She's brave
A beautiful apparition

If you ask her how she got tall she Will bend her own steel to a staircase so you can get the best Of you

She's perfect in the way she makes her presence a place where you can rest

She's strong enough to lead and rule With a refreshing smile

She swims in the ocean Of love and hope

She accept insults and serve With kindness

She wears the crown Of motherhood

She use her love to turn a house into a home and makes it glitters

She seeks opportunity when it doesnt seek her to open doors to leap forward in this uncertain world

Her gender give her the courage to roar

Her price is far above any currency

She's love in the purest form

She glows like the sun

She doesn't allow her fear undertake her strength

She brings goodness

She's a lioness

She's strong in her faith and firm in her belief

She Will scrape her fingers to the bone to reach her dreams

She's a listener and a teacher

She authors her cuvn life

She's the dictator and the culinary commander

She design her personal spirituality to inform her daily life

She sits in the circle Of women and tells her Story

When she speaks there's so much love in her voice

She's gorgeous even Without any pigment

She's the stardust and fabric Of the sky

She's a home builder

She's a patient gardener if you ask about her soil she Will tell you she nurtured it With love

She has the stamina and charisma that one would admire

Her heart is a chamber Of birth and love where dreams are revived

She value every content likea rare jewel

She doesnt complain, silently suffers and cries

She carries the burden Of the Whole generation on her shoulders

Her eyes sparkle likea bright Star in the sky

She conceal her scars for the sake Of humanity

Offer Of everything

She's patient and always forgive

She's beautiful inside and out

She's a mother Of the future and a sister Of the present

She's born to love and live

She's a woman Of million dreams

[Oluwamayowa Somoye]

Only In Africa

The male child is supreme,
The female, the spare,
Men are encouraged to remarry
sadly, by fellow women
because their wives birth girls,
Even though the father dictates the gender.

The girl child is taught to aim low,
For men hate independent women,
She must be a slave to the kitchen,
Only then can she find Mr. Right
bear his kids, forever find peace,
This is her destiny.

The woman is why there is no babe,
It is never the Man,
Even if his count is low
or his genes at fault,
She is to blame
She is the one to be disgraced.

The African woman is strong,
She can overcome prejudice,
Lead the nation
and still care for her family,
She is more than her beauty,

She is brilliant and talented.

We can be free,
Make our own decisions,
Choose our own path,
Dream as big as we can,
Pick our soulmate
at our own chosen pace.

We can decide to be single,
Not to have children
and still be fulfilled,
We can change the world,
Join powerful African women
to put Africa on the map.

Let us be united,
We can uplift each other,
Help each other grow,
We need not fight or
tear ourselves apart
for the favor of Men.

[Rutendo.S. Maturure]
Unforgivable

C aged within the walls and borders of her body; self-imposed to limits by culture. Tadadiswa embraced the coolness of her room as she threw herself on her unmade bed. Things were never going to be the same again. She knew it. She understood it.

Tadadiswa had committed an unforgivable sin.

One night Tadadiswa sat in her best friend's lounge sharing a drink and connecting in deep thoughts. A deep nudge of darkness raided her gut.

'Bukhosi something is wrong' Tadadiswa whispered.

'Tadi you are always edgy. Please let this pass' Bukhosi hissed with an expressionless face.

Tadadiswa had known Bukhosi long enough to understand problem-solving was an enemy, minding his business a priority. Ten years was long enough to know when he put up a mask of emotions and when he meant it. Trying not to dig her claws deep into his business, she stood up to stand by the window. It faced the Langa's bedroom, Bukhosi's neighbour. Something looked amiss. It was too quiet and organized for a home with people.

Giggling like a little girl 'He said I smell like coconut oil and mint'

'Is that a good thing?' Tadadiswa responded still searching deep at the Langa's for any
movement.

Bukhosi nodded with a loud sigh to try getting her attention. Suddenly a loud thud caught

Tadadiswa's attention. Bukhosi was having convulsions again, but this time it was different.

The room became strangely winter cold in October evening heat. Bukhosi spoke in various voices at once. The carpet vibrated his pain; his soft hands gripped and rayed the fur. Shudders galloped through Tadadiswa's body, she bit her tongue in fear. Everything froze and the horror began. Voices chattered away in echoes. Confused, Bukhosi laughed and whimpered in pain.

'You shouldn't have come here. You shouldn't have found us' a voice in Bukhosi cursed in IsiNdebele.

Suddenly in the intense silence of the night, Mrs. Langa screamed with her whole body. Tadadiswa turning to look through the window her eyes went wide with atrocity, leaving her mouth dry. The sky became overcast with dark clouds as Bukhosi let out a strange cry, forming clumsy fists that made him dig deep in his palms. Thunder rumbled and cracked, engulfing the drowsy sound of howling dogs and vehicles passing by. The skies threatened to outpour the same pain Bukhosi and Mrs. Langa held. Suddenly everything was wet and bleak.

Tadadiswa grew weak of the raging confusion paving through her body. An urge with power came over her. 'Who are you? What do you want?' she said keeping herself together. 'Respect your elders' child. Death creeps around you like the air you breathe. Your ancestors hover over you like flies on rotten meat.' A voice said from Bukhosi. 'We have been watching. We have been waiting but just not for you, for the one who resides in you.' Then they went silent leaving Bukhosi's body to collapse. He looked like an empty broken shell. Perspiration glistened on his brown caramel skin. Taking the zebra imprinted cloth on Bukhosi's table she wrapped it around herself and covered her hair with her orange scarf. She took the snuff in her bag put it in a metal kango plate she found in the kitchen. Then she set it alight allowing the smoke to cover Bukhosi. Then she began to sing his totems to appease his ancestors in his Isi

Ndebele 'Ngixolela Nxumalo (forgive me Nxumalo) Phola, Nxumalo (take it easy Nxumalo). Ndwandwe, Mkhatshwa (clan names).......' As she went on to sing praises.

This is an unforgivable sin in most tribes especially when there is bad blood in the past. One cannot sing praises of another's ancestors to appease them. A woman is expected to know her place. It bestows curses and unknown spirits hovering around you. They say it breathes bad luck on everything you touch. But Tadadiswa bends the rules to unlock her friend stuck in an unknown realm.

Do not go there Shumbakadzi, a voice whispered in her head. You are royalty we have bad blood with them. Come back Tadadiswa. He is not worth it fought the voice. Leaning against the wall Tadadiswa inhaled the fire and nightmares she fought as she tried to appease and beg. She felt a strange hand cover hers. It was

Mrs. Langa covered in bruises, eyes rolled at the back of her head, cold as ice.

'Baxolele Baba. (Forgive them, father) Baxolele Nxumalo.(Forgive them Nxumalo) Yingane lezi hawu Baba. (They are just children, father) Baxolele (Forgive them)' she screamed softly to appease Bukhosi's ancestors.

Tadadiswa woke up in the arms of sticky sweaty and exhausted Mrs. Langa who kept on chanting forgiveness and singing praises to the clan names. Unable to remember what happened she looked at Bukhosi who weakly smiled. Mrs. Langa was a distant aunt but closely related to the Nxumalo's clan, a daughter.

'You shouldn't have done what you did Tadi' she cursed scolding her. 'You angered them but they were amazed by your courage. No woman from your tribe has ever challenged these ancestors. I salute you, but you need to get going. You need to face who you are and accept your calling. Stop fighting them'.

Getting up with her weak body that felt like a stranger to her, she gathered her things and went home. A lot had happened but that night is to be never spoken of. The bruises imprinted on her body or the nightmares where her journey to finally embracing a gift she buried years ago. This was her place in the world. A story never told. Tadadiswa went home to embrace the coolness of her room. She threw herself on her unmade bed. Things were never going to be the same again. She knew it. She understood it.

Tadadiswa had committed an unforgivable sin.

[Chengetai Masalethulini]

Journey

Last year on international women's day, March 8th, I was mugged on my way home from work. I was walking with my sister before it got dark, quite a miracle as usually it's just me. She was coming back from meeting a friend at a nearby Pizza Place and had a box of the good stuff in her hands.

The ordeal started when a new looking silver Toyota Runnex with 5 men inside, pulled up from behind us as we waited to cross the road facing our house. We heard some yelling and suddenly they cut us off as it had come so close to me that I was sure my feet had been run over strangely. A man from the passenger's side suddenly reached out and grabbed my laptop bag and took off at high speed. I wish that's all it was but unfortunately the strap of the bag was hooked onto my neck leading to me being dragged remembering my last breath in that moment where the next thing I recall I was airborne.

I was being strangled by the strap and I couldn't get free. A big guy with short dreadlocks was hanging out the window, apparently trying to shake me off. I don't remember seeing him but I was told he was there. There must have been a mistake, I thought, as I beat the side of the car with my right hand screaming "Stop! Let me go!" Surely they didn't know I was still attached, or did they?

I saw the tar racing beneath my body. Alternating, seeing the side of their car and the grass opposite as my body bounced back and forth like a rag doll. My knees and hip grazed the ground and bounced up, then back down again. I heard my sister screaming "Let her go! Please God, Let her go!!!" I saw her running and crying after me, this broke my heart. They swerved to avoid a bag of maize that a gardener from next door threw onto the road to try and stop them. Vehicles passed by but I don't believe that they understood what was happening, although they could see us very clearly.

I knew it was over for me as our screams seemed to go unnoticed. Instead, they switched gears and accelerated. I couldn't breathe. I had no strength left within me so I stopped fighting. I could feel the tar against my arms and legs as gravity pulled me down thanks to the gear shift, I wasn't flying anymore. I was blacking out. Now all I could say was "Jesus, Jesus, Jesus..." My face was 10cm from the spinning wheel. I didn't want this to be the last thing I saw. The road ahead was fast approaching, we were going so fast. I chose to look back at my angel, she was running after me, growing smaller and smaller still. I wanted her to know it would be okay. I felt like someone or something was holding my head up, I had peace, I just wanted my family to be okay.

Eventually I heard a click, and rolled onto the tar. I saw them driving away recklessly somehow, much like an exaggerated cartoon sequence. My sister and the gardener rushed up and quickly removed me from the middle of the road and put me by the curb. One of our neighbours came out, and gave me first aid. It helped but they hadn't seen my side, my clothes were ripped and bloody, I was going into shock.

I was dragged almost a hundred metres uphill that day. I believe God saved me, they showed no signs of stopping. The months to follow I was treated as a burns victim, going to the hospital for daily dressing of my wounds which was torture. They needed to scrub and revive the dead flesh until it bled on top of scraping off tar and dirt from my wounds, and rubber from the spinning tyre from my elbow.

I screamed and wept like a baby because of the pain. Some of the nurses would shed tears as well as they tried to treat me. The wounds were too deep to do a skin graft. I could not feed myself, bathe, move my arms, bend my knees much or use my hands. Eventually mobility was returned to me through physiotherapy. I had to go for trauma counselling, this has been quite a journey.

I finally saw how beautifully strong my mother and sisters were as they watched me in agony fighting through the pain in my body and the pain in my heart, with grace shown in calm but with eyes that said, "You're in pain, we see it, we would gladly take it for you if we could but we need you to be stronger than you've ever been, this too shall pass."

Family 2

[Tamary Kudita]

Kuchengetedza Pfungwa:
Maintaining Memories
[Tamary Kudita]

My great great great grandfather was a white Anglo Boer War Commissioner who fell in love with a black plantation worker named Rosy, who worked for him at that time. Because of the political climate in Orange Free State they had to separate but before parting ways they had six children. Two of them were black (Sophie and Namasi), two of them were coloured (Martha and Lindy) and the other two were white (Peter and Ben). My great great grandfather Peter grew up to become a Boer soldier. He would occasionally sneak food to his siblings at night until he was caught and chased away to a black urban area with his wife. Years later they had a son named Harry who married a black woman. This cycle of inter racial union is the driving force behind this project.

Through investigating my family photo album, I have identified absences. There are no images of white people in my album because an aunt of mine found them and burnt them. She burnt them as a way of cutting cords of attachment to a painful past. The site of these images probably caused a relapse of pain. In my work I address these gaps by photographing individuals who have the same likeness to missing family members. These reconstructed portraits are based on oral reports.

My body of work is mostly self-reflective. Tracing back my genealogy, I wanted to find out where I come from and to know the people who shaped who I am today. Reenacting this storyline speaks to my identity and how I interact with the world. My work attempts to convey a truthful narrative and demonstrate how I engage with issues of invisibility, re-contextualization, appropriation and subversion to deflate white definitions of black personhood.

In Bell Hooks "In Our Glory: Photography and Black Life" she talks about the power of photography in the fight for representation. She views the field of representation as a site of ongoing struggle. This field of representation can be explained as how we see our selves versus how others see us. (Hooks 2010:1). How we see ourselves versus how others see us suggests that both the photographer and the viewer play a role in how the image acquires meaning and have total control over the image.

Using photography as a tool for resistance and reconciliation, I also use the same photographic processes colonizers used when they photographed Africans. For instance, Duggan Cronin who used the Camera Obscura to produce several collotype photographs of the Bantu Tribes of South Africa. Using these same processes as a black photographer, in a way subverts authority and allows me to take control of the narrative. It also disrupts a hegemonic system of thought by resurfacing visual omissions.

The process of transforming digital photography into film photography by using vintage filters mimic early photography photographs allows me to bring the past into the present - reenacting and retelling the love story of my great great great grand father and grandmother.

The individuals in my photos are carefully chosen. I chose them according to the description I was given by my grandmother when she narrated the story. This likeness extends beyond the physical it also has to do with character. To address issues of invisibility you have to make the content hyper visible.

Looking at my found images I found most of the people in the pictures to be in control of their own representation. They are not told how to sit or stand.

Although the people in my photographs are not passive recipients of the viewer's gaze there is one image that tells a different story. In fig 5 the individual plays the role of my great great grandmother Sophie who was a plantation worker during apartheid a time when black people were still discriminated against. Black people were measured by physical appearance and having a white father and black mother was not taken into account when it came to classification. It's a paradox that Sophie's father being a white man represented the very race that caused discrimination. In the photo I wanted the individual to embody Sophie. I also explore the notion of the colonial identity which is one that is not self acquired rather it is imposed upon in order to maintain appearances. Whereas the authentic identity is one that is practiced in private. Thinking about biracial identity in the abstract, highlights the need for discourse on the topic.

In addition to photographing individuals, my work consists of numerous found images of black working class families and students. In reading this collection it offers a new perspective on the life of black people. These images give us a way to see ourselves, a sense of how we would look when we are not wearing the mask trying to perfect the image for a white supremacist gaze. These concerns are similar to Santu Mofokeng's 'The Black Photo Album/Look at Me - an archival project involved in recovering existing images.

I am also recovering archival images but as the photographs do not exist, I am manufacturing them based on oral history. Subversion is implicit in my elected mode of practice and my choice of representation demonstrates a subject position congruent with that of Mofokeng. Mofokeng constantly subverts the comfort zones of racial and cultural memory, questions the politics of representation and the objectifying gaze of the photographer. In his images he seeks to tell a truthful narrative about black lives. When people looked at images of black people they do not see a human individual, rather the stories and legends attached to their blackness. In my work I rewrite these stories and legends starting with my family photo album

I see photography as the only way we can resist racist ideologies because a photograph brings the past into the present and facilitates the work of memory.

My body of work therefore responds to the disappearance of certain photographs and the bombardment of stereotypical representations. The images in my project serve to portray that African identities are complex. The album shows and depicts the various generations, the challenges and victories of each of those generations. Articulated within the discourse of race and racism my intent is to reclaim Black subjectivity and confront invisibility while reconstructing my family's story. My work makes salient what might otherwise would have remained obscure. When one opens a book or a magazine one is most likely to see images of black people that reinforce and re-inscribe white supremacy. I photograph black people in a different light in an effort to gain control over how we are represented, by challenging the conventional ways of seeing blackness - using photography as a tool to resist misrepresentation.

[Mojisola Esther]
Voiceless Storyteller

The piece of cloth left of her
Was her only protection,
Her laughter were mentally ill
Even momma won't believe her
She cried all evening in her darkness
Even as this pretty evil occurs every night

Papa and Johnnie drink all night
"I Knock on death's door she won't open!"
She draws her stories on her pad
Same womb breath live into Johnnie and her
Her momma busy schedule destroyed her
Momma the farm seeker, she plants her body everywhere

That same shadow, shadows, are here again
Pulls her hands out
Places her legs apart from themselves
Takes away her only protection - that piece of cloth
And rubs a thorn in her chest downward
And her waist and beyond.

Her tears are now dry from it's source
Johnnie and papa drink and drown into her skin
Every night this nightmares continues
Who shall I tell?
Who will believe her story?

"Momma won't believe either
Although I told her daily
Her snub goes beyond the devil's"
She tell her pad
She is 8 years with little or no voice
She needs a voice

[Sinenhlanhla Mlilowokunqoba Maphezabantu]

Ikhulukuthu

Khulukuthu that's what it was called, one of my horrid most unsettling memories. It had one small window with burglar guards, an un-flushable toilet, smelly worn out sponges with piss patches and a door that had a small transparent glass opening that was meant for the eyes of those who would scowl at me, after minutes (which felt like hours or maybe they were hours I am not certain) locked up in there.

There were no lights in the Khulukuthu so all the monsters came out to play.

I would stay confined at the Khulukuthu most times, because I was one of the most deranged.

I was hallucinating so therefore behaved irrationally and the nurses at Prince Mshiyeni

Memorial Hospital (D7) the psychiatric ward, thought it to be fitting and therapeutic to be confined in that dingy place. They would tell mama that it helps mentally disturbed people and I still wonder how?

You're already seeing and hearing things that are not there, the last thing you need is solitary confinement in a jail cell.

They would ridicule and imitate the gibberish I would say in my moments of utter bewilderment, calling and hand smacking each other while laughing hysterically at the comedy that I was.

To the irony, it was the security guards that were most understanding to my and the other patients situation.

We would be woken up at 4 o'clock to bath then go back to sleep, woken up again when break-fast came, then their circus would begin. Sphelele was a male that also spent most of his time at the Khulukuthu, he and I would kick, slap, spit and cry (simultaneously) in attempts to evade being thrown into the self-depraving room. The nurses did not care though, they rather seemed to enjoy dragging us to the dreaded room.

When I was consumed by a fit of sorrow he would come to me and ask what was wrong then placate me as I spoke my gibberish, which he understood.

Crying was second nature during that period, I am surprised my tear glands did not dry up.

When mama came to visit me, I always begged to go home with her, I shrieked, which would always be followed by the forcefully evacuation to iKhulukuthu.

During that time though, not once did I think of masturbating, which is proof that I really was disorientated mentally, back then when I was persistently and continuously faced with a predicament that was the first thing that arose in my mind.

Call me weak or meek for succumbing to life's harshness, I don't care.

Before I got psychologically challenged, I was enchained to the blackened, self-loathing, suicidal and volatile/ dispositions of depression.

I did not indulge in the rush of being a teenager, I did not converse with anyone, I never visited anyone, due to being afraid of the questions that might erupt (why are you so quiet which is something I struggle to answer up to this day, beside that one time in Riverside and that's because I had been practising for months). Even at home they said I had (still have) a short temper, they never bothered to look beyond the surface though.

So I locked myself, within myself.

The more I grew up, the tighter the locks became. As I encountered more conundrums, the more it became difficult for me to live with the other people but it was also a struggle to live with myself hence the suicidal thoughts and attempts.

Sometimes I long to go back to being a child, before I realised the depth of what sexual assault is, before I was even assaulted, which is majorly the reason why I am depressed today. And the fact that the antidepressants come with their own blues (continuous weight gain, tachycardia and vaginal thrush) makes me feel that I am stuck in the mud more.

I'm working for and toward peace now, eternal tranquillity so that I will live freely and merrily. I am sick and tired of being woeful, the frown embedded in my forehead is weighing my face and spirit down.

One day I will go back to Mshiyeni and enquire about their traumatic method of healing, it feeds the problem rather than solve it.

Now I am fighting the Khulukuthu that lurks inside me which I intend to conquer.

[Hlulani Sabela]
The Only Love She Knew

It rained an angry rain, an unforgiving rain, so unforgiving that it stole from the soil what it was supposed to provide. It was that day she came home early after hearing that her youngest child was not at school; her youngest child was not waiting to be picked up where she had been dropped off.

Upon arriving home, each step, each foot impression made in the soft clay of the wet earth, her heart filled with questions too difficult to answer and like an anchor it sank to the soles of her feet. When she sat down, she took a breathe deep enough to change the direction the world rotated and cried as though her heart caught alight and all she could do was watch it turn to ash.

She thought of the worst and darkest places only because it protected her weary soul from what she felt was inevitability. Then there came a sound so sweet, it reminded her of the first bite into a freshly baked cookie, so sweet it wrapped her wilted heart in a blanket of colour. It was the voice of her precious girl of 11 years old. It was her youngest of two daughters.

This would have been the best time to praise God, to hold her child so close each heart could touch and form an inseparable bond, to make her baby feel as though she was the only light source for all the lives she touched. Instead she took all her fear and torment and raised a belt to the delicate skin of her child. Each lash burnt to the ear and tore past her child's skin so fast that not even God could stop it. She punished her ingenuous child for taking her to every dark place. Rather than provide a warm and loving touch, she became the darkness she feared her daughter might come across.

That night she created a shale scar so big, it became all her child was because her child innocently visited her older sister at her high school and then walked home with her.

How can you console a child who screamed all her fear away?

Chazeni was a Zulu woman who bore the weight of her sorrows in her eyes and had cheekbones that made it seem as if the sorrow was not heavy enough. lower down she bore hips wide enough to birth a thousand sons and two daughters, yet her breasts appeared as if too small to fill up a bottle.

I cannot say I remember the exact day I met her and she became my step mother, but I can compare it to the type of feeling that engulfs your whole existence and fills you with the same discomfort of sitting on a bed of needles. I did not know this feeling in its entirety until that specific day. It was the day the sun forced its gift into the sanctuary of my father's home. I felt myself melting out of my skin. So Chazeni's children, Ngamla and Khazele suggested with an uncomfortable hesitation that we all attempt the forbidden. Go. For. A. Swim.

After submerging ourselves like paint brushes into a body of blue for several hours, everything went still. So still the silence was deafening. Soon the hum of the engine of a stark-night coloured car replaced the silence. Like a red mist, panic arose over everyone. Voices were raised to frequencies and volumes so high; it was like birds attempting to resolve conflict with fish.

The three of us walked in to find Chazeni seated dramatically in the armchair of the living room, like a scene from the Godfather. We were immediately told to return to the bedroom. Then Ngamla was called and a look possessed her face. She remembered a time once before when she was beaten for visiting her older sister t high school. It was as if she had seen death. Animosity beamed through as she opened the door. Then nothing but shrieks of horror and a slashing sound. Upon returning and minor examination I saw a painting of blues, purples and reds. Khazele was next and the same happened to her.

Although I was never one to have been called, I wondered if I would have felt better if I were. It was as if I was forcing myself into a box I never really fit in.

She was not my

[Ruth Kanu]
Afri – Femme: Am Strong, Bold And Beautiful.

"Please, can you lend me your note book after this class"?, I asked my course mate jane. I was busy arranging my books when I heard a statement from her : "what were you doing when your mates were going to school?"!. I felt very bad and remembered all I had been through to get to were I am today. It was a shock to hear such from her. She was just eighteen (18) years old and wouldn't understand.

I was a very brilliant girl In my primary school days and had it all. I was born with a silver spoon. My father was an aircraft engineer and my mother was a teacher, in a Government school in Port Harcourt, Rivers State Nigeria. I was the first daughter, having three (3) other siblings (all girls). My father wanted a male child and in his quest, he just walked out one day and didn't return. He left Rivers State to Lagos state with another woman. I was just nine (9) years old. My mother struggled from then on to train my siblings and I. She enrolled us into public schools and sure we studied hard. Her salary was very small and was never enough, but somehow we kept on growing.

I finished senior secondary school with very good grades but couldn't go to the university because my siblings had to finish secondary school too. I had to work as a sales girl with "D promise Fast Food" to help put food on our table. I needed the love of a father at that time. As a young girl of eighteen (18), there was a vacuum in my heart that needed to be filled. I knew I missed my father a lot and would search for him in the faces of people I meet.

I met a young Undergraduate student named Everest, who showed me love and I fell in love with him. We became intimate and at that time, the void in my heart was filled and I was happy. He went back to school and few months later, I discovered I was pregnant. I hid it for sometime but it was later discovered. My mother found out and all hell was let loose. She was angry and disappointed. I felt so ashamed as a first child. I had dreams but I saw it shattered before my eyes. I couldn't look at my siblings because I was supposed to set a pace for them. My mother later encouraged me after her anger had subsided. She had to assist, by then I had stopped working. Everest was told, he didn't deny it , and he said we should let his parents know. Mum and I went to his parents and his father, though a little bit angry, accepted the news in good fate. His mother refused bluntly , that her son was still in school and wasn't ready for such responsibility probably because there was a girl she wanted him to marry. Everest's dad insisted I move in with them, in the family house, which I did.

Few months later, I gave birth to a set of twin boys. My mum was so happy. I now had sons she didn't have. Everest's dad was happy and took good care of the children and I, but his mum was a torn on my flesh. She made life miserable for me, though she wasn't doing it in front of her husband. Everest's dad became sick and died few months later. My ordeal had just begun!

The mother increased her cruelty, with the support of his siblings. I planned going back to school when the kids were weaned at two years but Everest came back home. He was rusticated from school for allegedly been involved in cult activities. He never supported his mum's actions and always protected me from her. I got pregnant for my second child and gave birth to a son. Everest was later called back to school, after it was discovered he wasn't guilty of the crime he was accused of. He went back to school, graduated and went for the compulsory National Youth Service Corps (NYSC) Scheme.

During the time he was in school, I went into farming, sold my farm products to help me take care of our children. During his NYSC, things became a little bit easier. At least he could send us little money from his allowance. I was relived a bit. He started the traditional marriage rites

When Everest returned for holiday during his NYSC days, we decided to celebrate one year birthday for our second son. After the birthday party, I was cleaning up the house the following morning and heard voices. Everest and his sister were fighting and I tried to separate them but she bounced on me with a bottle in her hand. I ran away and later went to wash cloths. As I raised my head up, I saw someone running towards me with a gallon of kerosene and match sticks. Before I could stand up, she had poured the kerosene on me and was about striking the match stick, when I pushed her and she fell to the ground. Neighbors came and held her while I ran away with my children to my mother's house.

He went back to his base, returning after completion of NYSC . He had to look for a house, and we relocated. He wasn't working yet, but I was farming, buying and selling stuffs to put food on our table. He was also assisting by doing meagre daily jobs, since we had school fees and house rent to pay. My mother was also assisting in her little way not minding her other responsibilities. I still had dreams of returning to school. My siblings were already in university and were almost graduating. Mum was ready to assist me in my education. She was always talking about it but at that time, my children were my priority. One day, we heard a knock at the door. Lo and behold, it was my dad , standing at the door, begging for forgiveness. We forgave him and integrated him back into the family

Three years later, we were asked to return to the family house (because he was the first son). Initially I refused. I didn't want to go back to hell again, but he made me see reasons and I reluctantly accepted. We moved back to the family house and we were given an apartment there. Everest later got a job with a security firm and life became better. I became pregnant again and gave birth to another set of twins (a boy and a girl). I now had five children (4 boys and a girl).

Everest decided to go complete the traditional marriage rites since he now had a job. After the traditional marriage, the mother (a diabetic patient) started complaining of severe headache and was rushed to the hospital. She was diagnosed of diabetes and high blood pressure and was treated. Gradually, her sight started failing her and she eventually became blind. What a life!

Trouble brewed! She accused me of causing her blindness. She said I wanted her dead so I could collect her property. It was a big problem. Mother and son turned enemies while he was trying to protect me. His siblings all wanted my head. They started going to spiritual houses and even came physically to confront me. I told them my hands were clean and they should go any where. It was a battle and another phase of life.

One day, my mother - in-law told me that I would reap what I have sowed and I told her Let God be the judge and my witness". I went out that day, and purchased my JAMB form that would enable me continue my higher education. I processed it online and was waiting for the day of the examination. Few days later, my husband came from work and went to get us some litres of kerosene. While trying to pour it inside the stove, there was a ' boom" sound. The stove had exploded and he was engulfed with fire. From his neck down to his laps were burning. I poured water on him but he was in pains. It was a 3 rd degree burn. I managed him throughout the night and rushed him to the hospital in the morning. The little twins were just a year and eight months old. My dad became sick and was being admitted into the same hospital with my husband. I as shuttling between the two rooms, taking care of them both. I would still go home to make food and take care of the kids. It wasn't easy, the hospital was very far from home. My husband spent seven(7) months in the hospital. I became a wife, a mother and a daughter during this period. My dad died along the line, after so much money had been spent. I was forced to take my husband home because the burden was much for me alone. I became the medical doctor and nurse at the same time. I couldn't meet up to the time of the JAMB examination because I was coming from the hospital and it was too far from the venue of the examination. I lost that opportunity, but I never gave up. The company still retained his position and he joined them back after his recovery.

The following year, I bought the JAMB form again, wrote the examination and got admitted into University of Port-Harcourt to study Business Management. Right now I am in my second year. I went through a lot but I was never discouraged. Yes, course mates may make jest of me yet I come out tops in courses I thought they would do better.

I am an African woman, a wife, mother. I am strong, courageous, multi-talented and am living my dreams despite all the obstacles fate threw my way. I passed through a vigorous process and came out refined as gold. I know I will do something greater and better than before.

THE VAW JOURNAL

FEATURED VOICE

Noëlla Coursaris Musunka, is an international model and the founder of Malaika, a non-profit organization that believes in empowering Congolese communities through education. She was born in Lubumbashi, Democratic Republic of the Congo. At age 5, Noëlla lost her father and with her mother lacking resources she was sent to Switzerland to live with relatives.

After achieving a degree in business management, she moved to London and began a career in modeling,. In 2015, she was invited to speak about the future of Africa alongside President Clinton at the Clinton Global Initiative's Opening and Closing Plenaries in Morocco. In 2014, Noella was named one of the 100 most influential Africans by New African magazine. Since 2017, Noella has been a Champion for The Global Fund, the world's largest partnership combating these diseases with governments, civil society and the private sector. Today, Noëlla is also a wife, a mother of two, and leads operations and management of Malaika.

In a few interviews you mentioned your precious moments with JJ and Cara, reading them stories before bed. Are there any books by african writers you read to your children? Is it important to you that they connect with their African Heritage? Why or why not?

I am in an interracial relationship, so my kids are mixed. My daughter is five years old, and my son is nine years old. My kids learn about Africa with me everyday, and they go there as well. They know about Mandela, Patrice Lumumba, they know the presidents etc, and they follow the news in Africa. I don't want to over impose on them, I want them to naturally learn the culture of Africa, and their identity as an African. My son is nine years old and he has travelled 20 times to Congo and to different countries in Africa. So naturally, he understands the music, the food, all his friends are from the village, he goes to their homes all the time. So I am happier that he is learning all of this in this natural way.

My husband is white, I'm black. I don't have to explain Blackness and Whiteness to my kids but they understand, you know, and I think this is the best way for them for them to understand. We are based in England, so they understand English. There are some heroes that they're learning about at school, and they know that Africa also has her own heroes like Mandela, Lumumba, and so on.

There's already so much going on in the world currently, and it'll be too much for them to digest if I begin to impose it on them. When they go with me to the Congo, in the village, they themselves see the poverty, they will tell me "Mum, let's buy sweetened food for all these kids", or "Mum, I'm going to give my birthday cake to the kids in the village." or "Mum, let's buy a mattress for this girl, I went to see where she lives." I can understand parents that never go to Africa explaining through books, but my kids will go to Africa their entire life, they eat African food, and they're learning about the African culture in a natural way.

Your career in modeling seems to have started almost out of luck. You were originally on a track to a career in business then people were asking you to model and then your friend signed you up for the Agent provocateur competition, which then launched your modeling career. Were you reluctant at first about the opportunity especially since you had originally wanted to pursue a career in business? What was going through your mind around this time? And why did you choose modeling?

A lot of people were stopping me for many, many years, even when I was younger. I was a tomboy actually when I was growing up. When I started to grow older and develop my looks and my hair was growing longer, more and more people were asking me to model, but my mother sacrificed a lot, so my primary goal was to study. But, winning the competition was really good also. Modeling was a very quick platform where I met a lot of people, and travelled to different countries. However, I realized on time that it wasn't where my fulfillment was. What fulfills me is me being a mother, giving back to my mother and to my country through Malaika.

Like in many societies, modelling in Africa is still stigmatized, especially when done by women. Some of the reasons behind this not only confronts their

intelligence, but challenges their sexual freedom, which is one of our focus themes. Did you ever experience any disapproval and/or discrimination because of your modelling career?

Can you imagine that the first campaign is Agent Provocateur is a campaign in underwear? I probably gave a heart attack to all of my family. [laughter] But here's what I think, we Africans are changing. You can no longer impose on your kids that they have to be a lawyer, or be a judge, or be a journalist, or be a doctor.

That was what our parents wanted - these big titles and big jobs. Now, what is important for us as parents is our kid's relationship with their African identity. We want them to be happy, to fulfill their dreams. If they want to be a writer, if they want to be a singer, we do and should encourage them. Look at the amazing works of Tiwa Savage, Angelique Kidjo and the rest.

So, we want them to know that they can be whatever they want. Modeling for me was a door to different doors. It all depends on how you manage your career and your image. I think generally, we are completely changing, the world is changing. We need to constantly adapt. Even the modeling industry right now is entering into what I believe is a very important phase of the fashion industry, where the story and the substance behind the dress will matter more than the model. And we see that even more with what's happening with the racism in the US and all these people who have been dying. You cannot just think "Hey, I'm pretty, I'm black." No, it's more about what is your value? What do you stand for?

Another sub-theme of this project is "Her place in the world". What are some lessons you can share with young women out there as they embark or continue on their journey of self discovery in a world that already places them a couple steps behind?

I think women need to just go for it! As a young woman, you need to believe in yourself. You need to believe in your voice. It is important to know that you can be whatever you want to be; a judge, a journalist, a doctor, and so on. One thing I see nowadays is that a lot of women are changing careers. From being a makeup artist, then now they go back to school to become a journalist or vice-versa. And this is amazing.

I think the next few years will see a lot of women exploring different careers. And it's great because it might be uninteresting to stick to one career for 20/30 years. You would want to change and do something different at some point and that's fantastic.

You have stated that you felt FORTUNATE to have received good education in Switzerland after having to leave your home. You've also referred to the consequential separation with your mother as a loss. Considering both facts, how do you think we can make sure every girl in Africa feels as fortunate as you once felt without having to endure the great loss of leaving their homes?

When I lost my dad, I was five years old, and my mom didn't have resources to keep me. I was the only child. I grew up with my extended family in Europe and I went back to see my mum after 13 years. Now, my daughter just turned six years old. I believe that as children, one very important thing is to have parents until a certain age. Parents dedicate their time to read books to their kids, to go for a walk, to do sports with them, etc.

At my daughter's age, if she were to lose me or my husband, it would be tragic for her. I have a lot of admiration for my mum because if you asked me to give away my daughter now, I won't be able to do that. She lost her husband, and shortly after she lost me, but she moved on with life, and that's tough. At this time there was no Whatsapp, or zoom, so maybe we spoke two or three times. When I say I'm fortunate- what I'm trying to say is that my childhood was very tough on me, and on my mother. My education has made a huge difference today. Not everybody is strong enough to come out of tough times and become successful. I see some of my friends with that kind of have a similar story. They fell into drugs, they became suicidal, they developed mental health problems and the likes. You have to be very strong when facing challenges and for me, I'm a very determined person and helping my mum was my biggest dream and is the reason I just put all my effort into education.

You revolutionized girls' education in the RDC at a young age while acquiring substantial international support. Do you have any words of encouragement for young people with a similar ambition and a great level of uncertainty?

We need strong institutions in Africa, and I think something COVID-19 is showing us is that Africa needs to be self-sustainable and we need to work within Africa together. Each country, the 54 countries need to work together because we can not continue to depend on Europe or China for goods and financial aid. This also shows us that we need top quality schools, and top e-learning facilities. We need good hospitals because health too is important.

For 13 years, Malaika has been transforming this village. Despite the lack of water, electricity, and infrastructure, we were able to make a model, an ecosystem, that can be duplicated anywhere in any community in the world. It's called the Malika Model. We are finalizing the toolkit and we would love to share with individuals, foundations, and really advise them on how they can duplicate the school that we have, the community center, the water program that we have.

We are also into agriculture where we grow our own food and it goes to the canteen of the school, and this is an ecosystem you can duplicate. However, it is very important to have the input of the community so as to really serve the needs of the people.

Unfortunately, COVID-19 has been negatively impacting the whole world. You have stated that Malaika has implemented new practices to ensure students and the community are being safe. Tell us about these practices and how the girls are doing? How is the quarantine impacting their academic progress?

So, Malaika has been closed since the 19th of March - both the school and the community center. As a result of COVID-19, the President has ordered all public places to be closed. So our students don't go to school for now. Sadly we lost one of our students,

Leah. It's painful because if she were able to come to school, then we would have known she wasn't doing well and would have looked after her.

Beyond this virus there are a lot of challenges and problems. Food prices have gone up, some families don't even eat up to once a day. We recently did an emergency fund where twice a week we feed families in the community. We have impacted more than 2800 individuals. We have 20 points where there are basins for people to wash their hands. We give them soaps, we teach them how to wash properly, and we distribute food in the village. We have the team distributing homework at different points of the village too.

It has been going well, just that this is the first time the girls have been away from school for this long. School is a refuge for them sometimes, because we give them breakfast, lunch, and we look after their health. So right now I am not so worried about their academics, but I am more worried about their health and nutrition.

The VAW Journal is an artistic social action initiative. At I, AFRICA™ we believe in the power of expression through the arts. In Malaika's curriculum you not only focus on Math and science, but also the arts. Why do you think that's important? Are there any stories you could tell our audience about how art has personally and/or professionally benefited the girls at Malaika?

Well we are not all the same, we all love different things. I want the girls to feel fulfilled by doing what they love. One of our girls, Jolie, wants to become an architect. We have to realize that kids need to find what they love and what they want to do. For example, my son and my daughter are different. My daughter plays the cello while my son plays the piano. At the school we want to give our children a range of subjects where they can choose the areas they love. We have sports, music, coding, football etc, and we leave them to do whatever they love. Art is a massive component.

Malaika has been successful over the years, because we train our teachers. We work with technology and so our girls learn to code. We take care of their health and nutrition, we invite role models to speak to them, from the mother in the village to the big CEO. We have the American ambassador and other people here in the Congo with very good works who have come to visit the girls. If you observe our girls, you will notice that they are not afraid to speak to people, they're bold, they ask questions. These people come and speak about their success, the challenges they faced in their journey. It is important to instill values in our children through the schools they attend. The kids at Malaika are taught to look after each other, they work hard, show good leadership, and are honest. So when our girls start to work after school, they will exhibit these values.

An influencer is someone with the power to impact others. You definitely have such power. How do you aim to influence people? What is the number one thing you hope people take away as they scroll through your website and social media platforms?

For me it's Malaika. My family life is very private. I want people to know more about the kids in Malaika, what we are doing in the school, and to know that we have an amazing team managing things. I want them to know that together we can achieve so much more. I want people to know that we have so much in Africa and we really need to invest in education.

Last year, at the Global Education and Skills Forum, you said that "Congo deserves our attention because we are taking much from [it]" considering that 60 percent of the world's cobalt comes from the country. What would you say to companies unfairly benefiting from the use of this resource? And, what can the communities do to better protect themselves?

I think that in a way, we have let ourselves be exploited for too long in Africa. We need strong leaders who will truly serve the people, who will work for our benefits, who will fight for us, and who will work to promote equality for all.

We need to build Africa to a point where we will be able to travel and explore the beautiful beaches here, in Africa, rather than aspiring to go to other places. This is all a case for our leadership. One thing I am happy about is that the new generation of Africans are very awake. They don't like all the exploitation over the years and they are vocal about their displeasures.

Speaking of Congo, do you have any favorite African food? Tell us about it. And, since food and fashion have met on many occasions, some of them international, do you have a favorite female African designer?

Like I said earlier, I love fufu, beans, chicken, tomato sauce, peanut sauce, grilled fish and other lovely African dishes. My favorite African designers are; Duro Olowu, Keneth Ize and Studio 189.

You have Malaika, two children, an international modeling career, and many other hats. How do you manage everything? Do you have any help? And most importantly, how do you unwind?

Yeah, it's not easy because I'm a mother, I have two kids, and I want to be there for my kids. I follow their education and I follow everything they do very closely. Apart from this, I'm invited to speak to schools through a lot of conference calls etc, and because of my schedule, I choose my speaking engagements very carefully. I work around my kids. So when normally they go to school, I work. Then when they're at home, I'm with them and then I'm back to my work at eight o'clock. I like to work around their schedule.

I do a few campaigns a year as a model. Then there's also Malaika where I lead operations and yet I don't take any salary. I work six/seven hours on Malaika everyday because I love what I do. I make sure that I'm copied on every email. I lead it from fundraising, to marketing, the local teams, and basically from A-Z. I'm a workaholic, and so I'm very involved in everything. Also being a perfectionist I'm always looking for new ways to take Malaika to the next level.

This time where everything is closed we take time to reflect and adapt to any new changes, we have begun to train our teachers again, as well as the management team on leadership skills. We are also sewing and distributing face masks to the community. With the STEM program we run, our girls are doing face mask shields. We have been having lots of webinars with influential women at this time. They include Eve - our ambassador, June who is a journalist, and these women all share common traits: they believe in education, in empowerment, and they work so hard. I want the girls at Malaika to feel related to one of them or to all of them.

I unwind by baking, and I do some cooking. I love to watch TV, documentaries, read books, and magazines.

As a woman of African heritage, how do you understand, build and maintain your African identity?

Oh, for me, I'm very proud of my African heritage, and I say this many times when I speak. I was born in Africa and I grew up as an African woman. I know my roots, from my grandmother, to my mother who both lived in DRC, Africa. I take pride in wearing my African clothes. I go to Congo twice a year with my kids and I go to other different African countries as well. As a way of supporting African causes, I always give time when an African person reaches out to me. I believe we have to work together, we have to be united in order to create the new Africa we want. I believe that we should learn from the past too and move on quickly into our bright future. I also listen to African music, and I eat African food.

I understand and appreciate my African heritage. For instance, people often ask me who my female mentors are. While I have a lot of mentors, I love to go and sit with a mother in the village and have very enlightening conversations. They are so full of wisdom and they have lots of stories to tell. They are our heroes because they lived through most of Africa's troubled times and they're still here, laughing and sharing with us. This, for me, is the definition of the African identity. I love to work in the village because I learn so much from the people - their resilience and their beauty. I've been to South Africa, Ghana, Nigeria and many other African countries, and I hope to visit Angola soon and many more African countries.

SUBMISSIONS BY ARTISTS
—

21. **Sonia Jona (Sonita castanha)**
   - Raras Relíquias

22. **Lúcia Morais**
   - Soneto In Melodia (
   - Soneto Da Menina, Mulher Africana
   - Um Poema

23. **Hazvineyi Zinyowa**
   - Herstory 25years Later
   - My African Story

24. **Ifunanya Juliet Ottih**
   - Identity
   - Even With My Period

25. **Veronique Moore**
   - A Healing Break
   - Untitled
   - Life Goes On

26. **Patricia Musebah**
   - I Am Me
   - Call Me Zena Femme .Am A Woman.
   - Masks

27. **Sankofa Umbi Umbi**
   - Ventos De Igualdade

- Sobre Choros E Gritos

28. Tamary Kudita
- African Victorian
- African Victorian
- Mr. Luvie And Rosy
- Maintaining Memories
- Family 2
- Kuchengetedza Pfungwa: Maintaining Memories

29. Ammywrites
- A Tale No One Cared To Hear
- The Rapist Takes All The Blame (
- Freedom!

30. Paloma Peyron
- Untitled
- Untitled

31. Zawadi
- Casting Spells Of Pleasure
- Mountains, Vulvas And Rainbows
- Fountains Of Honey

32. Aisha Mohammed
- Reckoning
- Ode To A Mixed Girl's Homeland.
- Of Origins And Connections

ABOUT THE ARTISTS

—

Abigail Adigun: is a first generation Nigerian American high school student who loves serving her community, learning more about the mystery of the world, and living life to the fullest. In her free time, Abby enjoys hanging out with friends, writing, and watching TED talks.

Adedoyin Adebiyi: I love reading, writing and designing. I love trying out new food, writing challenges and making clothes. I have a wacky sense of humor and sometimes laugh at things that might not be funny but I am foremost a black woman and a Nigerian. I love telling stories and hope to make people happy with my creativity.

Liko: I am a 24 year old Namibian in the legal profession, and have always been passionate about writing however I have not written in a while or shared any of my work, I believe it's time to put my work out there and express myself on issues that affect women.

Aisha Mohammed: Aisha is Law student, poet and a writer. She is a mental health and SGBV who believes in the empowerment of women and children. When she's not studying Law and writing poetry she enjoys volunteering, watering plants and spending time with family.

aladywithapen: Aishatu was born and raised in northern Nigeria. A biochemist with strong passion for writing and works for eHealth Africa. She volunteers at Saving the Future Girls Initiative (SFGI) and Young African Leaders Initiative. Through SFGI, she works with other volunteers to bring girls off the street in an effort to minimize street hawking and enroll them in schools.

Aminat Sanni-Kamal: a lawyer, a blogger and an author. She writes fiction and non-fiction, her stories and articles are set mostly in Africa. She is a feminist who uses every medium within her capacity to speak against gender-based injustices. When she is not writing, she is either reading a book, watching a movie, practising yoga or chatting with friends, and family. She currently lives in Lagos, Nigeria with her family.

AriButtercup: is a lawyer, editor, poet, lover of pups and unicorns. She is ardent yogi, who is passionate about women's right and mental health awareness.

pen.cells: Benikranus Appaw is a Ghanaian born Writer, Editor, Blogger and Health Advocate. Her work was featured in the 2020 Ghana Writes Christmas/New Year Haiku and Senryū series. Growing up in a household full of boys, she kept a daily journal where she could let her mind run free and wild. She found it very soothing. She also believes that everyone has a story to tell, you just have to find the right audience.

Amandlovu: I've spent most of my life, stifling my voice, burying it deep so that it wouldn't get drowned out by the noise of the world - not knowing i was hurting it more than the world would. Now I'm ready to scream, cry , rant, laugh, as loud as I can.

Charanee Marimuthu: Someone once told me, "Charanee you do not think inside or outside the box, you have gotten rid of that box altogether." I am a firm believer of living life passionately, and without limits. It is only through our experiences (both good and bad) that we are able to create art that speaks to and moves the world. That being said, even if my work aspires just one person - then that would move my world.

Chelsy G. Maumbe: a firm believer in the influence that literature has on a growing mind, is passionate about sexual politics, especially when individual rights are undermined by another party. Though she is a sucker for romance and gets giddy anytime there is kissing involved, her writings have been described as 'guaranteed to leave one in a comfortable misery that makes visible the dark realities of this world.' She is a drama teacher at a prestigious high school in her country and spends the larger portion of her life at her local theatre (Reps Theatre) performing or at home, buried deep in the weaving tales of human experiences all across the world.

Chengetai Masalethulini: I am a self-taught artist and I've been passionate about it since I was 5. My work includes portraits, wildlife, murals, sign writing and set design. I love bringing smiles to people's faces through my work and interpretation of projects. I had a terrible encounter last year on international women's day, March 8th, that rocked my world. I was mugged and almost died during the process. For the longest time I was not myself and I could not do what I loved, making art and music as my body was still healing. At times I was unsure if I would able to do them again, it was so distant from the pain of my reality. But as my body grew stronger, I started to experiment, taking baby steps, from trying to play a simple scale on the piano to trying to draw a circle, I learnt to take baby steps at my body's pace and it helped me heal. Now I am fully recovered although I still have some scars on my body, I am grateful that I am able to do what I love. My style has shifted a bit as a result of my experiences but they have helped me to understand and process things in a different light.

Cláudia Cassoma: Since I started actively and intentionally working on defining my identity, I made it my purpose to assure that's true. Today, the arts are a great part of it. I am an author with nine titles published. I have also had the honor of being internationally recognized for my literary literary works. While writing is a great part of who I am, I also compose songs—with a few being already performed by portuguese and angolan singers. On top of it all, is my passion for service. I am the founder and a coordinator at SmallPrints, a non-profit organization focused on the holistic well-being of every angolan child. The recognitions extend to the aforementioned area as well. I currently hold six honors and awards in social action and a few others in leadership, academia, and health.

E'ta Foto: I am E'ta Foto. I am proud to be Nigerian and African. I enjoy everything Literary. I like reading, writing, speaking, and traveling. I am a serial volunteer because I have a desire to see Africans achieve their goals beyond borderlines. I am dedicated to making the SDGs a reality, especially numbers 4,5,6, and 16. Telling stories of Africa and Africans both at home and in diaspora, knowing our past and understanding our present, and cherishing our heritage and identity is a drive behind my studying English and Literary Studies. Contributing to the Voice of African Women anthology is a dream come true for me.

Dikun Elioba: Dikun Peace Elioba is a poet based in New York. Her poetry has been published in I Know Two Sudan's Anthology in London and in Sudan. Her poetry explores her grapple with memory and identity while trying to make sense of the duality of her culture and heritage across borders. She aims to piece together her heritage while exploring themes of desire, lust, and pain throughout her writing.

Ewuradwoa: My name is Elsie. I am from Ghana. Just out of spite...Ghana jollof all the way. I love other jollof's thought but Ghana jollof hits different. I write casually, as and when I feel led to write. It is a way of putting my thoughts on paper.

Sankofa Umbi Umbi: SANKOFA Umbi Umbi, Slammer. Nascida aos 02 de Setembro. Segunda Classificada do Concurso feminino de Spoken Word MUHATU (2016); Segunda Classificada do Concurso Angolano de Spoken Word Luanda Slam, dois anos consecutivos (2018-2019). Apaixonada por energias maravilhosamente positivas.

Eugenia Shaw: lives and works in the UK, and hails from Liberia, West Africa. She returned to the UK after her family were exiled due to the brutal Liberian civil war, in which her family lost everything. Upon returning to the UK she established herself as Healthy Hair

Consultant with her own hair care product line. She is passionate about writing and scalp and hair health, which led to the self publishing her 1st book Hair Is Hair (available on Amazon) in 2018, which combined both her passions. Writing, reading, learning, fitness, wellness, dancing and enjoying time with family and friends are a few of the things she is most passionate about.

EbeneAfrica: I am a black African woman from Cameroon. I spend my childhood in Cameroon. I lived in Cameroon, France and USA. I am proud to be Black, African, Woman.

f.gabdon: A Somali-British poet and writer. Author of my first poetry collection 'Breathing Just A Little.'

Felicia-Carol Manka: I am a mixed portraitist based in Pretoria. My work addresses issues related to identity and women.

Glennise Ayuk: is a medical doctor, humanitarian and digital health entrepreneur from Limbe, Cameroon. She is also a creative writer, with features of her work in Aaduna, African Writer, Parousia and Verbal Art. Her poetry is part of two anthologies; Bearing Witness: Poems From a Land in Turmoil, and Universal Oneness. Glennise is an ardent advocate for women's rights and empowerment, and for the creation of a self-sustaining, identity-proud Africa. She sings, orates and almost knows to paint. She is 25 years old, loves to jump rope and often describes herself as wild, soulful and sapiosexual.

Gugu Ngwenya: A selenophile and a lover of words. I honor my African lineage. I am entirely grateful for my ancestors who left me an inheritance of their gifts and for that reason, I am able to write. I am the anchor of their dreams and their chosen mouthpiece. I am vocal about my uniqueness and a fierce keloid warrior.

Harriet Mimi Uwineza:
1. Founder- WOPA
2. PhD Candidate (Peace Studies)
3. Former Country Director- Childcare Worldwide

Hazvineyi Zinyowa: Young African woman passionate about anything female ,from gender equality, feminism in the African space.Currently pursuing a career in community development and pro-women writings.

Henrietta Enam Quarshie: is currently a medical student at the University of Health and Allied Science. She comes from the Volta region of Ghana where she lives in its capital, Ho. She has been published by Praxis magazine, Tampered Press and in anthologies: To grow in two bodies and The yellow post. She writes micro poetry on Instagram under the pseudonym Poetbyimpulse.

Hlulani Sabela: I am a young South African teenager that holds a great passion for the performing arts and plans to pursue the performance arts as a career. Outspoken, unapologetic and filled with a humbled sense of pride. I was raised by a single mother who had little to keep quiet about. i am filled with nothing but an optimistic need to do what i was born to do, perform.

Ifeoma Onwuka: I am the youngest of four children. I was born in South Orange, New Jersey and I am currently in graduate school for my Master's. I was a middle school science teacher in Newark, and now I am an Academic Coordinator for a Non-profit organization. I mainly work with students of color and provide them with the necessary tools that they need to be successful in our society, and in my free time I love watching ROMCOM's and reading.

Ifunanya Juliet Ottih: is a talented creative writer, poet, storyteller, public speaker, and debater. Many call her a personality with myriads of talent because of her insatiable urge for knowledge. She is a 400 level student in the Department of Linguistics and Communication Studies, University of Calabar, Calabar, Crossriver state Nigeria. Her in-depth knowledge is born out of the unending concern for society and human behavior towards their environment.

Ivándra José: Ivándra Manuel José nasceu a 25 de Abril de 1993 em Quelimane província da Zambézia. Licenciada em Imagiologia e Mestre em Saúde Pública, escreve desde os 11 anos de idade. É apaixonada por leitura, gosta de ler romances e livros de auto ajuda. Activista social com interesses nas áreas de saúde pública e empoderamento feminino. Participou na colectânea de cartas de amor intitulada " Poemas e Cartas Ridículas de Amor " em Fevereiro de 2020.

Janice Allotey: is a recent graduate of the Johns Hopkins Bloomberg School of Public Health, where she earned a Master of Public Health degree. She is the Co-Founder and Administrative Director of the social enterprise Creation Care Concept, which produces functional items from plastic waste and advocates for environmental sustainability. Her goal is to use her skills and training to tackle environmental health issues in Ghana, especially those that disproportionately affect women and children.

Sepopo: My name is Jennifer Adjivon and I'm 20 years old. I was born in Lomé, Togo, and came to the US at the age of 6-7 years old. I am currently living in New York City, as an aspiring nurse. I have decided to participate in this project because I truly support the message - to give a voice to African Women. Frequently the voice of the female - and more so the African female - gets buried by the whims of society and solely labeled an oppressed voice. However, by labeling it so, it robs African Women of their beautiful stories, their wisdom, and their secrets. Just because the voice is oppressed, doesn't mean it doesn't exist. It is just not heard. I am proud to be participating in the Voices of African Women Anthology - a platform that allows for the voices of African women to be heard.

Khanysa Mabyeka: Sou luz, feminista e activista social interessada em contribuir para mudanças de normas sociais baseadas no patriarcado que mantém uma estrutura injusta de poder onde na maior parte das vezes nós as mulheres estamos em desvantagem. Faço isto através do meu trabalho como consultora de género e desenvolvimento e através do meu blogue www.mamilosanarquistas.com, onde reflicto sobre identidades, normas sociais, o corpo, a sexualidade, a política e a relação destes temas com a maternidade.

Kundai Muringi: Kundai is an African from Africa, who writes and creates chocolate art. She continues to passionately progress in Public Health and marries it all together, as a strong believer that nothing is ever separate.

Ladunni Peace: I am a lady in her teens, a lover of God, a poet, a linguist and a singer.

Lerato Makuwa: is an artist born in Port Elizabeth, Eastern Cape in South Africa. A qualified and trained performer, theatre award nominated actress, art enthusiast and overall creative. The rights and dignity of others serves of importance to her and notes educating oneself and being teachable as a necessity. "Material will be left behind for black children to delve into truthfully one day and some gems for black girls to be delighted in and unfold unto - that's quite something to imagine".

Lizelle van Dijk: was born in 1995 in Durbanville. Her writing has appeared in the student poetry collection Penseel. She recently graduated from the University of Stellenbosch, where she received her honours degree in English Studies.

Ana Mafalda Gonçalves Dias: My name is Lorna, I am a poet, proudly black. I have been writing since I was 11 years old. Poetry is my refuge, it's where I have a voice to express my feelings, shout, transform and change lives. I write because I believe it is possible to transform the world into a better world using literature.

Lúcia Morais: é uma poetisa Angola, Licenciada em Gestão de Empresas, MBA em Finanças e Negócios. Tem os seus poemas publicados em mais de 10 antologias e revistas por Angola, Moçambique, Portugal, Brasil e Itália. Possui os seguintes prêmios literários: Prémio Mundial de Poesia Nosside 2015, categoria Distinta [1] Prémio de Literatura Passos de Mulher 2015. Prémio Mundial de Poesia Nosside 2016, categoria Extraordinária. 27º CONCURSO LITERÁRIO INTERNACIONAL DE POESIAS, CONTOS E CRÔNICAS , categoria Destaques Literários – Poesia Internacional

Lucy Mwimbilizye: I am twenty three years old,I hold a bachelor of Commerce in Marketing.Currently I am an entrepreneur and a founder of a community Based organization named Woman To Woman organization which aims at empowering women and girls through education and training.

Mahafuza Abdulrahman : Am by name Mahafuza Abdulrahman am fulani by tribe and am also a student studying Agricultural science at Ibrahim badamasi Babangida university Lapai and I love writing its it's a part of me.

Michel'le Donnelly: A self-confessed drama queen. I live for telling stories and firmly believe creativity and storytelling have a key role to play in today's social justice movement. Apart from writing raging rants about my period and sharing the ridiculous choices I've made, I also run an online feminist newsletter that serves as a platform for women, non-binary, trans and gender non-conforming individuals of colour to share their creative work.

Mojisola Esthe: Mojisola E. Olatunji is a poet and poetry enthusiast who believes that poetry is not for the writer but for those who needs it. She have an educational degree in English language and have a flare for proofreading and editing aside writing. One of her major goals is to heal many through words and lines. In her journey to doing this - writing to heal- many friends have gone to her for constant help to write anything for them. This has made a great influence on the minds of readers of her poetry and their orientation about how words can heal.

Zawadi: is a self-taught painter and writer. her paintings are inspired by her poems and/or monologues and vice versa. She likes to indulge in topics about spirituality, queerness, mental health, gender equity and dismantling patriarchy.

Unique Bunny: I am a woman with a passion for writing who grew up in Rwanda in East Africa. I am currently a medical student at University of Global Health Equity. Writing is a hobby, therapy, and platform for my voice. I am highly interested in Mental health and Women's right.

Munira Maria Makerow: A creative coffeeholic pan-Africanist mother of two, autoimmune disease warrior, artist, and storyteller.

Nguseer Gavar: from Benue State Nigeria. I am a graduate of University of Mkar, Nigeria where I studied Food Science and Technology. I seek to resolve food insecurity in my country and Africa at large in respect to my discipline. I have deep passion for the speaking the truth through visual arts and poetry. I love reading, drawing, dancing and traveling.

Ammywrites: I love writing and burying my face in between the sheets of a book. My safest place, music and my notepad.

Khanyo Mandingo: My name is Nokukhanya Mtshali, 19 years of age. I am a student at Witwatersrand University. I started writing when I was 13 and it has been my form of communication ever since. My hobbies include listening to music, reading books, and spending time with my peers. I am unable to convey in words who I am and I am never able to articulate what is needed of me. I am very self-conscious about my writing and I'm very introverted.

Joselyne The Poetess: Having had once been a victim of exclusion and inequity, Joselyne Nzisabira grew in the Gasabo district in Rwanda with a passion for challenging the current existing health inequities. In a world full of cultural gendered paradigms and judgments, through writing and poetry, she found a voice; a voice for self-expression. At the age of 12 while she studied at Kigali Harvest school, she became a storyteller and a literature admirer with an ambition of bringing a sense of consideration, social disparities solving, and gender respect through literature. However, it was never easy when some of the people she expected inspiration from were the ones who weakened her. With the fear of criticism, the only choice she had was to keep the voice in her heart and notebooks. In 2019, she covered her nerves and presented her first poem about the Genocide perpetrated against Tutsi during the 25 Rwandan commemoration period in Kamonyi district. This motivated her and became a proceeding point of writing more small stories, inspirational, and self-esteem poems. Her poems include: She took her life for it, Pretty, That child, Born different, Karma is real..etc. Her current goal as a young medical student and poetess is to impact the lives of the younger generation facing criticism and inequity to speak up and rise.

Oluwamayowa Somoye: My name is Somoye Oluwamayowa. I am a poet,I write stories and articles. I see writing as a measure to express my emotions or help other people find healing. My Instagram handle is @mayor.ts. I am currently without a job.

Onyeka Nwabunnia: is an African feminist, writer, activist, and podcaster currently residing in the United States. She holds a Masters in Gender Studies and Law from SOAS University of London and works at a thinktank supporting research on education financing in international development. Onyeka is the Outreach Coordinator for Vanede, a sexual violence training and prevention organization in Washington DC, and supports the Cleopatra Broh's foundations efforts to provide access to education and sexual health resources to adolescent mothers in Liberia. Onyeka is the founder of the Blog Griotte: From Her Own Lips and is a cohost on the podcast From Her Own Lips. As a feminist, Onyeka is driven by questions concerning how we create knowledge and understand the world.

Oyindamola Adisa: is a medical project coordinator and a cancer awareness advocate who organizes programs to educate and inform the public on the importance of cancer awareness and screening in early detection. She is also a feminist and an avid advocate against gender-based violence in Nigeria; her volunteer work is primarily centered around this. She also freelances as a graphic designer @thecanvadesigner in her spare time.

Paloma Peyron: I'm a self-taught photographer. I'm Cameroonian, Spanish and French, born and raised in Cameroon. I started photography 9 years ago. Very versatile, interested in lots of different types of photography, I attempt to show my feelings by sharing her attraction for life through photography.

Patricia Musebah: I am a 25 year old vibrant feminist with a passion for literature.I use my voice through writing to fight bias a d challenge steriotypes. My dream is to convey a message through the art of poetry as it is a message inscribed forever on pages not lost .As an African ,my continent has exposed me to a significant amount of experience in what it entails to be a woman. I hope to entertain and educate through art as we tackle life as women in my region.

Rita Mbonika: Born in Norway to a Norwegian mother and a Tanzanian father. Spent most of my life in Africa. My passion for food,creating and discovering traditional food and trying to capture the moment with references to my daily life here at Ras Kilomoni ....

Rusud Makrim: Ruina Maksud Carim, nasceu ao 23 de Novembro de 1995 na Cidade de Quelimane Província da Zambézia. Nacionalidade Moçambicana. É empreendedora, criativa e activista social. formada no grau de Licenciatura em Administração e Gestão Hospitalar e actual Mestranda em Saúde Pública. Trabalha como docente universitária no departamento de Administração e Gestão Hospitalar. Pequena no mundo da poesia, em fevereiro de 2020 participou na coletânea nacional intitulada "Poemas e Cartas Ridículas de Amor" Gosta de leitura, desenho, escrever, fotografia, artes, natureza e ama viajar. Se inspira na mulher e criança, solidariedade, direitos de igualdade e no amor ao próximo.

Rumbidzai Zamukudzi: I'm a lady ged 26, an ecologist. I like writing so much and have followed my passion through all this corona virus pandemic. I have been through the hands of an abusive father and I hope and pray no child or woman should go though those difficult times.

Rutendo.S. Maturure: Words are a breath to my soul. I am passionate and in love with every word curved to put stories together. Because of this, it has given me a steady source of imagination driving me to build the best. This passion pushes me to be a voice, learn something new, and get better skills at what Ido.

Ruth Kanu: a beautiful African woman. I am a scientist, instrumentation technician, Educationist, writer, business and content developer and a social entrepreneur. I am graduate of Physics and mathematics from Imo State University. owerri , Imo State Nigeria. I am also the founder of Teens and Youths Enlightenment and Development Initiative (TYEDI- AFRICA), mentoring teens and Youths, teaching them life skills to use in impacting their society positively(especially teens with effects from Juvenile delinquency). I am an African mother, a wife, a career and a business woman. I invest in humanity and touch lives positively. I am an African woman. Am bold, strong , courageous and beautiful.i am proud of who I am and am living my dreams.

Ruwarashe Mukonyora: I am a 23 year old Zimbabwean girl studying medicine with the University of Zimbabwe. I love creating art because it is the purest and most accurate representation of the deepest part of my soul. A picture can say a thousand words...and the cherry on top? The eyes always remember!

Sephora Antaya: I was born and raised in France (Paris). I'm a 1st generation french of congolese parents. I started writing poems in November 2018. It is really therapeutic for me.

Siju Falade: I am a lawyer and a creative, two occupations that often seem to conflict. I am a first generation, Nigerian-American, black woman who loves all the complexities and multiplicities that come with being all of these things-- with existing at the intersection.

When I think of powerful, African women, I think of my mom. So this is for her.

Sinenhlanhla MlilowokuNqoba MaPhezabantu: I am a writing enthusiast who believes in the power of storytelling through words. I am a rape and molestation victim who is on antidepressants and I am just going through the motions of being a black woman in South Africa.

Sonia Jona (Sonita castanha): Sou formada em Ciências da Comunicação e a escolha do curso deveu-se mesmo ao gosto que tenho por comunicar com outros. Ensinar, aprender, ler, escrever. Sou activista social. Escrevo nas redes sociais, focada nos direitos humanos, igualdade de género e empoderamento da mulher. Na infância fui co-autora de um livro de poemas de Eduardo White e, com o conto "O Ritual de Águeda" obtive o primeiro lugar num concurso literário cujo prémio foi a edição do mesmo num livro de contos.

Stella Oduro: was born and partly raised in Ghana before she moved to the United States. Her transition from one culture to another was not always easy, especially being called an "African booty scratcher" by her peers and learning that the African continent was often referred to as one country Subsequently, she became very interested in how society shapes one's identity, specifically the identities of those from the African diaspora. She understands that different places and cultures assist in forming solidarity among people from the same diaspora. Being that more Africans and

African Americans are traveling, living, and working in East Asian countries, she particularly enjoys watching East Asian dramas and documentaries. These dramas and documentaries have given her the opportunity to see how these cultures perceive people of color and how these perceptions help create and encourage the different Black spaces. When she is not deep in her thoughts, Stella enjoys satirical political commentary shows like The Daily Show with Trevor Noah and Patriot Act with Hasan Minhaj. Stella graduated from SUNY Geneseo with a Bachelor of Arts in International Relations and a minor in Asian Studies. Stella's favorite writer and philosopher is the late Dr. Maya Angelou.

Tamary Kudita: A product of dual heritage, Tamary Kudita was born in Zimbabwe whilst her ancestry can be traced back to Orange Free State, historical Boer state in Southern Africa. She chose to study fine art at Michaelis School of Fine Art at the University of Cape Town. There, she graduated in 2017 with a bachelor of fine arts. Subsequently, she established herself in fine art photography thus beginning her artistic career. She maintains an active studio practice and has exhibited in Zimbabwe and outside the country. Her investigation looking at the legacy of colonialism on the family structure, has resulted in exhibitions delving into the history of the Post-colonial identity. Her first solo exhibition was held at the PH Center gallery in Cape town which explored notions of race and representation. Her previous exhibitions have been held at the Michaelis Galleries also in Cape town, titled, Maintaining Memories. Tamary, continued her investigation of history with an exhibition titled 'African Victorian' which was held at the National Gallery in Harare, Zimbabwe. Her most recent exhibition titled 'Representation' was held at Artillery Gallery also in Zimbabwe. This exhibition was an examination of how our unchosen histories shape our contemporary state. She has also been featured in Photo District News Magazine which is an international publication. Her future plans involve continuing and evolving her body of work by merging her antique processes with contemporary ways of photographing. Furthermore, she will be exploring themes that are tied to Black photography and Otherness.

Teresa José Taimo: "Entre gemidos da mulher casada e outros gritos mais" é uma crônica que visa expor a falta de liberdade sexual nos lares Africanos. Esta é uma temática que nos sufoca pois a nossa satisfação sexual está somente em agradar os maridos e procriar.

Thandokuhle Sibanda: I am a 20 year old female born and raised in Great Bulawayo, Zimbabwe. I was raised by a strong single woman and I owe most of what I have become to her nurturing hands and her loving heart. I started writing at a fairly young age, around 14,15 which is right about the time I started performing. Poetry is a way of life for me and I use it to communicate, speak out and pour my heart out. It is also some kind of escape from the ugliness of the worlds we create. I am poetry..

Tshepo Jamillah Moyo: has a strong background in development, human rights and communications. Tshepo has, throughout her career, gained extensive experience in consultancies for human rights and advocacy on Sexual Reproductive Health and Human Rights for women and adolescent girls and youth across the world and particularly the most marginalized in Africa. Through performing arts, public speaking engagements and her expansive writing works on digital and traditional media, Tshepo has, put a lens on critical issues around equal rights and autonomy for women and girls. She has gained experience in Southern Africa, including Botswana. She is driven by core values of feminism, commitment, diversity and integrity.

the.verve_: Ursula writes. Most times, she has trouble telling what it is she's written. Sometimes, she thinks it's poetry. She can't live without music, books or her laptop. In her spare time, which is usually stolen, not spared, she sleeps. When she does manage to control the voices in her head, she shares their ramblings on ursyrants.wordpress.com

Valerie Asiimwe Amani: is an artistic explorer based in Dar es salaam, Tanzania. Her multimedia approach includes incorporating textile, poetry, moving image and digital collage into her work. She has won an award in fashion and has co-authored a book titled Black Amara, a visual and literary journey of love, loss and healing. She experiments with the elements of memory and emotion, her art pieces having narratives around the changing complexities of identity and body, along with the nuances of daily existence through a neo-african feminine lens.

Veronique Moore: I am a world full of darkness. I always try to yearn for the light. This has always been a theme in my works. I am South African born with a wild imagination which usually excludes me from the general public. I aim to educate and make people aware of the hidden glimpses people sometimes fail to see.

Vimbainashe Takarwa: I have grown up in a world full of stereotypes, some of them well deserved but some are so far from the truth it hurts. I come from a country that is full of love but now the poverty and mistrust destroys it. I'm a queen of African heritage and wish our women would write for my children a different story. that society would re-evaluate, not to lose its spirit but to let the girl child grow. to empower the mother, sister, daughter, and wife in her to crave more. I am feminist but I guess in an age of equality I am radical, I want fairness for we are not equal. I am female and he is male and for that we are different but I do want my quarter, my due for what I give to society. I am a Queen, I acknowledge my King and I wish he did more than see me, I wish that the half I was created for heard me.

Vivian Ibemere: Ibemere Vivian is a Nigerian Writer and an Educationist. A graduate of English/History from the University of Nigeria, Nsukka. She loves to put all her feelings and experiences into writing with the belief that there is a thin line between life and fiction and hopes to give our complex reality a concrete form through her short stories.

Yvette Lisa Ndlovu: Yvette Lisa Ndlovu is a Zimbabwean sarungano (storyteller). She is pursuing her MFA at the University of Massachusetts Amherst where she teaches in the Writing Program. She earned her BA at Cornell University and was a finalist for a Tin House Young Adult Writer of Color Scholarship. She was the 2020 fiction winner of Columbia Journal's Womxn History Month Special Issue and a 2020 National Juror for the Scholastic Arts & Writing Awards. She received the Cornell University George Harmon Coxe Award for Poetry selected by Sally Wen Mao and is a 2020 New York State Summer Writers Institute Scholarship recipient. Her work has appeared or is forthcoming in the Columbia Journal, FIYAH, the Huffington Post, the Jellyfish Review, and Kalahari Review.

INDEX OF ARTISTS

—

Abigail Adigun

Adedoyin Adebiyi

Aisha Mohammed

aladywithapen

Amandlovu

Aminat Sanni-Kamal

Ammywrites

AriButtercup

Charanee Marimuthu

Chelsy G. Maumbe

Chengetai Masalethulini

Cláudia Cassoma

Dikun Elioba

E'ta Foto

EbeneAfrica

Eugenia Shaw

Ewuradwoa

f.gabdon

Felicia-Carol Manka

Glennise Ayuk

Gugu Ngwenya

Harriet Mimi Uwineza

Hazvineyi Zinyowa

Henrietta Enam Quarshie

Hlulani Sabela

Ifeoma Onwuka

Ifunanya Juliet Ottih

Ivándra José

Janice Allotey

Joselyne The Poetess
Khanyo Mandingo
Khanysa Mabyeka
Kundai Muringi
Ladunni Peace
Lerato Makuwa
Liko
Lizelle van Dijk
Lorna Zita
Lúcia Morais
Lucy Mwimbilizye
Mahafuza Abdulrahman
Michel'le Donnelly
Mojisola Esther
Munira Maria Makerow
Nguseer Gavar
Oluwamayowa Somoye
Onyeka Nwabunnia
Oyindamola Adisa
Paloma Peyron
Patricia Musebah
pen.cells
Rita Mbonika
Rumbidzai Zamukudzi
Rusud Makrim
Rutendo.S. Maturure
Ruth Kanu
Ruwarashe Mukonyora
Sankofa Umbi Umbi

Sephora Antaya

Sepopo

Siju Falade

Sinenhlanhla Londiwe Meyiwa

Sonia Jona (Sonita castanha)

Stella Oduro

Tamary Kudita

Teresa José Taimo

Thandokuhle Sibanda

the.verve_

Tshepo Jamillah Moyo

Unique Bunny

Valerie Asiimwe Amani

Veronique Moore

Vimbainashe Takarwa

Vivian Ibemere

Yvette Lisa Ndlovu

Zawadi

VAW AWARDS

—

- **VAW's Most Promising Female African Artist Award**
  Onyeka Nwabunnia
- **VAW's Most Outstanding Contribution to the African Arts Award**
  Chengetai Masalethulini
- **VAW's Most Inspiring Artist Award**
  Khanysa Mabyeka
- **VAW's Most Inspiring Piece of Art (in english) Award**
  Tamary Kudita — "African Victorian"
- **VAW's Most Inspiring Piece of Art (in portuguese) Award**
  Khanysa MaByeka — "A quem pertecem as minhas mamas?"
- **VAW'S Most Supportive of Other Women Award**
  Munira Maria Makerow
- **VAW's Arts Education Award**
  Nzisabira Joselyne
- **VAW's Most Influential Voice Award**
  Lorna Zita
- **VAW's Best Young Voice Award**
  Nokukhanya Mtshali
- **VAW's Best Wise Voice Award**
  N/A
- **VAW's Honorable Mention**
  Chelsy G. Maumbe
- **VAW's Cover Art Certificate of Recognition**
  Tamary Kudita — "African Victorian"

PROJECT'S STATISTICS

—

THE VAW JOURNAL

VOICES OF AFRICAN WOMEN

(2020)

77 Voices

160 artworks

by Sub-theme

- Sexual Freedom: 42
- Her place in the world: 96
- Storied the World Wouldn't Believe: 31

Printed by Amazon Italia Logistica S.r.l.
Torrazza Piemonte (TO), Italy

16672248R00259